CRAZY HOUSE

JIMMY PATTERSON BOOKS FOR YOUNG READERS

JAMES PATTERSON PRESENTS

Stalking Jack the Ripper by Kerri Maniscalco
Hunting Price Dracula by Kerri Maniscalco
Escaping from Houdini by Kerri Maniscalco
Becoming the Dark Prince by Kerri Maniscalco
Capturing the Devil by Kerri Maniscalco
Kingdom of the Wicked by Kerri Maniscalco
Gunslinger Girl by Lyndsay Ely
Twelve Steps to Normal by Farrah Penn
Campfire by Shawn Sarles
When We Were Lost by Kevin Wignall
Swipe Right for Murder by Derek Milman
Once & Future by Amy Rose Capetta and Cori McCarthy
Sword in the Stars by Amy Rose Capetta and Cori McCarthy
Girls of Paper and Fire by Natasha Ngan
Girls of Storm and Shadow by Natasha Ngan
You're Next by Kylie Schachte

THE MAXIMUM RIDE SERIES BY JAMES PATTERSON

The Angel Experiment
School's Out—Forever
Saving the World and Other Extreme Sports
The Final Warning
MAX
FANG
ANGEL
Nevermore
Maximum Ride Forever
Hawk

THE CONFESSIONS SERIES BY JAMES PATTERSON

Confessions of a Murder Suspect
Confessions: The Private School Murders
Confessions: The Paris Mysteries
Confessions: The Murder of an Angel

THE WITCH & WIZARD SERIES BY JAMES PATTERSON

Witch & Wizard
The Gift
The Fire
The Kiss
The Lost

NONFICTION BY JAMES PATTERSON

Med Head

STAND-ALONE NOVELS BY JAMES PATTERSON

The Injustice
Crazy House
The Fall of Crazy House
Cradle and All
First Love
Homeroom Diaries

For exclusives, trailers, and other information, visit jimmypatterson.org.

CRAZY HOUSE

JAMES PATTERSON

WITH GABRIELLE CHARBONNET

JIMMY Patterson Books
Little, Brown and Company
New York Boston London

Copyright © 2017 by James Patterson
Excerpt from *The Fall of Crazy House* copyright © 2018 by James Patterson
Excerpt from *The Girls of Paper and Fire* copyright © 2018 by Natasha Ngan

JIMMY Patterson Books / Little, Brown and Company
Hachette Book Group
1290 Avenue of the Americas, New York, NY 10104
jimmypatterson.org

Originally published in hardcover by JIMMY Patterson Books/Little, Brown and Company, May 2017
First paperback edition, May 2018

JIMMY Patterson Books is an imprint of Little, Brown and Company, a division of Hachette Book Group, Inc. The Little, Brown name and logo are trademarks of Hachette Book Group, Inc. The JIMMY Patterson Books® name and logo are trademarks of JBP Business, LLC.

The publisher is not responsible for websites (or their content) that are not owned by the publisher.

The Hachette Speakers Bureau provides a wide range of authors for speaking events. To find out more, go to hachettespeakersbureau.com or call (866) 376-6591.

The quote on page 117 is from Steve Jobs's commencement address at Stanford University, June 12, 2005, accessed at https://www.theguardian.com/technology/2011/oct/06/ steve-jobs -pancreas-cancer.

Library of Congress Cataloging-in-Publication Data
Names: Patterson, James, author. | Charbonnet, Gabrielle, author.
Title: Crazy house / James Patterson with Gabrielle Charbonnet.
Description: First edition. | New York : Little, Brown and Company, 2017. | "JIMMY Patterson Books." | Summary: In a future world where teenagers are taken, imprisoned, and forced to fight for their survival, well-behaved Cassie will do whatever it takes to save her rebellious twin sister from death row.
Identifiers: LCCN 2016050431 | ISBN 978-0-316-43131-6 (hc) / 978-0-316-51499-6 (pb)
Subjects: CYAC: Prisoners—Fiction. | Survival—Fiction. | Sisters—Fiction. | Twins—Fiction. | Conformity—Fiction. | Science fiction.
Classification: LCC PZ7.P27653 Cr 2017 | DDC [Fic]—dc23
LC record available at https://lccn.loc.gov/2016050431

10 9 8 7 6 5

LSC-C

Printed in the United States of America

In memory of my mother, Grace R. Charbonnet. Miss you.
—G.C.

PART
ONE

1

CASSIE

THANK GOD FOR PROGRAMMABLE COFFEEMAKERS, that's all I want to say. Actually, that's about all I *can* say until I've had that first cup. Right on time, 5:45 a.m., life's precious fluid starts seeping down to the carafe.

And thank God for coffee. Last year when we'd heard that a lot of coffee crops had failed, I thought the bottom of my life had dropped out. But this year coffee is back on the shelves at United All-Ways, and I for one am grateful.

Leaning back against the kitchen counter with my first hot cup, I looked out the torn window screen to see the barest hint of pink coming up over the tops of the trees by the Boundary. I guess people who live in cells by the ocean get to see the sun coming up over the water.

Actually, I don't know. I don't know if any people live near any ocean.

I felt the coffee igniting nerves throughout my body as I sipped and watched the sun come up. It was partly blocked by the carport where I kept my—

I bolted upright and peered through the ragged screen.

"No, she didn't!" I shrieked, wanting to hurl my coffee cup right out the window. It would have hit my truck *if my truck had been there.* Which it wasn't!

"Damnation, Rebecca!" I shouted, then wheeled and headed upstairs *just* to double-check. *Just* in case. Just in case my twin, Ridiculous Rebecca, was in fact still snoring in bed instead of *joy-riding in my truck.*

I slammed open her bedroom door, adrenaline making jumpy friends with all the caffeine in my system.

Becca's bed was empty.

Seething, I hurried to my room at the end of the hall, passing the door to our parents' room, which we kept shut all the time nowadays. In my room I threw on yesterday's jeans and a plaid shirt that I'd been too hasty in assigning to the dirty clothes pile. Jamming my feet into my perfectly worn cowboy boots, I started rehearsing what I would say to my sister when I caught up with her.

And I *would* catch up with her. There was zero doubt about that. Our cell was barely four miles across, a nice big crop circle. Becca had no place to run, no place to hide.

2

I PUSHED OPEN OUR SCREEN door so hard that one of the hinges busted, making it tilt crazily. *Watch it, idiot.* Anything I broke, I had to fix. It wasn't like there was anyone else to do it.

Halfway around the side of the house, I remembered to look at my watch. 5:55. Silently I mouthed *Crap!* I turned around, stomped up the steps, across the porch, through the broken screen door, and into our living room. Curfew wasn't over till 6:00 a.m., and I'd seen what happened to people who didn't think the Provost meant what he said about curfew. He really, really meant it. He meant *inside your house* from 10:00 p.m. to 6:00 a.m. Not in your yard. Not under your carport. Not leaning against your fence, enjoying the breeze. And he always, always knew.

My jaw was so tight it was starting to hurt. Since I had four—no, three—minutes left to kill, I went back into the kitchen and cut myself a couple slices of bread. I had a PB & J in my hand by 6:01, and I hurried out to the carport where Ma's dinky purple moped was leaning against a pole.

Just looking at it bummed me out. For one thing it reminded me of Ma, which, obviously: bad. For another thing it reminded me of Becca, because she's the one who used the moped now, and I was ready to skin her alive. Third, it had a top speed of twelve miles an hour. Twelve. Miles. An. Hour. And that was on a full charge, which it had only if Becca remembered to plug it in the night before. Fourth, the pickup had been Pa's, and he'd left *me* in charge of it. There were only a few pickup trucks left in the entire cell. We'd only been allowed to keep it because it was so ancient that I practically had to push-start it. But I still loved it, I was still the one who used it, and now Becca had taken it, had left before curfew, and was probably already getting high with her loser doper friends.

And who would have to come up with some lame excuse about her tardiness or absence at school? Me. Who had to hope that somehow she hadn't already been seen out before curfew? Me. As mad as I was, I didn't want to see her go through that. I never wanted to see her go through that.

Ma's moped started easily enough and I wheeled it around, then got on and steered through our gate with my non-sandwich-holding hand. The more I heard the gentle hum of its little engine pushing us down the road, the madder I got.

My sandwich was gone by the time I reached Murphy's crossroads—not that there are any Murphys anymore. I guess

"Forty-seven's crossroads" didn't have the same ring. At the big Healthier United sign I turned left to take the road to town, all the time searching the crop fields for the curved red roof of the pickup poking out above the wheat. Becca had several usual hangouts, and I circled down to the gully where kids went to smoke and generally be bad citizens. No one was there, and the tire tracks in the rutted mud looked a couple days old, at least.

By 7:30 I had puttered to all of Becca's lairs. Though I'd found several of her red-eyed friends, none of them admitted seeing Ridiculous, and no one had seen my truck. She'd done an excellent job of disappearing. Damnation!

3

IT ALMOST KILLED ME TO chug up to school on Ma's moped, but of course I did it because I'm not the twin who breaks rules. I'm not the twin who makes things harder for everyone. I'm the twin who shows up for school every day on time, rain or shine, and I'm the twin who then goes to my after-school job at United All-Ways because our family needs money. Ma was gone, Da was...gone-ish, and who kept Ridiculous from starving her skinny butt off?

That would be me.

School was school. We studied farming, mostly: planting patterns, current approved crops, harvesting tips 'n' tricks. Our cell was an ag cell, but of course there were other vocations, too. I'd hoped to be assigned to higher schooling, but at sixteen they had labeled Becca an electrician and me a mechanic. The irony there was that

Becca had clearly learned to hot-wire my truck, but she wouldn't know how to put the alternator belt back on once it slipped off its pulley, which it tended to do every couple hundred miles.

Becca wasn't at school. My truck was not in the parking lot. My anger flamed—not only would Becca risk getting herself into serious trouble, but she was *dragging my truck down with her!*

"Cassie Greenfield, please come to the principal's office."

I was so busy fuming that I didn't hear the first announcement.

"Cassandra Greenfield, please report to the principal's office."

Heads turned to look at me, and our teacher quit lecturing, her hand frozen on the slide that showed less-wasteful irrigation methods.

Slowly I got up, grabbed my backpack, and left the class.

Standing awkwardly in the outer office, I told the secretary that I'd been called. I'd never been in here before—one of the few kids who had never, ever done anything to warrant getting called to the principal's office.

The inner door opened and our principal, Ms. Ashworth, stood there frowning, her arms crossed over her chest. She was tall and sticklike, and no one I knew had ever seen her smile—not even my pa, who had gone to school with her.

I stood up and she motioned me into her office. My heart was beating fast, like a mechanical tree-shaker trying to loosen every last pecan. I couldn't even swallow.

"Sit down, Cassie," said Ms. Ashworth.

"Thank you, ma'am," I said, and took one of the seats that faced her big desk. I gave a quick glance around but it pretty much looked like what a school office should look like. In the corner hung the United flag on an eight-foot pole topped by a brass eagle. Our unit's flag with our mascot, a honeybee, on it. (A bee for Unit B, get it?) Our cell's flag, Cell B-97-4275. A framed photo of Ms. Ashworth with Provost Allen, shaking hands and smiling at the camera. A framed photo of President Unser, the one that was distributed when he'd celebrated thirty years in office.

"Where is Rebecca?" Ms. Ashworth got right to it.

I wished I could say "I don't know" and let Becca take whatever happened. But the stakes were too high, the outcome too awful. Even as mad as I was, I would never do that to my sister.

"She's home sick," I said.

Ms. Ashworth frowned. "Cassie, we don't get sick. Our cell enjoys perfect health, as you know."

Since I drove past the big Healthier United sign every day on my way to school, I did know that.

"No, not like sick with a virus or anything," I clarified, thinking fast. "I mean, sick from…overeating."

"Overeating what?" Ms. Ashworth knew that anyone having enough food to eat too much of it was as rare as someone coming down with a cold.

"Pears." It was like God had taken pity on me and dropped an idea into my brain. "We have a pear tree, and of course we pack up most of them for the Co-op. But when the pears get bruised, or have worms or something, we keep them and make pies or whatever. Can them for winter. The ones that aren't good enough for the Co-op." I spoke quickly now. "I told her not to, but Rebecca insisted on tasting all the ones I was cutting up. Some of them weren't even ripe. By lights-out she felt pretty bad, and this morning she was curled up moaning and wanting to throw up."

This was the best Becca excuse I'd ever come up with, and I congratulated myself silently. It was a shame that I'd only get to use it once.

Ms. Ashworth's pale-green eyes looked at me across her desk. "I don't believe you," she said.

4

MY HEART FELT LIKE IT was trying to climb out of my throat.

"I . . . beg your pardon, ma'am?" I stammered.

The crease between her straight pale eyebrows deepened. "It's just you and Becca at the farm now, right?"

Heat made my cheeks flush. Everyone in the cell knew about Ma, knew about Pa.

"Yes, ma'am," I mumbled.

"Your only sister is sick," said Ms. Ashworth. "I don't believe that you would just come to school and leave her."

All I could do was stare at her, my brain's activity crashing into a single, static line.

"I have a perfect attendance record," I managed to say, hoarsely.

"Oh. And you're trying to get a President's Star?" the principal asked.

I nodded. Any kid who never misses a day's school from kindergarten through graduation receives a gold star from President Unser himself. I was so close.

Her face softened the tiniest bit, as if she were a marble statue that had weathered for a hundred years. "I understand. I tell you what. You've already been marked present for today. I'm giving you special permission to leave school, go home, and keep an eye on Rebecca. But I expect you both back here tomorrow at eight a.m. on the dot!" Her face had toughened up again, but I nodded eagerly.

"Yes, ma'am! Thank you, ma'am! I'll stop at United Drugs, get some bicarb, and get right home."

"See that you do," she warned. "If I hear tell of you going anywhere else, doing anything else, you'll pay for it. Understand?"

"Yes, ma'am, I understand."

Thirty seconds later I was putt-putting out of the school yard. Of course I really went to United Drugs and actually bought bicarb; Ms. Ashworth would know if I hadn't. But then I headed home, hoping against hope that Becca had come to her senses. And that she had brought my truck back.

She hadn't. Now I had to wait until 3:30 to leave the house again, thankful that today was one of my days off from United All-Ways.

By 5:00 I started to actually be concerned. I'd made the rounds again, asking Becca's friends to give her up, but they seemed sincere when they said they hadn't seen her today. One of them was even mad because Becca had promised to help him rewire his burned-out soldering iron, and she hadn't shown.

Dinnertime came and went. At 7:00 I was pacing the floors,

looking through our windows to the darkness outside, praying I would see headlights bumping over the worn track to our house.

When the numbers on the oven clock changed to 8:00, I was sitting at the kitchen table, more afraid than I'd ever been. Becca wasn't playing hooky. Becca hadn't taken my truck to piss me off. Becca was missing. And Becca was the ninth kid to go missing this year. None of them had ever come back.

5

BECCA

WAS IT MORNING? AFTERNOON? NIGHT? No clue. They'd gotten me at 3:00 this morning. How much time had passed? I didn't know.

"Goddamnit!" I muttered, and tried to yank my hands apart for the hundredth time. They didn't budge, and the zip tie dug more sharply into my skin. I felt the slight, warm stickiness of blood seeping down my hand. "Goddamnit to hell!"

"You!" said a woman's voice, and my head swiveled blindly toward the sound—I couldn't see anything through the black hood. I hadn't seen anything since 3:12 a.m. "You! Swearing is forbidden!"

"Bite a scythe, asshole!" I snapped, and something big and solid slammed against my head. Sparks exploded inside my eyes as I gasped and fell sideways onto a cold concrete floor. "Oof!" I swallowed, tasting blood, trying to stave off a sudden urge to puke my guts up.

Someone leaned over me. "Swearing. Is. Forbidden," said the woman's icy voice. "Repeat that after me: Swearing is..."

"The only appropriate response to this shitty sitch!" I wanted to spit blood out but it would have just hit the hood.

A hard, pointed shoe kicked me then, right in my gut, and I almost screamed. Acid rose in my throat as a heavy, burning pain filled my insides. I quickly coiled up as best as I could with my hands tied behind me and my ankles lashed together. What in holy hell was going on? For about a minute this morning, I'd thought it was a prank, at best, and at worst, a warning from Big Ted, who I owed a measly thirty-two bucks. But after the first punch that had knocked my lights out, it became clear that this was some other shit altogether.

Rough hands scrabbled at my neck and I promised myself to bite the hell out of the next asshole who got too close. They untied the hood and yanked it off, making my head snap against the concrete again.

My eyes blinked painfully against the sudden, too-bright light. I wanted to throw up, then get my hands on the strongest pain-killers I could find. A shadow blotted out the light, and I glanced up warily. A woman frowned down at me, but all I could do was gape at her. I'd never seen anything like her. Her brown hair was coiled on top of her head, like braided Easter bread. Her eyes had thin dark lines drawn around them, reminding me of those Egypt people who had failed because their system was bad. Her mouth was painted with barn-red paint, and I wondered how she could stand it. Wouldn't the paint dry and crack? Didn't it taste terrible?

Shifting a bit more onto my shoulders, I simply looked her up and down, not even caring if this got me kicked again. She was wearing a navy-blue suit, like a man's suit, but with a skirt. Her shoes were...thin, totally useless for walking in fields. Her shirt was white and almost shiny—not cotton, not linen, not wool. I wanted to touch it.

"My name," she said in a voice like an icicle, "is Helen Strepp. You may call me Ms. Strepp."

My mouth has gotten me in trouble my whole life, and it didn't stop now. "As long as I don't call you late for dinner!" I said, remembering when my pa had laughed at that.

Ms. Strepp nodded at someone behind me; there was a slight sound, and then a rocklike boot kicked me in the back.

I couldn't help sucking in breath with almost a whimper. My eyes squeezed shut against the pain and I realized that every part of me felt bruised and broken. If I'd been home by myself with no one to see, I would have cried. But I hadn't cried in front of Careful Cassie in years, and I sure wasn't going to give these assholes a show.

"Now," said the woman, "what is my name?"

"Ms. Strepp," I mumbled, not opening my eyes.

"Good," she said, and I hated the satisfaction in her voice. Well, I hated everything about this, no doubt about that.

"Now you know my name, the fact that swearing is forbidden here, and you've gotten just a slight taste of what happens when you disobey the rules," Ms. Strepp said. "The last thing you need to know right now is that you're in prison. A maximum security prison for enemies of our system."

That made my eyes pop open again, and I stared at her in disbelief.

"Are you shittin' me?" I blurted, and was rewarded by a kick so hard I passed out.

6

A POEM by Rebecca Greenfield

Yellow is the color of the sun
Yellow is the color of ripening wheat
Yellow is the color of the hawkweed flowers in
*   summer*
Yellow is the color of corn (certain varieties—
*   not Silver Queen)*
Yellow is the color of this goddamn freaking
*   goddamn son of a bitch goddamn*
*   freaking jumpsuit that they make me wear*
*   in goddamn freaking prison*
The end.

• • •

They took my pa's watch, which almost killed me. They took my clothes. They were my third-best jeans, the one T-shirt I had with no holes in it, and the soft plaid shirt with the shiny pearl snaps that I'd stolen from Careful Cassie last night. Looked like she wasn't ever going to find out. Silver lining.

My loose yellow jumpsuit closed with a plastic zipper. There were no shoes of any kind. The one good thing was the Band-Aids they'd put on my wrists where the zip ties had gouged channels into my skin.

And, son of a bitch, this really was a freaking prison. Which meant we weren't in our cell anymore. I knew every building, every house, every shed, every barn in our entire cell. Everyone did. None of those buildings had high concrete walls topped with cattle wire. None of them had windows with bars.

I was out of my cell for the first time in seventeen years. *It was not an improvement.* Which meant that the Provost was right *again.*

"Move!" A man in a gray uniform pointed his wooden billy club at me and motioned me through a barred gate. I walked through, shuffling because I still had ankle irons connected by a chain. The gate slammed shut behind us.

In addition to the huge, swelling bruises all over from being punched and kicked, my head hurt so much that I felt sick. When they'd moved me from the first room I was in to this big building, it had been dark outside. I hadn't eaten all day and was hollow with hunger, dizzy with fatigue, and nauseated. So far, being out of my cell *sucked.*

"You will obey all the rules," Ms. Strepp was saying, spitting out her words like gunfire. "You will try to fit in. You will do what is asked of you. You will speak only when spoken to. Is this clear?"

Pretty much a yes or no question, but my reply flew right out of my head as we moved down the hallway. There were small rooms on either side, like the ones we'd seen in history books about pre-system times. Jail rooms with people in them.

And all the people lining up to look at me, holding on to their bars, were *kids*.

7

KIDS. TEENAGERS, LIKE ME. WERE they all enemies of the system? I still didn't understand what I had done to get myself thrown in prison. I mean, what thing *in particular.*

"Is this clear?" Ms. Strepp repeated more loudly, smacking me on the arm.

But I had stopped dead, because not only were the prisoners all kids, but they were...different from people in our cell. Some of them.

When I saw a slender girl with dark-brown skin and soft-looking, puffy brown hair I couldn't help staring.

My skin is colored like vanilla ice cream. Ms. Strepp's skin was chalky white, like cow bones left in the sun. The guard had a red face and neck, like a lot of men in our cell. Every single person that

I'd ever seen was some shade of those basic three colors. My skin got tanner in the summer—most people's did. But nobody in our cell had that smooth dark skin. Nobody had puffy brown hair like lamb's wool.

The guard *thunked* me in the back with his club, and I kept shuffling forward.

"You will obey the rules," Ms. Strepp said again. "You will try to fit in. You will do what is asked of you. You will—"

"Oh, my God!" I exclaimed, stopping again. A boy was holding on to his bars, watching me go by. He was different, too! His eyes were shaped like pumpkin seeds. His skin was golden, like corn silk at harvest. His hair was short and black.

This time the billy club hit me hard against my hip bone. It really hurt and knocked me sideways so that I crashed against the bars. The kids inside took quick steps back, their eyes big.

When I regained my balance I shouted, "Goddamnit! Quit hitting me! What the hell is wrong with you?"

This pushed Ms. Strepp over the edge, and she whirled, punching me in the stomach as hard as she could. I doubled over, and then the worst happened: I puked all over her fancy, impractical shoes.

8

THIS WENT OVER LIKE A hay bale off a truck. The entire jail block froze in silence. I was thinking Ms. Strepp had lucked out, because I'd skipped breakfast this morning and hadn't eaten anything since then. It wasn't like after the pie-eating contest, which had been a rainbow of bad.

"Ow!"

Ms. Strepp grabbed my braid and yanked up on it hard enough to pull me off the ground. I pressed my lips together, trying not to say anything more. A crisp white handkerchief floated down to the floor.

"Clean. That. Up." Ms. Strepp's voice was shaking with fury.

I did, thinking that now I was the lucky one.

When her shoes were shiny again, she pulled up on my braid

until I was standing. Muted whispers had begun among the prisoners. My head swam and I blinked several times, gritting my teeth. The guard pushed me forward with his club, and this time I kept my mouth shut until we stopped in front of a jail room. I gave a quick glance sideways and saw four colorful kids already in there. The guard unlocked the bars and shoved me inside, then slammed the gate closed and locked it.

"Bring your feet over here," he commanded, and I shuffled forward. Reaching through the bars, he unlocked one ankle iron, then the other, and swiftly pulled the cuffs through the bars.

Ms. Strepp stepped closer and almost hissed at me. "You will follow the rules, you will fit in, you will do what is asked of you, and you will speak only when spoken to. Is this clear?"

I gave an unenthusiastic nod. With a sharp, satisfied grimace that I realized was her version of a smile, she and the guard marched back down the long hallway, her shoes clicking loudly against the floor.

I was in prison. I was an enemy of the system.

And I had no idea why.

9

CASSIE

BY THE TIME I'D SUSPECTED that Becca had been taken, it was 8:00. I'd immediately gone out again on the moped, and this time I went all around the cell on the ring road that follows the cell boundary, all twelve miles of it. No one I knew had ever gone across the Boundary—all we could see were thick, dark, dense woods. One road led into our cell, and the same road led out, but I'd never seen anyone come or go on it, either on foot or in a vehicle.

We'd been taught about the dangers beyond the boundary woods—there were many, many ways to die out there. Inside was better. Still, we'd heard stories of people who had tried to cross the Boundary—no one we knew, just people in the past. There were sensors, so the police and the Provost would know. And it would be bad.

At twelve miles an hour, it had taken me an hour to circle our cell. It was already a little past 9:00, and I still had to get home. But when I reached the boundary road leading out of our cell, I paused for a minute, peering into the darkness. I turned off the moped and looked on the ground, wondering if I would see my truck's tire treads. They were distinctive because the front left tire had been patched, and the patch made a smooth spot in the middle of its treads.

I didn't see them. But vehicles had obviously been here, and recently. I was still pondering this when I heard the 9:30 siren.

"Crap!" I jumped back on the moped and gunned it, which made me go slightly faster than a cow walking. The road leading in and out of the cell was in the northeast; I lived in the southwest. With any luck, I would get home with ten minutes to spare.

The moped's weak headlight picked out the dusty roads I knew so well. I could probably close my eyes and still find my way home.

As it was, I had a problem. Stupidly, I hadn't charged the moped during the day while I had to stay inside. With all the driving I'd done this morning, and then again tonight, its battery was pretty much drained. I was still a mile and a half from home when it went dead completely, the headlight flickering out and the small, quiet motor sputtering to a stop.

"Crap!" I said again. "Dammit!" I was usually more careful than this. Now I had a choice: abandon Ma's moped here on the road and race for home, definitely getting there before curfew, or trying to push it all the way as fast as I could and risk missing curfew.

I hesitated for several moments on the dark, empty road, pulled by both choices. Then I grabbed the handlebars, kicked up the stand, and began wheeling it toward home.

I'm a strong girl. I had to be to keep on top of all the work since Pa—

I'm strong. But after only half a mile I was exhausted. My legs ached, it was hard to catch my breath, and I had to keep switching sides because of how the weight of the moped pulled my muscles.

I checked my watch. I had twelve minutes. I had another mile to go. If I left the moped by the side of the road and the police found it, it would be confiscated. People take care of what's important to them. If I left it, it would mean it wasn't important to me, that I didn't really need it. And it would be taken.

If I still had the truck, we could get by without the moped. With no truck, the moped was the only thing that kept us from having to walk everywhere.

Also, the moped had been Ma's.

"Dammit!" Hot tears made tracks through the dust on my face. "This is Becca's fault!" Then I remembered that Becca might have been disappeared, and found I couldn't blame her—I was too worried.

I tried to go faster.

I was just slogging through our gate when the curfew siren sounded. From our yard we could see four other houses; the closest was half a mile away. I saw their lights blink out.

Barely able to breathe, every muscle screaming, I shoved the moped under the carport, letting it fall, and then I scrambled into the house as fast as I could, hoping with all my heart that I hadn't been seen in the yard a minute after the siren.

I climbed upstairs in the dark and fell across my bed in all my sweaty, dirty clothes. This was the first night that my sister hadn't slept under this roof. The first night in my entire life that I was totally, completely alone. Tears came then, and I fell asleep while I was still crying.

And I slept about twenty minutes that night.

10

BECCA

I LOOKED AT MY FOUR roommates with equal amounts of curiosity and caution. There were two brown people, one tan person, and one cream-colored person like me. They were all staring back at me, but maybe they'd never seen quite so many bruises on a girl.

Did we all introduce ourselves now? Shake hands? Was there a prison etiquette? If there was, I was sure I'd be forcibly educated in it momentarily. As it was, I was left being me.

"What the hell is this crazy house? And who was that evil woman?" I demanded.

The kids seemed startled, one of them laughing nervously, and then the dark-brown girl glanced up and to the left, very quickly. I followed her line of sight and saw a tiny camera mounted high on the wall on the other side. As I watched, it swung in an arc, then swung back.

A surveillance camera. We were being watched all the time. How prisonlike.

"My name is Becca," I said. "I don't know why I'm here. I don't know what this place is. I don't know how to get out of here. Like, can my fam—can my sister come bail me out or something?" Despite our differences, I knew that Cassie wouldn't hesitate. If it was possible, she would already be working on getting me out. I hoped it was possible.

This time all four of them looked solemn.

"I'm Robin," the dark girl said.

"I'm Diego." The tan boy bit his thumb and then dropped his hand, as if he was trying to break the habit.

The tall dark boy with straight hair stepped closer. "I'm Vijay."

I'd barely noticed the other girl, except to see she had the same color skin as me. Now she nodded at me shyly. "I'm Merry. Like Merry Christmas. Not like Virgin Mary."

Vijay pressed his lips together and Robin held up a warning finger. "Don't even," she said.

"She's got to find some other way of describing it," Vijay said defensively. "It leaves her set up perfectly, and it's unfair that I have to suppress every humorous instinct I have."

"Not this again," Diego muttered, while Merry crossed her arms over her chest and gave Vijay a look I recognized: fed-up impatience. Having often been on the receiving end of that look, I sympathized.

"Maybe just spell it?" Vijay suggested helpfully. "Leave the Virgin out of it?"

"What *is* this crazy house?" I said again, a little louder this time to get their attention. "Why are we here? Why are you here? What's going on?"

Their faces fell again. I sure was a killjoy.

"This crazy house, as you call it, is a maximum security prison for enemies of the system. Strepp is the deputy warden." Vijay had a dry, precise way of talking, as if he'd been picked for higher schooling.

"To answer your other questions," Robin said, "we don't know why we're here. We don't know where 'here' is. And there's only one way out."

"In fact," Diego said, his voice tense, "kids get out that way all the time."

"What is it?" I asked eagerly, ready to sign up for good behavior or whatever.

Merry sighed. She was younger than me, with light-brown hair we call "mouse-colored" in our cell. "Diego is...kidding," she said. "Sort of. What he means is, this isn't just a prison, and we're not just prisoners. This is death row. We've all been sentenced to die. And that's the only way out."

11

CASSIE

AT 6:00 A.M., I WAS awake and dressed, gritty-eyed and shaking with panic, perched on the edge of a kitchen chair. The moment curfew was over, I tore outside and plugged in the moped. It had rained during the night, and even now fog and mist shrouded the world, blurring outlines and muffling sounds.

My old bike was leaning against the house—I hadn't ridden it since Pa had let me use his truck. Pa. I knew I had to tell him about Becca. I also knew he wouldn't hear me. Wouldn't understand me. Those days were over.

What a weird thought: I used to have two parents. But Ma was taken away for a mood-adjust. She hadn't come back. And then I'd been stupid enough to leave Pa home with the rifle. Even though I knew—

By pedaling furiously, I was outside my best friend's house at 6:20, throwing pebbles up at her window. Steph finally opened her window and peered out. After one look at my white, frantic face, she blinked and whispered, "What's wrong?"

"Becca's still gone!" I said, and saw the instant fear in Steph's eyes.

"Just like Kathy," she said, putting her hand over her mouth. I nodded. Kathy Hobhouse had been in our class at school. Four months ago she had simply disappeared, and hadn't returned.

"But I still want to look for Becca—just in case."

After a moment's hesitation, Steph nodded. A few minutes later she was downstairs, dressed, and armed with her mother's car key.

"Maybe she's just…staying with a friend," Steph suggested, pushing the ignition button.

"I hope so," I said fervently. "I really, really hope she's just being a jerk and making me worry."

Steph's dinky little electric Hopper wasn't much, but it was all we had. We picked up two friends I could trust: Sarah and Ted. I wanted to race up and down the fields of wheat, sweep every road, check every house. Rebecca—ridiculous as she was—was my twin sister, and we'd *never* been separated. Shouldn't I be able to sense where she was? Shouldn't there be an invisible twin beacon that would call me to her?

"Did you go to the Provost's office?" Ted asked as we headed down the road to town.

"Not yet. They didn't help when Ma disappeared," I said bitterly.

Lines of worry creased Sarah's forehead. "But people don't

disappear," she said. "Not in our cell. I mean—even with Kathy. I'm sure there's some explanation."

"Like what?" I asked. "We've all seen the flyers around town: MISSING PERSON. They stay up for a day or two and then get taken down. But the people don't come back!"

Sarah looked unconvinced. "But this is our cell," she said. "Maybe they just…moved to a different house."

"We would know!" I pointed out, losing patience. "We know everyone! We know every house!"

"I don't," Sarah said stubbornly.

My teeth clenched at her blind loyalty, but before I could argue, Steph spoke up.

"You better…you better do things by the book," she said. "Go file a missing person report and meet us back here. We'll start in the square and work our way outward."

"Since this is Becca, we'll hit all the bad citizens first," Ted said. "No offense."

"None taken," I said, and got out.

The Hopper drove off silently as I looked up at the Management Building with dread. This was the center of our cell: where you got marriage licenses and licenses to have kids or to move, where you registered your moped or got permission to buy another cow or horse. Where you filed a missing person report with the Provost's office. Like I had done three years ago for Ma.

They hadn't helped then and I didn't think they would help now. But this was Becca. With my stomach already in a knot, I went up the white marble steps.

Inside the Provost's office was a waiting room full of uncomfortable wooden chairs. Five or six people were sitting patiently. I didn't have time to wait, and instead went up to the counter where the Provost Secretary sat. Behind her was a screen scrolling messages: **LIFE IS HAPPINESS UNITED! OUR PEOPLE ARE HEALTHIER UNITED! CRIME IS AT AN ALL-TIME LOW! WE HAVE CONQUERED DISEASE!** It was the same stuff we were taught in school. It played on screens everywhere—in the few restaurants, the drugstore, the grocery stores, the hardware and feed store.

The secretary looked at me over the top of her glasses. "Missing? Our citizens don't go missing," she said.

"My ma's never come back," I pointed out. "And Becca's not the only kid who's disappeared."

The secretary's chilly gooseberry-colored eyes narrowed. "Your ma went away for a mood-adjust," she told me, like I didn't know that. "She didn't disappear. And neither did your sister. Or the other teenagers."

"How did you know they were teenagers?" I said, gripping the edge of the counter.

Two pink spots of anger colored her face, and she sharply rapped a pile of papers against the counter. Picking up a cube of Post-it notes, she wrote "Rebecca Greenfield—missing?" on it, and stuck it on the sheaf of papers. "There. I'll give this to the Provost. Even though you're wasting his time on this." Then she banged a little bell and shouted, "Next!"

Feeling helpless, I leaned over the counter. "My sister is missing,"

I said, my voice shaking. "And we need to find her. Having kids disappear is *not good for the cell*."

The secretary looked at me coldly and banged her bell again. *"Next!"*

Near tears, I left the office. What had I expected? When I, a terrified fourteen-year-old, had reported that my ma wasn't at home, wasn't at church, wasn't anywhere, that same secretary had flipped through her files, glaring at me. Finally she'd told me that my ma had been chosen for a mood-adjust. And would be back soon.

She'd been lying then, and she was lying now.

But I wasn't fourteen anymore, and now my whole family was gone. I wasn't going to go away and shut up. Not this time.

12

"I GOTTA GO HOME," STEPH said, apologetically. "It's dinnertime."

"It's Becca," I pleaded. *"My sister. The only one I have."* My voice broke. It had been a long, hard, stupid day. Sarah and Ted had gotten more and more uncomfortable as we searched, and had finally bailed before lunch. Now it was getting dark, and even my best friend couldn't take it anymore.

"I'm sure she'll turn up," Steph said, but her eyes were worried.

"Yeah, okay," I said, letting her off the hook. Inside, I felt like a tornado: shrieking, whirling, unsure of what else I could do but desperately needing to do something. I would do anything to get my sister back—even talk to Mr. Harrison, our history teacher. *Try not to throw up when you see that jerk.*

Steph dropped me at home. The house was dark, silent. Not

even bothering to check inside, I just grabbed the moped and took off again. We'd searched everyplace I could think of . . . except one.

Our cell, B-97-4275, is the best cell I know. Actually, it's the only cell I know. When you have a cell as great as ours, you really don't need anything else. All the same, there are still some people who don't follow the rules. Like Ridiculous Rebecca. And her loser friends.

A half mile away from the town square was a sector that I'd never been to. Most people lived on farms with at least a couple of acres—our cell had over eight thousand acres, so there was plenty of room. But people in this sector worked in offices as lawyers or doctors, or at one of the mills for grain or wool, or at the Co-op, which gathered all our crops and distributed them to our United All-Ways grocery store and even other cells. These people had no land. They lived practically on top of each other. *I would hate living here,* I thought as I cruised up and down the crowded, narrow streets. You could hear everything your neighbors were saying, hear music playing or someone hammering. You could smell the food your neighbor was cooking.

I parked the moped by a lamppost and looped its chain around it to show that it hadn't been abandoned. Then I started going door-to-door, my tension building with every dead end. Finally the only places left were houses with few lights on, peeling paint, some windows that had been boarded up.

This is for Becca, I thought as I looked at the first forbidding house. Maybe she was sick inside. Maybe she'd been kidnapped, nonexistent crime or not. It took everything I had to go through the rusty gate, up a weed-choked sidewalk, and across a porch that was not an example of a good citizen porch. (Not swept, not painted, no flowers.) I knocked on the door. No one answered. I knocked again.

Finally a woman opened the door a bit and peered out at me. Cigarette smoke swirled around her lank hair.

"I'm looking for Becca Greenfield," I said. "Have you seen her?"

The woman's eyes narrowed meanly. "I ain't seen nobody but me and my husband. Get lost!" And she slammed the door on me.

My knees were rubbery when I went to the next house. There was no answer at all, though I knocked three times.

The next house was under a broken streetlight. The Provost's office was usually really strict about keeping the cell tidy and in good repair. With my heart in my throat, I crossed the porch and knocked on the door. A tall guy opened it and looked out with one eye.

"I'm looking for Becca Greenfield," I said again, no doubt pointlessly. "Do you know where she is?"

The tall guy stroked his scraggly goatee. "Becca isn't here anymore," he said. "She's gone."

13

I GAPED AT HIM. "BUT you've seen her? When? Where is she now?"

It seemed to take the guy several moments to process my words. Then he leaned back and bellowed into the house, "Hey! Where'd Becca go?"

A girl came and opened the door wider, then gave the guy a scathing look. "You idiot. This *is* Becca. Hey, Beck."

The guy squinted at me. "No, it isn't."

"I'm not Becca," I said. "I'm her sister. I'm looking for her. I have to find her! Please, can you help me?"

The girl blinked and stepped closer, looking me up and down. "Huh," she said.

"Where's Becca?" I almost shrieked.

"If you ain't her, then she ain't here," the girl said flatly.

"When was the last time you saw her?" My fingers were twitching by my sides. Finally I had a clue, but these two morons were in the way!

"Yesterday?" the guy suggested.

The girl shook her head. "Nah. She came here...not last night but the night before. Around midnight."

I almost choked. *Becca had been driving around in the middle of curfew.* And I hadn't known about it. "Then what?"

The girl shrugged. "She hung out here."

Somehow I managed not to grab her shoulders and shake her till her teeth rattled. "Then. What," I said tightly.

"She left," the girl said. "Like around two, two thirty."

"Where did she go?"

The door opened wider and another guy stood there. He had shaggy blond hair and needed a shave.

"Lookin' for Becca? I heard her say she was going to the Boundary, man," he said, shaking his head.

"*The Boundary?*" I felt like I'd been punched. "Why would she do that?"

The guy shrugged. "'Cause she's Becca."

Well, he had me there.

"So at two in the morning she headed out to the Boundary?" I asked. "Did anyone see her actually try to cross the Boundary?"

The blond guy nodded. "Taylor went with her. Like they were daring each other. Egging each other on. He was on his moped, and Becca had the truck."

My truck.

"Did Taylor come back, or is he missing, too?" My heart was beating fast and my mind was racing.

"Naw, Taylor's back," said the first guy.

"Where is he?" I demanded.

The first guy opened the door wide enough for me to go in.

"Taylor's here?" My voice was thin and screechy.

"He's downstairs," said the girl, and drifted into another room toward the back of the house.

Inside, the house was just as creepy as outside. The tall guy led me through one dark room after another. I was aware of several people sitting on broken-down furniture, either sleeping or drinking silently, or watching a Cell News show with no sound.

The tall guy opened a door and gestured down: these were cellar stairs, and they led into total blackness. And it was only then that I realized that there might not be a Taylor at all, and that maybe I'd made a really stupid mistake.

14

BECCA

OUR PRISON ROOM HAD FOUR narrow metal beds. There were five of us in here. As the newbie, I was elected to sleep on the cold concrete floor. I was already in so much pain that it didn't really make it worse.

Another fun thing: we had a tiny metal sink that dripped constantly. Around 2:00 in the morning I decided they made it drip on purpose to drive us totally batshit. And it was *working*.

There was one toilet, just a metal bowl attached to the wall. No seat, no lid. One toilet out in the open, and there were three girls and two aim-deficient guys in here. It was enough to make you want to hold it, like, *forever*.

I'd been gone a long time. Cassie must be frantic. Frantic and super pissed. If *she* were missing, I'd be flipping out. Since it was

Cassie and *I* was missing, I knew she was doubly flipping out. That's how she is. *Sorry, Cass.*

Anyway, between the concrete floor, worrying about Cassie, and my various bruises and injuries, I got almost no sleep last night.

Around 6:00 the big gate down at the end of the hall screeched open. The noise woke Robin, and she quickly leaned down to me. "I meant to tell you," she whispered, "the first thing they'll do is test you."

"On what?" I whispered back.

"Everything," she said urgently. "Do as best as you can. How well you do determines how you're treated."

The footsteps were getting closer. Maybe two guys with boots? Three?

"How you're treated, how much you get to eat, and how long you get to live," Robin hissed, then turned her back and pretended to be asleep.

Oh. So, no pressure.

Sure enough, the guards stopped in front of our rusty sliding door. One of them pointed a beefy finger at me.

"You. Get up. It's time."

I pretended not to know what he meant. "Time for breakfast?"

"Just get up."

He unlocked the door and pulled it open wide enough for me to get out. The other guard immediately spun me around and clamped handcuffs around my wrists. I saw Robin, and the other kids now, too, watching silently. Robin gave me a very, very tiny thumbs-up. I didn't react—didn't want to get her in trouble.

Then the guards were hauling me down the row to...I had no idea what.

15

THERE WAS THAT FAMILIAR PRE-HURL feeling—the sudden clammi-ness, the extra spit in my mouth, the tunnel vision.

I stopped walking. The guards clamped onto my arms and dragged me forward. I pressed my lips together and swallowed a bunch of times.

Robin had said we were on death row. Were they taking me to be executed? Was I going to die without knowing why, without saying good-bye to my sister, or even Pa? Suddenly I felt like I had wasted a lot of years.

Actually, it turned out to be worse than death: I was strong-armed into a *classroom*.

I wasn't an enthusiastic student when *not* in prison, so death row wasn't going to up the scholarly factor. Still, the guards plunked me down in a chair behind a desk and took the cuffs off me. I rubbed my wrists, feeling the zip tie cuts start to bleed again.

Everyone's favorite warden, Ms. Strepp, strode into the classroom and motioned for the guards to stand in the back. Today she was wearing an olive-green suit with pants and looked sort of military.

She gave me a good glare, then turned and wrote on the white-board at the front of the room. "Education is the most powerful weapon which you can use to change the world." - Nelson Mandela.

My eyes narrowed. I had no idea who this Nelson Mandela guy was, or what he had to do with life at home in the cell.

"You will now be tested on some core subjects," Ms. Strepp said, handing me a test booklet and a pencil. "Science, technology, engineering, and mathematics are crucial for our society today. Let's see how much you were paying attention during the years you received free schooling at the United's expense."

Robin had said that how well I did on these tests would determine how long I lived. Well, I was already dead, because none of these were my strong suit. Sure, I had passed the initial testing for my electrician's license, but basically the only good that did me was teach me how to hot-wire Cassie's truck. The truck that had been abandoned on the boundary road, and had no doubt been confiscated by now. If these tests didn't kill me, if I wasn't executed, then I knew my sister would definitely have my head on a pike when she found out I'd lost her truck.

Things were not looking up.

I met Ms. Strepp's eyes calmly. "I haven't eaten in more than a day. There's no way I can concentrate on this stuff."

Her face turned to concrete. She motioned one of the guards to come up, and my heart started pounding as I braced to get hit. "This man has a Taser," Ms. Strepp said icily. "You will start taking the test, or he will tase you. Have you ever been tased?"

I shook my head.

"It's terribly unpleasant," she said with a sneer. "I suggest you start writing..." She took out a stopwatch and clicked it. "Now!"

I opened the test book and almost started crying when I saw the first question had to do with figuring out the area of a circle. Shit. Careful Cassie had bugged me about this stuff, like, my whole life. I could just hear her voice: *I told you this was important! I told you and told you and told you! You have to know about your own cell! It's four miles across!*

Frowning, I sat up straighter and tried to get a couple of synapses to ignite. Okay, if a circle is four miles across, then its radius is two, then there's some kind of formula...

Sweat dotted my forehead. I brushed it away. No idea if I'd remembered correctly, calculated correctly, or did anything correctly. But I started thinking that if I did okay, I would get to eat. And maybe live longer—long enough to see my sister again.

The next question had to do with how much fertilizer to use on seven acres of crops, given the application rate of fifty pounds of fertilizer per one hundred square feet.

Oh, my freaking God.

My stomach rumbled. I hunched over the book and started writing.

16

"To educate a person in mind and not in morals is to educate a menace to society." - Theodore Roosevelt.

Another weird quote from someone I'd never heard of.

The morning had not gone well. In addition to having Cassie saying *I told you so* in my head, I had Ms. Strepp pacing noisily around the room, distracting me. Not to mention the huge guard with the Taser looming over me.

I was hungry, nervous, scared, and angry, none of which was adding up to the cool ability to think straight. I did the best I could on questions about mitosis and photosynthesis and weather predictions. Vague math formulas floated around my brain like moths circling a sputtering candle. There was a section on electrical engineering, which I was reasonably confident about. But as the testing went on and on, I got tireder and tireder and hungrier and hungrier until I was almost willing to be tased just to take a nice break and be unconscious for a while.

What was happening to me? I'd lived my whole life in the cell with hardly any problems—I mean, besides Ma being carted away, and then Pa—

But I had no idea what I was doing here.

Wham! I jumped as the heavy wooden stick smashed down on my desk half an inch from my hand. Ms. Strepp had approached without me hearing her. I wondered if she'd meant to break my fingers.

"You better get your act together, missy," she said in a voice like iron. "After this you'll be tested on all the other subjects they tried to drill into you."

Oh, holy hell.

The next test booklet wanted me to write five hundred words about the importance of a group work ethic and how that related to our unit's mascot of a bee. I put my head down on my arms and braced to get tased. But as I heard Ms. Strepp rapidly walking over, I suddenly exploded in rage.

Standing up, I snapped the pencil in half and swept the test booklet off the desk.

"This is all bullshit!" I yelled. "I'm on death row! Who cares about any of this school shit? Why are you doing this to me?"

Ms. Strepp held up one hand, as if to stop the guard who was advancing on me. She met my eyes and said calmly, "We're all on death row, ultimately. Are you so stupid that you don't see that?

Sure, you kids in here, as enemies of the system, will assuredly die earlier than most. As well you should. But all of us everywhere have a one-way ticket to death."

I gritted my teeth. "Then what's the point of all this?" I asked, waving my arm at the classroom.

"The point," Ms. Strepp said, "is to find out what you know. And what you don't know." She gave a nod to the guard, and before I could leap away, I felt a horrible jolt, like a million watts of electricity streaking through my body. I went rigid, unable to move, and fell over face-first, headlong onto the floor without being able to catch myself.

The electrical feeling only lasted a few seconds, but even after it stopped I lay there quivering like jelly for who knows how long. Drool seeped out of my mouth but I couldn't stop it, couldn't raise my hand, couldn't even curl up into a sad little ball.

"Take her to the ring," Ms. Strepp said, and the two guards hoisted me up.

With great effort I stumbled along between them, too fuzzy to worry about what "the ring" might be, but unwilling to be dragged like a sack of feed. I noticed we were in another prison hallway with rows of jail rooms on the side filled with kids, and high windows that let sunshine in.

Little black dots floated above me like sunspots. I blinked over and over, trying to make them go away, figuring they were just another effect of the Taser.

They didn't go away. Gradually my eyes began to focus. One of the black dots fluttered closer. It was...a dragonfly. In the cell, some of the older folks called them darning-needle flies, because of their long, thin tails.

Mesmerized, I watched the dragonfly flit in and out of the sunlight, its glassy wings looking like tiny blue fairy lights. Then there was another one, cruising next to it. And another. All in all, I counted six of them, dipping and swirling in circles high above me.

The guards paused before a pair of tall gray metal doors, and my brain started to slowly *ping* back to life.

What now?

17

CASSIE

THEY DON'T LIGHT COUNTRY ROADS. At night after lights-out the whole world is dark—dark enough to see the amazing glitter of a trillion stars overhead and the filmy gauze of the Milky Way moving slowly across the sky. Even if there's no moon—especially if there's no moon—the stars cast enough light for me to pick out the shapes of our neighbors' barns, the haystacks in Pa's fields, the shiny outline of a cow's back as it dozes.

This cellar was much darker than that.

At the bottom of the steps I hesitated, feeling for solid ground with my foot. I glanced back to see the guy close the door at the top of the steps, leaving me in blackness.

I turned to race up the steps, ready to break the door down, but then my gaze was caught by the dimmest blue light. I couldn't tell what it was or how far away it was.

Swallowing, still holding on to the stair railing, I said hesitantly, "Taylor?"

No one spoke, but I heard the scrape of a chair across a floor. I cleared my throat and said more strongly, "Taylor?"

"Yeah?"

So there was a Taylor. I didn't know whether to be more scared or relieved. Maybe he was a psychopath, and those kids upstairs just threw new people down to him every so often. Sweat broke out on my palms and my throat felt like it was closing. I couldn't help blinking, though it did no good.

"Um...where are you?"

Another sound, and then the blue glow became clearer, as if a very weak lamp had been uncovered. I simply stood still, letting my eyes get used to the dimness, keeping in mind where the stairs were and how I would get out of here if Taylor turned out to be a serial killer.

Not that there were any serial killers in our cell, of course.

At least, not that anyone had ever heard of.

"What do you want?" Taylor asked, and now I could almost see enough to pick my way across the cellar. Around me were dusty, cobwebby wooden shelves that held dusty, cobwebby glass jars of fruits and vegetables: home canning. Very slowly, trying not to knock anything over, I headed toward the blue light. Taylor turned out to be just a guy, maybe a little older than me, slumped on a couch, drinking from a bottle. The blue light was from the cracked screen of his cell phone, beside him on the couch.

When I came close enough for him to see me, his eyes flared open and he jumped up.

"Becca! Thank God! I thought you were—"

"I'm not Becca," I said. "I'm her sister, Cassie. I'm looking for her. Someone told me that you two were playing chicken out on the boundary road."

After staring at me in disbelief for a moment, Taylor's face crumpled and he sank back down. He picked up his beer bottle and drained it, then wiped his mouth on the back of his hand.

When he didn't say anything, I came closer. "Taylor. Tell me what happened."

Now he looked sullen, not meeting my eyes. "Nothing."

That was enough to push me over the edge. It was late, I was in a bad neighborhood, my sister had been missing for more than a day, and I snapped for the first time in my life. Lunging forward, I grabbed his beer bottle and slammed it against a table, breaking off the bottom. Holding the unbroken end, I leaned over a shocked Taylor and waved the jagged glass, trying to look mean.

"Listen...*dipshit*," I ground out. "My only sister is missing. People say you were with her. Now you tell me what the hell happened out on the boundary road or I'm going to carve your face up like a...like a Halloween pumpkin! You got that?"

Taylor drew away from me. I waved the broken bottle.

"We were racing," he said reluctantly. "Seeing who would go the farthest. But it was too far."

"You chickened out," I said coldly, and he looked at me with loathing.

"It was too far. I turned around and headed back on my moped. I thought Becca was right behind me. But she wasn't."

"What happened then? You just left her out there?" The thought made me feel frantic.

"No!" Taylor said. "I turned around. I was going to tell her okay, she won. But when I went back, all I saw was the truck by the side of the road. No Becca."

I wanted to scream. He'd left my sister out on the boundary road to die. I threw the broken bottle down on the couch, making him flinch. Then I stomped across the cellar and up the dark steps, and burst out the door. Outside I grabbed my moped and got the hell out of that sector. I knew what I had to do now. I had to go see Pa.

18

I HATE GOING TO HEALTHCARE United. Hate, hate, hate it. And every time I go, I remember that someday I won't have to come here anymore. Then I feel both glad and guilty.

The receptionist on duty recognized me, of course. For the first month I'd come every single day. Then every other day. After that the neighbors had faded away, and there was no more help in the fields or people bringing food by for me and Becca. Once I started having to work the farm and feed us and keep the house going, my visits dropped down to a couple times a week.

On the second floor I passed the baby nursery and couldn't help glancing in. Today there were three babies in their little plastic bassinets. Which meant that roughly nine months ago, three people had died. Balance is everything in the cell. On the side of the Management Building was a public screen that kept a running tally of how many people had died that month. So if five people had died, then the next five people on the waiting list for babies got their licenses approved. They had three months to make good on it, then they had to cede their place to the next couple in line. A few times in my life, more people had died than there were people on the baby-license waiting list. Then the Provost visited couples who had only one child so far and encouraged them to have another.

Again, balance is everything. To help with predictable population planning, there was System-Assisted Suicide. You didn't even need a license for it. You just called them up and a black van showed up at your door. They made sure your papers were in order, and then the nurse hooked you up, the preacher stood there and prayed with your family, and you died.

Of course Pa, being Pa, had chosen his own way out.

He'd been in the Lingering Wing for a while now. His room looked out over the memorial garden, not that he saw anything. I pushed open his door and was greeted as usual by the soft beep and whir of machines. Not extreme measures to keep him alive, of course—that would throw the balance all out of whack. No, just machines to feed him, monitor him, let the nurses know if anything happened. Anything like him dying, for example.

When Becca and I were little, Pa had been the strongest, handsomest man we knew. He could carry both of us on his shoulders at once, while we shrieked and clung to his hair or his ears. Ma would laugh and tell him to put us down before we fell. I was never afraid of falling. I knew Pa would catch me.

He was neither strong nor handsome now.

Behind me the door opened and one of Pa's regular nurses came in quietly.

"Hey, Sandy," I said.

"Hey, Cassie," she said softly.

I moved to the bed and took one of Pa's hands. It was warm, and the skin was softer and smoother than it had been when he was working the fields. Well, months in the Lingering Wing could do that.

I needed Sandy to leave so I could tell Pa about Becca, but I knew why she was here.

"Cassie," she began. "I need to tell you again—"

"About our options for System-Assisted Suicide," I finished for her. "Pa won't ever get better. He's dying, but slowly. He has minimal brain function. He'll never be able to work again. He'll never come home. I should let the system lovingly help him find his way to his final rest. It will be fast, painless, and is a service offered for free to our citizens."

With a look full of compassion, Sandy nodded. I knew this wasn't her idea. I knew she was required to tell Pa's relatives about Murder United.

"I'm sorry, Cassie," she said gently. "I know it's hard. But it really would be better for your father now. It's been three months since . . . the incident. His lungs are slowly filling with fluid, and his kidneys are shutting down. We don't want him to suffer anymore, do we?"

I shook my head, trying not to cry. Sandy was probably right, but I just couldn't sign the order that would take my pa away forever. Not yet.

"I'll think about it," I said, which was more than I usually agreed to. I saw surprise in Sandy's eyes, and then she squeezed my shoulder and left as quietly as she had come.

I leaned against Pa's bed and held his hand. "Hi, Pa," I said, and then my voice broke. I cleared my throat and tried again. "It's me, Cassie. You won't believe what I'm going to tell you about Becca." I took a deep breath. "She's actually at home studying. *Studying!* Becca! I asked her what she had done with the real Becca." I gave a small fake laugh and held his hand tighter. "Well, maybe she's changing, Pa. Maybe she's growing up at last. That would be good, wouldn't it? Anyway, I'm sure she'll come visit you soon. And so will I."

Leaning over, careful not to dislodge the sensors, I kissed Pa's cool forehead. "I have to go now, but you get better soon, you hear me? I need you at home. You get better immediately, if not sooner. Okay?" Then, clamping my jaws together so I wouldn't start bawling, I turned and got out of there as fast as I could.

19

IF PA WERE HIMSELF, HE'D have seen through my lies in a jackrabbit second. These days, I could get away with anything.

The moped and I were both running low on juice by the time I came up on the town square. The streetlights showed a crowd of people standing around the Management Building's steps. Maybe they were handing out extras of some kind, like milk or apples— they did sometimes. I parked the moped and glanced at my watch: 9:00. One hour till curfew.

I'm pretty tall, but I still had to peer over people's heads and edge my way into the crowd before I saw what was happening.

"When else in the history of this great union have we achieved such impressive goals? But we have, neighbors! Our cell—and every other cell—reports one hundred percent literacy!" Provost

Allen said, opening his arms wide. A spotlight made him look like he was glowing against the dark backdrop of the Management Building. The crowd cheered and clapped, all the cellfolk nodding and smiling at each other.

The Provost of our cell—whose word was literally law—stood at the top of the steps, looking down at us. He was like everyone's uncle, everyone's strong shoulder to lean on—that's what his office said. He came to company Christmas parties, grade twelve graduations, sometimes even baby namings. My pa had told me that the Provost and his family had moved here fifteen years ago, sent here by the system.

"Under my guidance, and thanks to your strength and work ethic, our cell has reached an all-time high in wheat production, feed-corn production, and milk production!" the Provost went on as people clapped more. "We are Stronger United!"

Cheers. Claps. My parents had always taken me and Becca to these rallies, and we'd always cheered and clapped as much as anyone. But today, looking at Provost Allen, knowing how little his office had helped to bring back my ma, and now to find Becca, I saw him with new eyes.

Critical eyes.

"We are two hundred and fourteen days without a serious accident!" the Provost boomed. "Our population is in almost perfect balance! We are Healthier United—our cell barely ever has a cold!"

The crowd erupted again in cheers, with some cellfolk hugging each other joyfully.

"No one is hungry! Every citizen has a vocation!"

I thought about the people I'd seen in the dark part of the sector, the people sitting around, drinking beer. What were their vocations? They hadn't even looked all that healthy. I thought about how I had wanted to be a teacher, and Becca had wanted to be an artist. Instead she was an electrician and I was a mechanic. I mean, I didn't *mind* fixing engines. It was interesting, and a critical skill in the cell. But I'd wanted to be a teacher. I'd almost forgotten that.

"But now, I hear of unrest," the Provost said, and even though I was just one face in a crowd of hundreds, I felt like he was looking right at *me*.

20

THE CROWD QUIETED, LOOKING AT one other with raised eyebrows as the Provost went on.

"I hear of Outsiders, bad citizens, who don't want to live by the cell rules!" he said. "Rules that help and protect everyone!"

Like...most of Becca's friends. I wasn't naïve; I'd seen her friends. In the dark sector I'd seen people *even worse* than her friends. Were they Outsiders? Were they actually a problem?

The cellfolk murmured to each other, and a few shook their heads.

Provost Allen lowered his voice dramatically and leaned over the microphone, his icy blue eyes scanning the crowd. "I hear stories about kids 'disappearing.'" He made air quotes when he said *disappearing*, like it wasn't real. Like it hadn't happened to my sister.

"Disappear?" he shouted suddenly. "I don't think so! Not when every last corner of our cell is a little paradise! No, these few kids didn't disappear. They've joined the Outsiders! These kids are *choosing* to lie low! To not participate in our cell!"

I glanced around his rapt audience. Several people were frowning angrily, and the murmuring increased. Then I got it: The Provost was turning the people away from anyone who disappeared. He was making it *not real*, not a problem.

My voice rose up and burst out of me before I even realized it. "That's not true!" I yelled. "My sister isn't an Outsider! She *did* disappear!"

Heads turned in surprise. Several of my neighbors looked at me in confusion. But I couldn't stop myself.

"She's not just some kid!" My voice seemed to have frozen the whole square. "You keep saying *these kids!* But her name is Becca! Rebecca Greenfield!"

Ridiculous Rebecca.

The Provost peered out into the streetlamp-lit gathering, as if he heard a mosquito buzzing and wondered where it was coming from.

"You be quiet, girl!" said an older woman, shaking her finger at me. "How dare you speak like that!"

"Don't interrupt the Provost!" a man said angrily. "Unless *you're* an Outsider!"

I took a step backward in shock. "I'm not an Outsider! I'm Cassie Greenfield!"

"Cassie," said a woman, and I turned to see Mrs. Tanner, my

grade three teacher. "This isn't like you. I know you don't mean to make trouble." Her eyes were sympathetic.

"But Becca's missing!" I told her pleadingly.

After another long look at me, she simply turned away and faced the Provost.

These were my neighbors and fellow cellfolk. And none of them were going to help me. Were they... were they all heartless jerks... or were they *scared?*

21

INSIDE, I WAS SHAKING. I'D never had people look at me like that before. I was the *good* twin. With everyone frowning at me suspiciously, I turned and headed to the moped. Becca was missing, and I had maybe just broken the law. I had to get out of here before my heart pounded through my chest. It was getting close to curfew, anyway.

When a finger tapped me on the shoulder, I spun, my hands up, ready for who knows what.

But not ready for Nathaniel.

Tall, good-looking Nathaniel Allen was the son of the Provost. We'd been in school together since kindergarten. And I'd hated him for just about that long. In kindergarten I'd seen him clobber another kid with a wooden truck. He hadn't improved since then.

"What do you want?" I snapped, getting on the moped.

"I just want to say...well, I'm sorry about Becca."

My eyes narrowed. For the last twelve years he'd tormented Becca and me, pretending to not be able to tell us apart, calling us by the wrong names. He'd been a ponytail-puller, a lunchbox-cookie-stealer, and a bully. If he weren't the Provost's son, he'd be considered a bad citizen.

"Well, *I'm* sorry you're...an *asshole*," I said, and pressed the ignition button. I had just spoken out in public, I had waved a broken bottle at someone a few hours ago, and now I was swearing. Losing my sister was turning me into someone else.

Nathaniel opened his mouth to speak, but just then the roar of motorcycles drowned everything out.

Motorcycles were even more rare than trucks. I'd never seen one in real life, though I'd heard about them—as really souped-up mopeds.

There were two of them, big and loud, with two people riding them, wearing leather jackets and helmets with dark faceplates. If the cellfolk had been shocked when I spoke out, they were about nineteen times more shocked now. The cyclists *vroomed* through the crowd, making the cellfolk draw back and press together like sheep. The Provost at his podium gestured to one of his aides, shouting an order that I couldn't hear.

Then, as the cyclists passed in front of the Provost again, they pulled out guns.

I gasped, and I'm sure I wasn't the only one. Even over the sound of the engines I heard a faint *pop! pop!* and the Provost staggered backward.

69

More than one woman screamed, and I had my hand over my mouth, stunned. Two police cars, lights and sirens blaring, screeched around the corner. The cyclists gunned their engines, the growling rumble seeming to mock the quiet electric police cars as they all raced away from the square.

In the silence, all eyes turned toward the Provost, but instead of lying on the ground in a pool of blood, he was standing upright, furiously shouting at his aides and several other cops who'd run up. Spoiling his fancy suit—no worker's overalls for him—were two bright green splotches.

He'd been shot with paintballs.

The paint had splattered up over his neck and face, and was dripping down his legs. He looked like he'd had a run-in with an angry salad.

Using every bit of self-control I had, I managed to get several blocks away. Then I had to pull over and stop just to process the image of the Provost covered in green paint. Oh, my Lord. This had been a weird day. A horrible day. And I was no closer to finding Becca than I'd been this morning.

Which reminded me. With just eight minutes left till curfew, I made a hard right on Weaver Road, and soon pulled up at a horribly familiar house. Coming here made acid rise in the back of my throat. But he was my last hope for finding Becca. He always knew where Becca was. And for all the wrong reasons.

I leaned the moped against the fence and went to ring the doorbell.

"Are you home, you jerk?" I muttered, trying to peer into the window.

There was no answer. I wanted to pound on his door, wanted to yell in frustration. But I had to accept the fact that I wouldn't be able to confront Mr. Harrison until tomorrow. Scowling just thinking about him, I went back to the moped and raced toward home.

At twelve. Freaking. Miles. An. Hour.

22

BECCA

THE GUARDS HAULED ME THROUGH the big gray metal doors. The effects of the Taser were wearing off, but static still bounced around my brain, making it hard to think. Warden von Strepp had told them to take me to "the ring."

What the hell was "the ring"? Like, a running track?

It wasn't a running track.

It was...a boxing ring. There was a raised canvas floor, and ropes making up the four sides of the ring. Technically, it should be called a boxing *square*. I plan to write an angry letter about that.

The guards pushed me forward, and cheers broke out. The bleachers were full of kids. Prisoners in bright yellow jumpsuits. Jeez. Okay, so I was here to watch some stupid fight. I started to shuffle toward the bleachers, but the guards stopped me.

"You're not a spectator, scum," one said.

"You're the main event," said the other one, and I decided my brain must still be scrambled from the Taser.

"Here! Quick!" A tall girl with dark hair shoved something at me. Instinctively my hands shot out to grab it.

"What the f—" I began, looking at it, but the girl interrupted me.

"Take off your jumpsuit and put this on!" she ordered. "Fast!"

Yes, because *ordering* works *so well* on me.

"No?" I tried, and then I recognized her. "Kathy? Kathy Hobhouse?"

"Yeah," she said shortly. "Surprise. No time to chat. Okay, it'll be worse with the jumpsuit. But whatever." She grabbed my shoulders and spun me around, dropping something heavy over my head. It was...armor. Not fancy, knight-in-shining-armor armor—more like someone had taken a couple of garbage-can lids and riveted straps to them.

"What in the name of—" I started, but again Kathy shushed me. I stood there like a dummy while she fastened a helmet onto my head.

"This will be bad," she said rapidly, hooking pieces together. "Just try to get through it. They always start with the one to break you down, so go ahead and get broken down. But the two of you will be stuck in a tiny room together afterward, so don't piss him off."

I understood each individual word, but strung together like that, they made zero sense. And I was still shocked to realize that I wasn't the only one from our cell here.

"Who else is here?" I asked her. "How long have you been here? Who took you?"

"I saw Livvie Clayhill a month ago," she said quickly. "But she's gone. Now quit talking. And keep your tongue in your mouth. I mean, literally. Last week some poor schmuck lost his tongue."

I stared at her. "Lost his—"

Kathy jammed my hands into something like a cross between boxing gloves and a robot hand. I couldn't even wiggle my fingers. Finally she gave my helmet a couple of sharp raps, and met my eyes for the first time.

"Sorry," she said, almost looking like she meant it. "Just...try to get through it. We're all going to die soon anyway. Doesn't matter if it's now or later."

She pointed to the steps. Feeling like I was swimming through a bizarre, disturbing nightmare, I climbed up them clumsily and stepped between the ropes. I stood uncertainly on the canvas, giving it a couple of experimental bounces.

The crowd roared as my opponent stepped into the ring. Clamping my jaws shut so I wouldn't scream, I stared in horror. It was a guy, and he was almost as tall as Mr. Butcher's prizewinning wonder horse. He was probably as broad, too. Maybe weighed about the same. This was who I was supposed to fight.

Time to die, I thought.

23

FIGHTING GOES AGAINST THE GROUP work ethic, so it's strongly discouraged in the cell. However, I'd had a lifetime of not taking kindly to people teasing Careful Cassie for being a lily-livered chicken. So I braced my feet and scanned my opponent for weak spots.

Um, apparently none. And that was the last semi-coherent thought I had for quite a while.

As soon as the bell dinged, the guy lunged at me. He was huge, but I'm fairly nimble, so I ducked and tried to punch him in the kidney. In an instant, he spun the other way and gave me an uppercut to my jaw that lifted me clean off the ground, then laid me flat. The ref stood over me, counting, while I blinked up at the black stars spinning over my head. I tried to breathe and couldn't. I tried to move my jaw and couldn't. I couldn't feel my face. My mouth tasted like blood, and blood filled my nose, making me feel like I was drowning.

As the crowd screamed the countdown with the ref, a white-hot surge of fury made me scramble awkwardly to my feet. I had a moment to see surprise in the guy's eyes before I roared and walloped his head as hard as I possibly could. He staggered.

"You asshole!" I screamed, and spat blood onto the canvas. "You goddamn son of a bitch! I'm going to kill you, you shit-eating asswipe!"

Bruiser hesitated, then his eyes turned to steel and he came at me. That's when I found out what the girl had meant about it being worse with the jumpsuit on. The guy had claws on his gloves, and he raked them down my arm, shredding my sleeve. The fabric got caught and he gave a sharp tug. The hateful yellow cloth ripped as he yanked again and again, pulling it off me. The seams cut into my skin, my shoulders, the tops of my legs. It felt like he was tightening tourniquets around me, scraping my skin raw. I tried to break his grip, punched at his hand and his arm and anything else I could reach, but he was determined. Soon the jumpsuit was gone and I was there in my underwear and a bunch of rough-edged armor. My skin was scraped and bleeding, my nose was trickling a mixture of snot and blood, and now that I could feel my jaw again I could tell that one of my teeth was loose.

The next mouthful of blood I spat right into his face. His eyes flared, and after that it was no holds barred—not that there had been any holds barred before. He was, as the girl had put it, breaking me down. I punched and kicked whenever I could, but he was so much taller and stronger and more of a douchebag than I was, and he kept slugging me long after he had clearly won.

An eon later I heard the bell ding, followed by the muffled roar of the crowd. I was lying facedown in a puddle of blood, feeling like every bone in my body was broken. Blearily my gaze wandered past the ropes to see Deputy Warden Strepp standing there, frowning at me, her arms crossed over her chest.

That gave me enough of a spark to struggle onto my hands and knees. A tooth had actually been knocked out, and I took a deep breath and spit it at Strepp. It barely made it to the edge of the canvas.

Her eyes narrowed. "There's something wrong here," she said.

I stared at her. "Yeah? Which part? The fact that I'm in *prison?* That all the prisoners are *kids?* This freak show of a fight with a muscle-bound moron? Like, be more specific!"

Strepp nodded briskly at the guards. "Take them to the pen," she said.

The girl had said that the guy and I would be stuck in a small room together after the fight.

So, just great.

24

MS. STREPP

HELEN STREPP KNEW WHEN TO speak and when to keep silent. You didn't get as far as she had without that skill. So Strepp waited patiently while Warden Bell finished what she was doing. After several minutes, during which the Warden didn't hurry one bit or even acknowledge Strepp's presence, she finally looked up.

"Yes, Ms. Strepp?" Those three words were enough to make a lesser person tremble, coming out of the Warden's hard slit of a mouth. She was the scariest, most imposing woman Helen had ever met. Even the Warden's thinning white hair, cropped into a crewcut, seemed to stand straight at attention. Her large, fleshy body overpowered her desk chair, her bulk spilling over the sides. Helen tried not to mentally calculate its weight load, tried not to picture the metal legs bending slowly and then snapping.

Actually, the chair probably wouldn't dare, she decided.

"There's a problem." Ms. Strepp made her face carefully expressionless, admitting neither guilt nor concern.

"Do tell," the Warden replied, lacing her thick fingers together on top of her desk. Her cold black eyes waited and watched, like a spider's.

Ms. Strepp breathed in slowly. She knew not to prevaricate, not to pretty it up, not to use words like *might* or *seemed*. Instead she spoke firmly, meeting the Warden's glittering gaze.

"We took the wrong twin."

25

THE WARDEN LOOKED AT MS. STREPP with a coldness that seemed to penetrate Ms. Strepp's very bones.

Resolve, Ms. Strepp thought. *You knew this wouldn't be easy. Nothing worthwhile ever is.*

After a moment, the Warden spoke, her voice sounding like car tires rolling over gravel. "Refresh my memory, Ms. Strepp. I know we've gathered several sets of twins for our…experiments. Of which twin do you speak?"

"Cassandra Greenfield. We have Rebecca Greenfield instead. From B-97-4275. The agricultural community. The girls must have switched vehicles that day."

The Warden drummed her fingers on her desk as she digested this information. "Well, *fudge,*" she said.

Again Ms. Strepp waited.

The Warden sighed and moved some papers from one pile to another. Birth certificates, death certificates, autopsy reports, experiment data. It all piled up.

Then, having reached a decision, she shrugged. "Execute her. Get the other one."

"That was my thought exactly, Warden," Ms. Strepp said. "Then I thought, what if I use her as an example to the others? Her testing scores are dismal, as you know. Her fighting ability is pathetic. But if I whip her into shape, if she starts to perform as expected…well, the other prisoners would see what was possible. Even with clay as unpromising as Rebecca Greenfield."

"Hm." The Warden looked at her shrewdly. "Don't get attached to this girl, Strepp. She won't be with us long. You know that."

"Of course!" Ms. Strepp looked offended at the very suggestion. "That's why we're here. That thought is foremost in my mind at all times, Warden. I see this as simply another experiment."

The Warden gave a brisk nod. "Very well then, Ms. Strepp. Carry on."

"Thank you, Warden Bell."

Ms. Strepp lost no time leaving the office wing of the prison and returning to her own domain. She was grateful that the Warden was allowing her this experiment. It was going to be very interesting indeed. Of course, first she had to whip Rebecca into shape. With real whips, if necessary.

26

BECCA

THE PEN WAS A SMALL box of a room, about four feet across and four feet deep. No bars, just solid concrete walls and a metal door with a tiny window in it. There was no furniture, no benches, no nothing. Into this pen they put me and Bruiser, together, only minutes after he beat the stuffing out of me. Too late I remembered the gist of the girl's words: "Don't piss him off—you'll be locked up with him later." Well, maybe he hadn't taken offense to me calling him an asshole and a son of a bitch and whatever else I had said. Maybe me spitting blood in his face was all water under the bridge.

One thing was for sure: in this little pen, with no armor, this guy could end me in about two seconds. And maybe that was his plan.

The door clanged behind us with chilling finality. Bruiser and

I stood there and looked at each other. My swollen, abraded hands automatically clenched into fists, not that they would help me at all.

The guy stuck out his hand and I instinctively flinched. When he didn't touch me I gave him a quick glance. He was waiting there, his hand held out. "I'm Tim," he said.

Quickly I replayed the last several minutes in my mind: (1) Forced to fight, check. (2) Got totally and completely "broken down," check. (3) Had my tooth knocked right out of my jaw by this hulking freak, check. (4) Was now locked in a pen with him, check. (5) He had just introduced himself and offered to shake hands, double check.

One of those things didn't fit.

Shaking my head, I blinked a couple of times, as if that would help snap me back into reality.

"What?" I managed, and wiped blood off my face.

The little window in the door slid open, and a yellow jumpsuit was pushed through it. Then the window shot closed again.

I was now thrilled to see the garment that I had detested so heartily just an hour ago. The crazy-house uniform. It hurt to bend down to pick it up. Leaning against the concrete wall, I shakily put one leg in, then the other. Trying to get it up over my shoulders and my arms into the sleeves was the worst pain I'd ever felt, and all I wanted to do was groan loudly, like a horse foaling. But I wouldn't give Bruiser the satisfaction.

Finally I was covered up, which was much better than not being covered up. The fabric instantly began to stick to the places that were bleeding, and I pulled and plucked at it so it wouldn't fuse to the scabs.

Bruiser leaned against the door and crossed his arms. "What's your name?" he tried.

"What do you care?" Slowly I let myself slide down the wall until I was sitting. Bruiser did the same thing, sitting with his back to the door. Like I would even think about trying to get past him.

"Did you want to fight?" he asked.

"Sure," I said wearily. "I get a kick out of it."

"Well, I didn't," he said, looking away. "I hate fighting. My vocation was to be a house-builder. That's what I wanted to do. But they took me and put me here and they make me fight."

Now I looked at him. His brown hair was about a quarter of an inch long. He had brown eyes that seemed warm now, but in the ring they had been cold and hard. With pleasure I noticed a bruise on his cheek and a scrape on his face. I had done that.

"Congrats. You're awfully good at it," I said.

"I have to be," he said. "I pay if I'm not. When I first came here, I refused to fight." He held up his left hand. Two of his fingers had odd angles to them, as if they'd been broken and not set. "They convinced me."

I didn't know what to think. Maybe he was lying. Maybe he wasn't. He could be a spy. Or he could be just a kid, like me, who was in the middle of a heinous situation through no fault of his own.

"How long have you been here?" I asked.

"Four months." He looked bitter. "I guess I've lasted so long because I'm entertainment in the ring. Most kids don't last this long."

"They really do execute people here?"

Now his eyes looked sad, almost haunted. "Yeah," he said. "All the time."

27

"BECCA!"

"Mmmph," I mumbled.

"Becca! Wake up!"

"Five more minutes, Ma," I said, squeezing my eyes shut.

"I'm not your ma," someone said, and I opened my eyes. The ceiling above me was unpainted cinder blocks. In one horrible second, it all came back to me: I was sleeping on a floor in prison. My jaw ached where I'd lost a tooth to my pal Tim. Ma hadn't woken me up for school in three years.

Right then I hated reality so much.

Blinking a couple more times, I focused on the friendly face above me. Robin. It was still dark in our prison block, and there were no sounds of movement or activity.

"Robin," I whispered. "What's up? What time is it?" It felt like only minutes since I had been escorted from the pen back to my prison room, where I had promptly passed out.

"It's two thirty," she said apologetically. "But they're going to be coming for you soon, and I thought it'd be better if you were on your feet."

"Who's coming for me?" I said, scrambling to stand up. Pain after pain assaulted my sleep-deprived brain as every bruised muscle strained to hold me upright. I swallowed moans and groans and tried to control my breathing.

"You said you'd done badly on the tests," Robin whispered, patting her bunk next to her. I shook my head; if I sat down, I'd never be able to get back up. Not without crying. "And you got beaten in the ring."

It was a kindhearted understatement, and I nodded again.

"When that happens, they put the kid through lessons and training," Robin went on. Her head turned involuntarily, as mine did, when we heard the doors at the end of our block screech open.

"More lessons, more training," Robin went on in a whisper. "Starting now." Quickly she lay down on her bunk and pretended to be asleep. Heavy footsteps marched toward me, getting louder and louder. When the guards reached my room, I was standing there, awake and clear-eyed, looking at them calmly.

They seemed startled, disappointed—no doubt they'd been looking forward to hauling me up from the floor and dragging me down the hall.

"Let's go!" one guard said roughly, and she yanked my hands behind me to put handcuffs on my wrists.

I kept my balance, walking quickly between them, and amid the almost detached awareness I had of every single cell in my body screaming in agony, I thought: *Thank you, Robin.*

28

SCHOOL, FOR ME, WAS MOSTLY about seeing my friends. If any facts and figures filtered into my awareness, well, that was just a bonus.

School *all by myself* at 2:30 in the morning was not a situation guaranteed to bring out my good side.

"Sit!" A woman—not the Strepp, but definitely of the Strepp breed—frowned at me and pointed to the rows of desks. I chose one and sat down.

"Your math scores were abysmal!" she snapped, pacing at the front of the room. "Since your English scores were also bad, I'll explain that *abysmal* means very low! As if they'd been found at the bottom of an *abyss!*"

I nodded, wondering how the hell I was going to stay awake through this.

"Now tell me," she went on, "what kind of word is *abysmal?*"

This had "trick question" written all over it. "Um, depressing?" I guessed. "Or...embarrassing?"

A vein in her neck started throbbing, and her face got red. If she had a heart attack, it would definitely perk me up for several minutes.

"No!" she shouted, and threw a marker at me. It glanced off my shoulder and fell to the floor with a clatter. "What *part of speech* is it?"

Part of speech—I'd definitely heard something like this before. Verb? No. I tried to channel Cassie, who would be trotting out this info like there was no tomorrow. Verb, adverb, present perfect, no—

"Adjective!" I said.

The teacher nodded reluctantly, then started writing on the whiteboard, stuff about nouns and pronouns, blah blah blah. A couple of minutes later she must have noticed my eyelids drooping because she suddenly yelled, "Give me thirty!"

"Thirty what?" I asked.

"Thirty push-ups, right now!" she shouted, pointing to the floor. "Drop and give me thirty. That will help you stay awake."

Well. Push-ups are actually *really, really* hard, even for a farm girl. Push-ups when every muscle was already close to its breaking point are just crazy. But she had a fervent, take-no-prisoners expression, and I got down on the chilly linoleum floor. My arms were shaking after ten. Sweat beaded on my forehead, and I gritted my teeth as I somehow got out another five.

After twenty my arms felt like noodles, and at twenty-two I paused, panting.

Thwack! I yelped and bolted up as a thin wooden cane whipped the backs of my legs.

"You're weak!" the teacher yelled in my face. "Let's see if this will help." She nodded at the guard, who kicked a board in front of me. A board covered with fine, sharp nails. Pointing up.

"Now finish those thirty, before I change my mind and ask for fifty."

Oh, my God. Slowly I lowered myself right above the board. My arms shook and the sweat on my face was as cold as pond ice. If I fell, if my arms didn't hold me, I would be a Becca-kabob in about two seconds. Shit.

Okay. Goddamnit. Goddamn this stupid freaking place to hell, I screamed inside my head as I grimly pushed back up. *I hate these freaking assholes! I hope they all burn in hell forever! I hope they all get run over by a disk tiller!*

I lowered myself carefully again and again, trying not to look at the sharp nails right below me. *These assholes would get churned right into the ground! I would* drive *the disk tiller! I'd be laughing! I'd love to see their terrified faces getting sucked beneath the tiller's churning blades! These scum-sucking goddamn sons of bitches, yellow-bellied shitwads, stupid douchebags!*

Annnnnd, that was thirty. My chest heaving, I sat back on my heels and looked at the teacher. Her eyes narrowed, and all I wanted was to shoot the bird at her.

Without a word she turned back to the whiteboard. She wrote "Active Voice" and "Passive Voice," and drew a line beneath them. Determined not to cry, I practically crawled back to my desk and took my seat.

29

THAT WAS HOW IT WENT for the rest of the night. After the English teacher with anger issues, there was a guy, then another woman, then a guy. They had clearly been recruited from some asylum for the criminally insane, and lectured at me about various types of math, more language and writing, and a couple of different sciences. When I looked the slightest bit less rabidly alert, they made me do heinous physical training.

Math, then a hundred sit-ups. I almost threw up after those. Chemistry, then jumping rope for fifteen minutes. Again, nausea inducing. More push-ups, and let's just say they did not end well. Physics, then punching a heavy bag, which was the most fun I'd had since I got here. I worked out a lot of aggression, slamming the bag again and again until my knuckles bled.

By 8:00 in the morning I was seriously fatigued and starving—but the fun really began when Ms. Strepp showed up. And by "fun" I mean a soul-crushing nightmare of pain and fear. Turned out those were all just *practice* classes, *practice* warm-ups. She had a whole program of her own, and she was eager to get started.

As soon as she wrote, "I've got a woman's ability to stick to a job and get on with it, when everyone else walks off and leaves it." - Margaret Thatcher, I knew I was in for a rough time. Who asked this Margaret Thatcher, anyway?

Finally, at dinnertime, Strepp let me go. "You're a disgrace," she said sharply. "You're one of the worst kids I've ever seen—and I've seen a lot."

It was amazing, but I managed not to scream back at her. Somehow I staggered toward the mess hall, almost delirious. A tiny buzzing sound filled my ears and I shook my head to clear it. The buzzing was still there. Blinking wearily, I looked up and saw evidence that the outside world still existed: a dragonfly. My dragonfly. It was a tiny harbinger of freedom, and I suddenly loved it fiercely—this insect who could come and go at will.

"Hope," I murmured to it. "Your name is Hope." I smiled as it flitted away.

"Becca!" It was Vijay, looking concerned. It was the first instance of empathy I'd seen all day, and it almost destroyed me. "Go sit down," he said. "I'll bring your tray."

Diego pulled out a chair for me. I sat down so hard I almost tipped over. Robin and Merry were already eating their watery bean soup and wilted vegetables, and gave me furtive, understanding smiles. Nobody said a word about the hundreds of pinpricks in the front of my jumpsuit, each one outlined by blood.

I was too tired to eat, could barely feel my hands. My four friends—and they had become my friends—took turns carefully pushing food into my mouth, funneling water into me. Amazingly, the food and water revived me, and after a while I took my own spoon and finished the meal myself.

"Thanks, guys," I managed.

Robin looked apologetic. "I wish you could go back and just sleep," she said. "But we have to read this tonight—all of us." She held up a battered paperback book. It was called *The Beautiful Struggle* by someone named Ta-Nehisi Coates.

"Oh, just kill me now," I moaned.

Merry shook her head. "If only it were that easy."

30

"LET'S GO OVER THE PLOT again." Diego's voice was barely audible—his face was buried in his arms as he stretched out on his bunk.

Robin made a fist and punched his leg.

"Ow!" he said, raising his head.

"I told you not to lie down!" she said. "You can't fall asleep now!"

"I'm paying attention!" he protested.

The rest of us—Merry, Vijay, and me—watched this play out. It was late; we were all wiped. I, in particular, was a quivering mass of sore muscles and mental exhaustion.

But Robin said this book was important. She said we'd be tested on it. In two short days, I'd learned not to doubt Robin—not ever.

"We've read this book before," she explained to me. "When we talked about it in class, Strepp exploded. She said we'd misunderstood everything, that we'd missed the whole point of it. So we're rereading it. Trying to figure it out."

I leaned back against the cool cinder-block wall. "It doesn't make sense," I said. "It's written like it really happened, and it says 'Memoir' on it. But it's like, totally made-up. A totally made-up world."

Robin nodded. "I know. That's what we said. Strepp says we're wrong."

"Where's his cell?" I demanded. "What was his vocation? Not a single person in that whole book was contributing to the United! And what kind of cell name is Bal-ti-more? It's ridiculous!"

For a second I flashed on my twin calling me Ridiculous Rebecca, and my throat closed up. Cassie. Would I ever see her again?

"Maybe it took place in the past," Vijay suggested. "Just... somewhere else."

I looked at him, seeing the intelligence in his dark-brown eyes. It hit me: All these kids were smart. Every one of them would be assigned higher schooling, or some brainy kind of vocation. Why were they here? Why were any of us *here*?

"Maybe it's a cell just for bad citizens," Merry said.

"Oh, God, who knows?" I almost wailed, and closed my eyes just for a moment.

"Uh-oh—sorry, guys," said Diego, lunging to our one open toilet.

"No, Diego, no!" we all yelled, but it was too late. There was a horrible squishing sound, like a hog rolling in mud, and then our

small space was filled with a noxious stench much worse than when Cassie and I found Mrs. Simpson's dead cow. So much worse.

I clapped my hand over my nose and mouth. Vijay desperately pressed his face to the metal bars, trying to suck in clean air from the hall. It was too late: the kids across from us were now shrieking, pulling their jumpsuits up over their heads, pressing their faces into threadbare blankets. The nuclear cloud of evil and beans rolled down the hallway, and the cries of horror grew as it traveled.

"Whew!" Diego said cheerfully, flushing for the third time. "That was intense! Sorry, guys! Wow! When you gotta go, you gotta go!"

We glared at him in mute protest, unwilling to uncover our noses and mouths to speak.

Then his face fell, and he jiggled the handle of the toilet. "Hm," he said. "Think it's clogged."

31

CASSIE

HAVING TO GO TO SCHOOL again was awful, but with Pa at Healthcare United and Becca missing, there was no one to write me an absent note. Could I write myself one?

The bell rang right as I was grabbing my social studies book out of my locker, and I almost jumped when I shut the locker door and saw Nathaniel Allen standing there.

"Jeezum! What do *you* want?" I asked, pushing past him to get to class.

He took hold of my arm, and I stared at him. "Let. Me. Go."

"I just need to talk to you," he said.

"I don't want to hear anything you have to say," I snapped, and jerked my arm away.

"You don't understand," he began, but I cut him off.

"*You* don't understand that you need to leave me alone!" I said. "You're the son of the Provost! You don't *talk* to me! You don't even *look* at me! Got it?" Leaving him standing in the hallway, I spun and hurried to my last class. I'd never spoken to anyone like that in my life, but I was walking on the edge, my emotions getting frayed like the end of a wheat stalk.

Like I said, having to go to school while Becca was still missing was awful, but you know what real torture was? Having to sit in Mr. Harrison's class. I'd tried to get Mrs. Woodrow for history, but she'd left midterm. So every day, I had to sit in a classroom while that jerk stood at the front of the room and lectured.

Now I had to talk to him on purpose, to ask about Becca. So instead of leaping up the instant the bell sounded, I lingered by my desk while the rest of the class filed out. "Mr. Harrison? Can I talk to you?"

"Of course, Cassie. What is it?"

"Becca is…missing," I said, and watched as his smarmy face turned to concern. "I was wondering if you'd heard from her."

"Why would I have heard from Becca?"

I crossed my arms. "You know why."

Mr. Harrison frowned. "Now, Cassie, that's no way to talk to a teacher," he said sternly. "You better watch your attitude—you know what happens to citizens with bad attitudes."

I froze, my eyes wide.

"They go away for a mood-adjust," he said smugly.

I actually felt the blood draining from my face. "Don't you talk about my ma," I said in a low, shaking voice. Something inside me came undone and I went on, not sounding like myself at all. "You're not the only one who can make threats. Remember when you pushed me into the supply closet? Remember shoving your tongue down my throat?"

Mr. Harrison got red, his eyes narrowing.

"I'm sure you do, because I bit the heck out of it," I went on. "But Becca wasn't so lucky, was she? No, you actually got her alone that time. And you forced yourself on her! You're just a rapist! Not any kind of teacher."

"You listen here," Mr. Harrison began, striding toward me angrily. "That girl had it coming to her! Just like you!" He was reaching out to grab me when pure, adrenaline-laced fear shot me into autopilot. As if from a distance I saw myself take a step back to grab my backpack from my desk. This new, braver Cassie took another step back and swung the bag as hard as I could. It connected, snapping Mr. Harrison's head sideways. Arms flailing, eyes rolling up into his head, he staggered backward and fell over several desks, where he lay, out cold.

Panting, I stared at him in horror. What had I done? Had I killed a teacher?

The classroom door burst open, and who should come in but Nathaniel. He took in my pale face, my white-knuckle grip on my backpack, and then Mr. Harrison lying like a lox on the floor.

He was standing by Mr. Harrison when two more teachers rushed in.

"What in the world happened?" Ms. Jenkins gasped.

"We heard a crash," said Mr. Moore. "Oh, my goodness, is that Harrison?"

They looked back and forth between me and Nathaniel, and I waited for him to turn me in, like the bullying jerk he was.

"Mr. Harrison fell," Nathaniel said. "I saw him. I think he fainted. Maybe he had a heart attack."

My eyes widened as Ms. Jenkins and Mr. Moore ran off to call a cell ambulance.

"Why did you do that?" I asked. "You know I clobbered him."

"I doubt he'll admit that to anyone," Nathaniel said. "But I really do need to talk to you."

We heard the sounds of running feet, and a far-off siren.

"Let's get out of here," he said, and for once I listened to him.

32

"LOOK," NATHANIEL SAID AS WE walked quickly to the school parking lot. "I need to show you something. I promise if you come see it, I'll never bother you again. After you see this, if you tell me to never talk to you again, I won't."

I stopped by my moped. "See what?"

"I can't talk about it here," he said quietly. "But please, it's important."

"Why should I trust you?" I asked, thinking of the hundreds of times he'd been a jerk to me or Becca.

He paused for a moment, and finally said, "Well, I can't think of any reason you should."

Oddly, that made me trust him—a tiny bit.

"Okay, I'll go see this whatever," I said. "But if this is a double cross, I will hunt you down like a rabid raccoon and put you out of my misery."

"Got it," he said, and we both started our mopeds and headed away from school.

Like I said, our cell is four miles across, pretty much a big circle. There's the town part and a factory part, but those are pretty small compared to all the rest, which is farmland. Nathaniel led me to an outer road that I'd only been on once or twice, with Pa.

"Where are we going?" I called to Nathaniel, but he didn't answer.

No one lived out here—these were the far reaches of other people's farms. We passed acre after acre of fenced pasture, saw herd after herd of soft-eyed dairy cows, and still we kept on, heading toward the edge of the cell.

Cassie, you're being stupid—again, I told myself. *You know you can't trust him! Why are you so willing to follow him out to the edge of nowhere? Maybe this is what he did with Becca.* Maybe he'd found her out on the boundary road, after she played chicken with Taylor. Maybe he was the reason she'd disappeared.

Maybe it was my turn to disappear.

Crap. I almost stopped and turned around. If I got a bit of a head start, he might not be able to catch me—his moped was brand-new and shiny, but I'd tinkered with the engine on mine, and could probably squeeze a bit more power out of it.

Nathaniel seemed to sense my hesitation; he looked at me then, caught my eye, and pointed off to the distance. Barely visible, surrounded by wheat fields, stood a building. A farmhouse. Suddenly

Nathaniel took a sharp right. It looked like he was plunging right into the wheat, but as I clumsily turned and followed him I saw we were on a narrow dirt track.

It would be easy to dump a body here, I thought. *There wouldn't be anyone around to notice a cloud of buzzards circling overhead.* Drying heads of wheat stalks whipped against me, and I kept my face down. I couldn't turn around here—the track was so narrow that the only way out was forward with Nathaniel, or backward. My mouth went dry as I accepted the fact that I'd made a huge mistake.

Then suddenly we were out of the wheat field and right in front of the house. It hadn't been lived in for a long time—windows were broken, the porch was rotten, and there wasn't even a bit of paint on the worn weatherboards.

Nathaniel stopped his moped and kicked the stand in place. I stopped, but kept my engine running.

He came over and took hold of my handlebars. Keeping his eyes on me, he reached forward and pressed the ignition button off. The slight vibration ceased, and then the world seemed silent, empty of people, and there was no one except me and the Provost's son.

"Get off the moped, Cassie," he said softly. "We're going in back, to the barn."

33

IF I QUICKLY STARTED AND gunned the engine, I could putt-putt back toward the wheat field and pray that I could find the track that already seemed to be gone. If I jumped off the moped and ran, I would no doubt get lost in the wheat, and Nathaniel would just follow me and drag me back. Either way, I was totally out of luck. I'd been stupid to follow him out here.

I got off the moped. Nathaniel took my arm lightly, as if to tell me not to even think about running. My brain was spinning, trying to come up with a plan for escape. Maybe in the barn there would be old farm tools, like a scythe or something.

The only sound out here was the wind. I heard no birds, no insects, no rodents scurrying. Soon there would be no sound of Cassie. My throat was tight. One week ago my life was the new normal: no Ma or Pa, but me and Becca and regular everything else. So far today I had decked a teacher and was now with the Provost's son, wondering if I would have to kill him to escape.

He kept hold of me as he pulled one of the big barn doors open. It ground on rusty hinges, revealing the dark inside an inch at a time.

When it was wide enough for us to slip through, Nathaniel pushed me gently forward. I blinked, unable to see anything after the bright afternoon. Behind me, Nathaniel pulled the door shut with a groaning crunch. I tried to swallow and couldn't, blinking wildly in the faint light let in by cracks in the boards.

On the count of three, I was going to whirl, stomp on his instep, and then throw myself at the door, I decided. *One, two—*

"Hey, Cassie," said a girl's voice. "Long time no see."

"Wh—who is that?" I said.

A shadow moved toward me, and then another. And another. The nearer they got, the clearer their features became, and my mouth opened in surprise as I saw Rachel Detweiler, Russ Mickelson, and Tony Hanson. Kids from school.

Nathaniel let go of me and went to stand next to them.

"What is this?" I demanded. "Why am I out here?" I backed up, heading for the door, and glanced around to see if anyone else was coming at me. My eyes fell on a couple of rifles sitting on an old bale of hay. I tensed, but then realized that they had green paint splattered around the ends of their barrels. They were paint guns. The paint guns used to shoot the Provost the other night.

Nathaniel held his arms open wide. "Welcome to the Outsiders," he said.

34

"WHA—?" I MANAGED.

"We're some of the Outsiders," Rachel said.

"Some of the kids that disappeared were Outsiders," Nathaniel said. "We didn't take them—we don't know who did. Maybe my father. Maybe the police. Believe me, we want to find out just as much as you do."

"But . . . what do you do, as Outsiders?" I asked, sitting abruptly on a hay bale before my legs gave out.

"Mostly we try to learn what we're not being taught." That was a voice I didn't recognize. A girl with straight black hair, shaved off on one side of her head, stepped out of the shadows.

"Who are you?" I asked.

"Tara Nightwing," she said. "And guess what—I'm not from your cell."

I'd never met anyone who wasn't from our cell. Not in seventeen years. "Uh…where are you from?" I asked.

"B-97-4270," she said. "It isn't that far from here. It's a manufacturing cell. We made your moped, and most of the tractors here. Kitchen appliances."

Obviously I knew that people went to the store and bought new ovens or whatever, but I'd never wondered where the ovens *came from*.

"I know," Tara said, nodding at my expression. "I never wondered where our bread came from."

"I never wondered where our cars *or* our bread came from," said another voice.

Now that my eyes had adjusted, I saw at least a dozen kids standing among the rusting equipment and old piles of bales. I recognized six of them from school. But the others I'd never, ever seen. I'd remember someone with such dark skin, or such different-looking eyes.

One by one they stepped forward and introduced themselves. Two of them came from the same cell as Tara. One came from B-97-4274, practically next door. One from B-65-1001. And one girl, tall and skinny with a mostly shaved head except for a tightly curled broad stripe of hair that ran from her forehead to the nape of her neck—she came from Cell F-14-27.

I'm supposed to be so smart—not smart enough for higher schooling, I guess, but I usually get the best grades in my classes. But it had never occurred to me that B-97-4275 wasn't just a name. It was a designation.

"The United is divided up into six big sections, from A to F," a guy named Jefferson explained. "Each section is divided up into a hundred smaller sections. Those smaller sections are divided up into anywhere from sixty to five thousand cells."

All I could do was stare as connections started to click in my brain. How could I not have even thought about this? How had I never wondered? Everyone thought—we were all taught—that the cell was everything. We were cells united. But all I knew about was mine.

"How come you shot paintballs at the Provost?"

"We're slowly educating people," Tara said. "Showing them that the cell way isn't the only way. That they can dissent. They can rebel against the Provost. Like by shooting paintballs at him, for starters."

"What good is it for them to be bad citizens?" My whole worldview was shifting, and I felt like I was going to fall off the face of the earth.

"Bad citizens aren't always bad," a girl named Cecily said. "Sometimes they are—if they steal or hurt a neighbor—but sometimes the United calls someone a bad citizen just because they want to know more than the United wants them to know, because they won't blindly accept everything that they're told."

Like I'd always done.

All this was fascinating and overwhelming, but really, the only thing I wanted was my sister back, safe and sound.

"But why am I here? What does any of this have to do with Becca?" I asked Nathaniel.

He looked surprised. "Because Becca was an Outsider, of course."

35

BECCA

IT FELT LIKE I HAD just closed my eyes to sleep when I was awoken again by the all-too-familiar clumping of heavy guard boots coming this way. Swearing bitterly helped me to not start weeping in despair, so I pulled myself to a sitting position and started screaming inside my head.

These 2:00 a.m. classes/torture were killing me, probably literally. My chest and stomach were a pincushion of painful dots, relics of my last failure to execute a successful push-up.

Gritting my teeth, I got to my feet. I hadn't given up yet. I wouldn't give in. When they came to get me, I'd be ready.

Sure enough, the guards stopped in front of our bars. My fists clenched as I prepared to have my wrists cuffed.

"Robin Wellfleet!"

I'd already taken a step forward, and stopped in confusion.

The mean-faced guard bellowed the name again: "Robin Wellfleet!"

My roommates woke up quickly and completely, as prisoners do. Robin was already standing, blinking in the dim fluorescent light.

"Here," she said.

"Time to go!" one guard said roughly, and rapped his billy club against our rusty bars. Robin stepped forward and was immediately grabbed, her hands twisted behind her back.

"What's going on?" I demanded. "Why are you taking her?"

Ignoring me, the guards yanked Robin out into the hall just as the prison-wide comm system crackled into ear-shredding life.

"Prisoners! Report to the ring!" Strepp boomed.

"Oh, shit," Vijay breathed, his brown eyes full of dread.

"What?" I asked. "What's going on?"

The guards dragged Robin down the hallway, her bare feet scraping the cold concrete floor. She looked back at me again and mouthed, *Be strong.*

"Prisoners!" the comm system blared again. "Report to the ring!"

"Oh, my God," I said, as I followed Diego and Merry out into the hallway. "Is this another fight? Jesus! They're going to make us watch a *fight* in the middle of the freaking night? What is *wrong* with them?"

They didn't answer me, just followed the stream of prisoners who were being released one room at a time.

Vijay bumped my shoulder. I was startled to see tears forming in his eyes. "It's not a fight," he said, his voice breaking. "It's an execution."

36

THE OTHER PRISONERS LOOKED SLEEPY and disgruntled as we streamed down the hallway and into the clammy stairwell. Myself, I was almost hysterical, grabbing my roommates' arms, chattering questions, praying for someone to tell me that it was just a fight after all.

"What do you mean, execution?" I asked Diego. "They wouldn't—they took Robin for something else, right? This doesn't have anything to do with her, right?"

Diego met my eyes for a second and shook his head. "You know we're all on death row," he said.

"Okay, but not *Robin*, right?" I pleaded. "Not *Robin?*" In the short time I'd been in the crazy house, Robin had saved my life over and over—telling me what to expect, how to survive. There were kids at home I'd known my whole life, but in just a couple days Robin had become a real friend—and everything I needed to survive.

I couldn't be about to watch her die. I just couldn't.

In front of me, Merry was openly crying. Kids were whispering about another kid—a boy named Tomás. Inside I was frozen, every bit of life draining away. What would I do without Robin? For years I hadn't needed anyone. I'd made do without my ma. I'd made do without my pa. I'd always had Careful Cassie, but tried not to depend on her: who knew how long she would be around?

But in here, in this hellish nightmare, I'd let my guard down. I'd desperately needed help. I'd needed a friend. Robin had stepped up. She'd risked her own safety to help me.

She couldn't die. Not now.

Numbly I followed the others into the big auditorium where Tim had beaten me to a pulp. The raised ring was still there, but this time there were two gurneys parked on the canvas surface, and two monitoring machines, like the kind they had Pa hooked up to at Healthcare United.

Strepp was standing in the ring, wearing—get this—a white medical coat. Like she was a doctor. Didn't doctors promise to do no harm?

Our prison block sat in one section of wooden bleachers. I felt like I was going to be sick. I clung so tightly to Vijay's hand that he pulled it away and shook his fingers to get the feeling back. But the four of us—Diego, Vijay, Merry, and me—Robin's roommates and friends, sat together, pale-faced and with tears streaming down our cheeks.

Guards pulled Robin up into the ring. On the other side, two guards pushed a boy toward the gurney. He was small, young, and clearly terrified. Robin's dark skin was ashen. I saw her scanning the bleachers, looking for our section. I jumped up and yelled, "We're here!" only to have Diego and Merry grab my jumpsuit and slam me back onto the bleachers.

"Shut up!" Diego hissed. "Do you want to get us all tased?"

Guards were patrolling the aisles, Tasers out. I'd been so freaked I hadn't noticed them. Now I huddled down between my friends, my fist pressed to my lips so I wouldn't get them in trouble, too.

In the ring, Strepp's nurse minions fastened Robin and the boy onto their gurneys, locking their ankles and wrists into thick leather straps. The lit billboards on either side of the auditorium flashed: **ROBIN WELLFLEET. TOMÁS RIVERA. ENEMIES OF THE SYSTEM.**

I wanted to scream that they weren't enemies! That it was the system that was the enemy! Instead I bit my knuckles so hard that I broke the skin.

My breath stuck in my throat as an assistant pushed a needle into a vein in Robin's arm. They attached monitors to her chest, and the small screen showed my friend's scared, rapid heartbeats racing from one side to the other.

"This can't be happening," I whispered, and Merry clenched my hand tightly. She, Diego, and Vijay had all known Robin longer than I had. This was hurting them, too.

Tomás was hooked up as well, his heartbeats flying across his monitor.

This had to be a bad dream. I couldn't be sitting here in some secret prison, about to watch my best friend die right in front of me.

Strepp dropped her hand, as if starting a car race. Many prisoners around us were stone-faced, silent, or even bored-looking. I saw one girl chewing her thumb, another playing with her hair, not watching the scene at all. They were coping. I didn't judge them.

The assistant pushed a button on the IV machine. It took only two breaths before Robin's eyes closed. Almost immediately the green blips of heartbeats slowed and lengthened. Merry's nails dug into the back of my hand. I grabbed Diego's jumpsuit so hard the fabric almost ripped.

It took less than twenty seconds. In just moments the green blips had flattened into a straight line, repeating over and over. Robin's chest quit rising and falling. Her lips went slack.

Robin was dead.

37

PAIN IS HAVING YOUR MA disappear for a mood-adjust and never come back. Pain is your pa propping his rifle up between stacks of farmers' almanacs and pulling a string tied to the trigger.

Watching your good friend be murdered right in front of you is worse.

Robin, who had whispered instructions that helped me survive; Robin, who had been the first friendly face I'd seen in this insane freak show; Robin, who was strong and brave and loyal and beautiful—was actually *dead*. Really and truly dead. I had seen it.

"Prisoners! Report to the chapel!"

I winced as the crackling, fuzzy words assaulted my ears. Kids around me stood up and shuffled into the aisles. Diego took my arm and pulled me to my feet.

"Report what to the huh?" I whispered through my tears.

"The chapel," Vijay whispered back. "Sometimes we go to the chapel after an execution."

This was the most outrageous thing of all. The guards marched us across a barren expanse of hard-packed gray dirt, and then suddenly an incredibly beautiful church rose out of the bleakness like a peony blooming in a salted field.

I was still crying, but once inside the church a hush fell over all of us. I blinked in amazement—our plain, serviceable little church at home was nothing like this. This was...grandeur, a ridiculous flight of fancy, with stone carved into elaborate arches overhead, large stained-glass windows, and behind the white marble altar, a rose window so ornate and stunningly beautiful that my mouth went dry.

"What is this?" I managed to whisper to Diego. "Where did this come from?"

He shrugged slightly—he didn't know.

Line after line of prisoners filled the polished wooden pews, our dusty feet almost silent on the deep-red carpet. I saw Kathy again. She met my eyes for a second, then looked away. I remembered that she said she'd seen Livvie Clayhill, but that she was gone now. Did that mean Livvie was dead? Who else from our cell had ended up here? Every kid that had disappeared? Only a couple of them?

The air was still and faintly scented with something spicy. My sobs slowed to hiccups as I looked around, taking in every miraculous detail.

Then Strepp stood in front of the altar and began to speak.

"'No one wants to die,'" she said. "'Even people who want to go to heaven don't want to die to get there. And yet death is the destination we all share. No one has ever escaped it. And that is as it should be, because death is very likely the single best invention of life. It is life's change agent. It clears out the old to make way for the new.'"

She paused, letting the words sink in. "A man named Steve Jobs said that. And he was right." Her eyes raked the rows of prisoners, teenagers in grubby yellow jumpsuits, some spattered with blood.

I was numb, trying to process that Robin was actually gone. Gone forever.

"Death is necessary. Death is the means of change that is necessary for every society to achieve its full potential." Strepp paced back and forth, her heels sounding like crickets on a summer night.

"There is good and there is evil in the world," she went on. "Evil will always try to suppress good. 'When good people in any country cease their vigilance and struggle, then evil men prevail.' A woman named Pearl S. Buck said that, and she was right, too. What choices have *you* made against evil?" She stopped suddenly and stared right into the crowd. "I'll tell you! None! You have made *no* choice against evil! You have supported evil, you have facilitated evil, and you have excused evil, every day of your lives!"

My eyes widened at this crazy diatribe, but no one else seemed surprised. No doubt they'd heard it all before. The Strepp went on like this, sprinkling in quotes to support her whole good versus evil schtick. I mean, *good* versus *evil*. Had she looked in a mirror lately? Irony much?

Despite my being wracked with grief and horror, something about this place still felt soothing. The stained-glass windows were so beautiful, showing different scenes of people I didn't recognize.

There was a tiny detail in one corner of a window, barely noticeable; basically a couple of dots at the border of a much larger scene. I blinked as I realized it was...a dragonfly. A green-and-blue dragonfly with crystal-clear wings, made of glass who knew how long ago.

Something caught fire inside me. The shock of Robin's death, the brutality of being here, the absurd but life-threatening tests I'd been put through—my senses exploded.

I am a dragonfly, I thought. *I can be a dragonfly.*

With no more coherent thought than that, I stood up and shouted, "This is bullshit! You're a *murderer! You're* evil! This place is evil! *Murderer!*"

38

THE GUARDS DIDN'T WAIT FOR orders. In moments they had seized me, dragged me out of the pew, and shot me with their Tasers. My body jerked and twitched as the electrical current shorted my brain out.

It took a long time for me to join the pieces of myself back together, but right at the moment that I understood I was drooling onto the deep-red carpet, a guard pulled back a heavy booted foot and kicked me so hard in the stomach that I gagged and retched. A terrible, seizing agony gripped me; surely my insides had exploded. A coldness swept over me, and then my system just shut down.

When I came to, I was on a stretcher. I heard someone murmur, "The blood," and my consciousness slowly swam above the pain to realize that my legs were covered in a sticky warmth.

The lights overhead were bright. I was in one of the hallways with the high windows. I had to throw up and tried to lean over the edge of the stretcher, but didn't make it.

Well, this day couldn't possibly get worse, I thought hazily, and tried hard to pass out again—anything to escape this burning, searing pain in my gut. A weird, animal-like moaning reached my ears, and it was a while before I realized it was me.

Blinking, I saw my dragonfly flitting above me. "Hope," I mumbled.

"It's too late for that, I'm afraid," said Ms. Strepp, and my heart sank. She leaned over and motioned to the guards to set the stretcher on a gurney.

"Get her an IV!" she yelled. Turning back to me, she said, "I think you're having a miscarriage. When were you going to tell me you were pregnant?"

Gasping, I opened my eyes wider. "What?"

"Were you planning to have a baby without a new-birth license? Is that how you were going to rebel against your community?" Her face looked cold, and her jaw twitched with anger.

"No!" I moaned, closing my eyes. "I didn't know...I'd hoped not...it was a teacher. A teacher forced himself on me. I didn't want this!"

My mind was reeling, unable to deal with everything— anything. I'd tried to be strong for so long. But this...on top of Robin...now...now I broke down. I couldn't even pretend to be brave. Not anymore. My raw, ugly, heavy sobs broke free and filled the room. Crying felt like dropping bricks onto my shattered insides, but I couldn't control it. This was the worst pain I'd ever felt in my entire life, so total and complete that I couldn't imagine a time that I wouldn't feel it. Pain was my whole world, and I was living in it.

"I want my ma!" I sobbed. "Why is this happening? Why are you doing this? Robin—I watched her. You killed her! And now you're telling me..." I ended with a screech of agony, both physical and emotional. I was broken inside. My body was broken, bleeding, rejecting the life I'd refused to admit was growing there. My brain was seared, severed, any ability to think destroyed. *Maybe I belong here in the crazy house,* I thought hysterically.

I lay there and howled, uncaring of anything, praying that I would die, that they wouldn't be able to stop the bleeding, that this wretched, ridiculous wreck of a life would finally be over and I would be at peace. A nurse came and started a drip in my arm and the pain eased slightly. Still I sobbed, getting out every last bit of misery, terror, and shame. And right before I drifted off into blessed unconsciousness, my gaze fell on the hateful face of Ms. Strepp. She looked...her eyes looked...her mouth...she looked sympathetic. Caring.

No. That couldn't be right.

And then I was out.

39

CASSIE

I'D HAD THE REST OF the day to absorb the fact that my sister had been an Outsider and I hadn't known about it. All the times I'd thought she was out somewhere, hanging out with bad citizen friends, she'd actually been with Nathaniel and the others, coming up with plans to turn the cell upside down.

Why hadn't she told me?

I pressed my lips together and unpacked my ma's field glasses from my shoulder bag. She hadn't told me because I would have been horrified, I admitted to myself. I would have fussed at her, warned her, been scared for her—for us. I would have thought she was making bad, stupid decisions.

My chest hurt, thinking about all this. I'd been a bad sister. I hadn't meant to be. But I'd been so caught up with being good for the cell that I hadn't even noticed I'd let Becca down.

Now it was almost dark, and I was out by the boundary gate.

"You shouldn't be here." Nathaniel Allen crossed his arms over his chest, long legs supporting the moped he sat on.

"Look who's talking," I retorted, and raised my ma's field glasses to peer into the distance.

"You're too close to the Boundary," he pointed out unnecessarily.

"Oh, really? Is that what all the barbed wire is about?" I scanned the horizon, peering as far down the boundary road as I could. I'd been good for so long. All my life. Even extra good, like I had to make up for my ma and my pa. But being good wouldn't help me find Becca. If I wanted to find my sister, I was going to have to start breaking rules.

I lowered the glasses with a sigh. All I could see from here was bare dirt, rocks, and tire treads.

"And you're loaded for bear," Nathaniel observed, gesturing to my pa's hunting rifle. "What are you even looking for?"

I knew now that he wasn't my enemy. He was just extremely closely related to my enemy. But that wasn't his fault.

"A guy named Taylor told me that he and Becca had been playing chicken out on the boundary road, the night she disappeared," I told him. Nathaniel looked convincingly shocked. "In my truck, I might add. So I've been searching along the boundary, hoping to at least find my truck—and maybe some clues about what happened to Becca."

"Jeez," Nathaniel said. "I had no idea she was doing stuff like that."

I frowned at him. "Why would *you* have any idea of *anything* she was doing?"

He gave me a too-patient look that I'd seen him use on teachers. It made me want to sock him in the jaw. "Becca was an Outsider. We told you."

My eyes narrowed. "Yeah, you told me, but hang on: she hated you. And you were an asshole to her at school. I saw you."

Nathaniel grinned, and I blinked at how different it made him look. "That was so fun," he said. "We had to keep our cover up. It was hard to be such a prick without falling over laughing."

I digested this information. "I bet. Anyway, what—"

"Oops, one sec," he said, and held up a finger. A small radio was duct-taped to his moped, and now he fiddled with its dial until he got a clear signal. "Time for the daily rant."

It was 6:00, when the main edition of Cell News aired.

"There has been more bad citizen activity from the Outsiders," our newscaster announced. "Provost Allen is here with encouraging words. Provost?"

"What is happening to our community?" the Provost asked. "What are we?"

Voices in the background cried, "Stronger United!"

The Provost went on, "Exactly! Our cell works, and is the best cell ever, because we are united. We are one. We support each other. So what is happening with these so-called Outsiders? Their very name means they're *outside* of being united! They are not of us! They are *choosing* to not participate in our cell! Do we have the time for that? Do we have the space for that? Do we have the *resources* for that?"

The voices in the background cried, "No!"

"If you're not with us," said the Provost, "then you're against us!"
The crowd in the news station booed.

"My friends, we must hunt them down," said the Provost. "We must discover who these Outsiders are, and we must put them outside of our cell—our happy, united cell."

"Yes!" cried the people.

"Oh, my God!" I said, and ripped the little radio off his moped. "I can't listen to this!" With the right arm that won our middle-school baseball championship, I heaved the radio as far out into the boundary as I could.

"Hey!" Nathaniel said. "That was my radio!"

I raised my pa's rifle to my shoulder and took aim. *Bam!* "Now it's dust," I said, and lowered the gun.

In twelve years I'd never seen obnoxious Nathaniel Allen at a loss for words, but I was seeing it now. It was the best feeling I'd had in a long, long time.

40

MS. STREPP

"THIS IS THE PLACE." HELEN STREPP nodded curtly at her driver, who pulled over to one side of Weaver Road. Out of habit Ms. Strepp glanced up and down the street. Though Harrison lived in town, not on a farm, the houses were far enough apart here that there shouldn't be any trouble.

"Drive around the block and meet me in back," Ms. Strepp instructed, and the guard nodded, just once. With no hesitation Ms. Strepp got out of the car and headed up to the porch. She rang the doorbell as the black car turned the corner, out of sight.

A curtain over a window twitched, and then the front door was unlocked. Christopher Harrison stood there, his sandy hair backlit by the living room lamp. For a second he wore a bland, questioning smile, and then his eyes flared in alarm.

"You!" he blurted, already stepping backward to slam the door in her face. But Ms. Strepp was ready for that and blocked it with her foot. She shoved it open as Harrison backed awkwardly into the room.

When she pulled out the gun, he became belligerent. "Wait a second," he began angrily, holding his hands up. "There's been some misun—"

The silenced pistol shot made a faint whistling sound, almost simultaneous with the sound of Christopher Harrison hitting the floor as hard and heavy as a sack of feed. His eyes blinked up at her as the red stain on his shirt spread rapidly.

"I don't think there's been any misunderstanding, you bastard," Ms. Strepp said. "That was for Becca. And for me. And no doubt for other girls as well. Love the black eye, by the way."

She allowed herself to watch as the life faded from his eyes. One less asshole in the world. About a million more to go.

Ms. Strepp walked through the house to the back door. She crossed the yard to the alley, where the black car was waiting. She slid inside, oddly breathless. Then the car glided away, taking her back home.

41

CASSIE

OUR USUAL ALARM IS FOR tornadoes. Every once in a long while, for flash flooding. Sometimes I heard fire trucks—almost everything on a farm is flammable. Do not throw flour on a grease fire.

On my way to school the next day, I heard a different siren, a different alarm. I was early anyway, so I turned off the east road and headed toward it.

And I wasn't the only one. The nearer I got to the wailing sound, the more people I met heading the same way.

"What's going on?" I called to Mr. Henry, who lived north of me.

He spit tobacco juice into a bottle. "Don't know!" he said. "Gonna go find out!"

The feeling of dread started when I realized we were approaching where Mr. Harrison lived. A crowd had already gathered in front of his house. There was an EMS truck, a fire truck, and two police cars. Uniformed officers were already stringing up yellow crime scene tape along his fence.

"What happened?" I gasped, as two EMS techs walked out of Mr. Harrison's house carrying a stretcher. Someone was on the stretcher, covered by a white sheet.

"It's Christopher Harrison," an older woman told me, her hand to her cheek. "He's dead, they say."

Icy alarm swept me from head to foot. I had hit him really hard—was it just *yesterday?* Maybe he had gone home and had an embolism or something. Maybe his brain had bled out. Oh, my God—was I a *murderer?*

"Relax, it wasn't you." Nathaniel's quiet voice almost made me tip my moped over.

My head whipped around. "Quit sneaking up on me!"

His light-brown eyebrows raised. "I apologize for sneaking up on you in a big crowd of people outside in broad daylight with a lot of drama happening."

"Well, you snuck up on me yesterday!" I was upset and slightly freaking, and Nathaniel Allen was the last thing I needed. He made me feel off-balance, unsettled.

"Yesterday, when you shot my radio to smithereens?" he asked mildly. "Would that be when I drove up to you in the middle of nowhere where you could see and probably hear me coming from half a mile away? Was that the time?"

I pressed my lips together before I gave him more ammo.

When I flashed an irritated look at him, he smirked and patted the brand-new radio he had *chained* to his moped. I wouldn't be grabbing that one any time soon.

I exhaled and tried to get a grip on my emotions. "Do you know what happened?"

"Well, he's dead," Nathaniel said, making my heart sink.

"Do you . . . do you know how he died?" I asked in a small voice.

"He was shot!" A woman had overheard me. "Someone shot him!"

My jaw dropped.

"Do they have any idea who?" Nathaniel asked, casually.

"Outsiders, no doubt," said an older man, looking disgusted.

Sure enough, at that moment a large car pulled up, its rare, non-electric engine sounding weirdly loud. A young woman in a suit jumped out and opened the rear door, and Provost Allen got out. The woman handed him a megaphone.

"Neighbors!" The Provost's voice made me wince. "Cellfolk! This tragedy is upsetting for all of us! And once again, it shows our increasing need and determination to rout these Outsiders!"

The crowd yelled their agreement; several people raised fists in the air.

"He's saying that Outsiders did this?" I whispered to Nathaniel.

Nathaniel kept his public, "outraged" face on, but spoke out of the side of his mouth. "Yep. We didn't, of course."

"The same Outsiders who have been taking our children!" the Provost went on. "But fear not, citizens!" He lowered his voice and leaned forward as if about to tell a secret. "We have discovered who these Outsiders are!"

130

People around me roared their approval. Nathaniel punched his fist in the air and yelled, "Yes!"

I stared at him. What a hypocrite!

"Start yelling your agreement," he said in a low voice only I could hear.

"No! I—"

"Cassie. Start yelling your agreement."

Everything in me protested even *looking* like I agreed with the Provost and his thugs. Becca was still missing, for God's sake! And my folks—

"Do. It. Now." His voice was quite definite, and his elbow pressed into my ribs.

He'd survived as the leader of the Outsiders for a long time, all while looking like the best son the Provost could hope for.

"Arrests are imminent!" the Provost cried.

With bile rising in my throat, I punched my fist in the air. "Yes!"

PART TWO

42

BECCA

DEFIANCE AND A LACK OF regard for rules has always been part of my personal charm, but let me tell you, they were long gone. After my miscarriage, they sent me back to my prison room as soon as they were sure the bleeding had stopped. I shuffled between two guards, knowing that this was my absolute lowest, both physically and emotionally.

The guards pushed me through the sliding door of metal bars, and I went to a lower bunk and gingerly sat down. My roommates knew enough to wait until the guards had gone before they gathered around me in support.

"Oh, my God, Becca," Merry said, hugging me. "I was sure you were dead!"

"Almost," I agreed dully.

"What happened?" Vijay asked.

"The guard kicked me, and it made me miscarry." No point in prettying it up. "But it wasn't complete, so they aborted the rest of...it."

"Oh, Becca." Merry's face, already blotchy from crying, crumpled again.

"You were pregnant?" Diego knelt in front of me in concern.

I let out a breath. "Yeah. I guess so. I didn't want to admit it—even to myself. But I was." I met my roommates' eyes. "A teacher back home—he raped me. I wanted to tell the police, but right then my pa tried to kill himself. Things were crazy, and by the time Pa was stable, in the hospital, I couldn't think about anything but him. Anyway. I got pregnant. Well, now I'm not."

Gingerly I lowered myself onto the bunk and curled up, my back to them. It occurred to me that I was on Robin's bunk, and I could stay here, sleep here, because Robin was gone. And so was my baby.

I started to cry, muffling it in Robin's blanket.

"Becca Greenfield!" A guard was waiting for me out in the hall.

Diego, Vijay, and Merry looked shocked that I wouldn't be given more time to recover, but I wasn't. I knew not to expect special consideration. I knew not to expect anything anymore.

43

THE GUARD CUFFED MY WRISTS and took me to the classroom. I
walked as slowly as I dared, my insides burning with each step.
Glancing up at the windows, I longed to catch a glimpse of Hope,
but not even my dragonfly was with me now.

The Strepp was already in the classroom, pacing as she always
did, rapping a wooden ruler against one palm.

"Sit," she said.

I did. Obedient Becca. Becca in pain.

Strepp wrote on the whiteboard: "Despite my discouragement, I
shall rise again; I will take up my pencil which I have forsaken in my
great discouragement, and I will go on with my drawing." - Vincent
van Gogh.

Did she want me to draw something now? An art test?

But she wasn't done. Her next quote was: "Defeat should never be a source of discouragement but rather a fresh stimulus." - Robert South.

"Do you know what these quotes mean, Becca?" she asked.

My brain was hardly working well enough to know my own name, but what the hey. I took a stab. "Don't give up?"

"Yes!" Ms. Strepp pointed her marker at me. "Yes! Truly great people do not see their defeats as steps backward, but merely as steps along their journey."

Whatever. Okay. I kept quiet, wishing I could get my hands on a bottle of ibuprofen. A whole bottle.

"Do you feel defeated, Becca?" she asked.

For the first time, I met her gaze. Maybe she wanted a rote answer, like, "Never!" or "Yes, I'm ready to do anything you say," but I gave her question serious consideration. What did defeat mean? On the one hand, I felt pretty damn banged up and abused. I didn't care if I woke up tomorrow. On the other hand, would I try to break out of here if it meant I could see Cassie again? Hell, yeah.

"Um, I guess not totally?" I hazarded.

Her face took on an expression that I couldn't fathom. But she said nothing and instead handed me a sheaf of papers: today's tests.

I did them all as fast as I could and turned them in in record time.

Ms. Strepp glanced at them. "Be careful, Becca," she said, flipping pages. "Remember—there are executions all the time. You're on a short list."

"Yep. Got it," I said.

She nodded, still looking at me thoughtfully. "You have to do your best."

"Yes," I said, praying I could go back to my room and sleep, but strongly suspecting I was about to do thirty push-ups over the nail board instead.

Ms. Strepp stood up briskly, tapped the papers into a briefcase, and seemed like her usual cold, hateful self. "Okay. Good job, Becca," she said, and left the room without looking at me.

Mouth open, I just stared after her.

Then it hit me: This was another one of her crazy-house games. She was keeping me off-balance, unable to know what to expect.

It was working very well.

44

CASSIE

"ARE YOU SURE ABOUT THIS?" Nathaniel's voice was low in my ear.

"No," I said. "But I don't know what else to do." It was still weird, hanging with the Provost's son—I'd despised him for so long. But I knew he hadn't ratted me out about going to the Boundary yesterday, and this morning he'd been looking out for me, at Harrison's house. It was still hard to believe that schmuck was dead. As soon as I had a minute to feel glad about it, I intended to.

Now it was dark, but we still had a couple of hours till curfew. I should be at home doing schoolwork—my grades had suffered since Becca had disappeared—but instead I was out here, preparing to break the law for the first time in my life.

"This is the only boundary road, right?" I asked quietly. "There's not some secret entrance hidden somewhere that only the Outsiders know about?" I was pretty sure it was, but wanted to double-check. Before last week, I would have said I knew the cell like I knew my garden tools. Since then I'd found out that it had a lot of secrets.

"Yep," Nathaniel said. "Our crew has been all over the Boundary. There's one way into Cell B-97-4275, and one way out."

"Okay," I said. "Let's go."

We'd left our mopeds behind—even their small electric engines would make more noise than us walking. With Pa's rifle over my shoulder, I followed Nathaniel through a hole in the barbed wire, about two hundred yards from the open boundary gate. Cellfolk are so used to following the rules that the Provost doesn't even bother closing or guarding the gate.

"This way." Nathaniel's voice was very low. He stepped carefully over rocks and avoided the clumps of wild roses that made a thick and effective thorny barrier. There was a big ditch, a gully, about a hundred yards in, and he climbed down one side and offered me his hand. After a moment of internal back-and-forth, I took it. He motioned for me to go first up the other side, I guess to catch me if I fell. I scrambled up the boulders, my feet sliding only a bit, and then I was up and holding out a hand for him.

"You've been out here before." I wasn't asking.

"Yes. We've done as much exploring as we could."

"What for? I mean, what's the point of knowing people from other cells?"

Nathaniel paused for a minute, the moonlight making a sculpture of his face, his cheekbones. "There's a bigger picture," he said finally. "There's a whole world. There are tens of thousands of other cells. And that's just in the United! There are other Uniteds out there—where people speak different languages, where they look different. There are oceans—bigger than you could possibly imagine. Not just one ocean. Five of them. All of the United is on one landmass, one huge chunk of land. But there are six *other* enormous, gigantic chunks of land."

We walked in silence for a bit while I tried to wrap my mind around this. Was he just making it up? Maybe. What if he wasn't? What if there really were oceans and huge lands besides the United? What would that mean for me? For any of us?

"Your ma got taken for a mood-adjust," he surprised me by saying.

My brows came together and I got ready to lash out at him.

"Mine did, too."

That was the last thing I expected him to say, and I gaped at him. In the night shadows, he gave me a half smile. "But they brought her back."

"Yeah," I said in confusion. "I've seen her standing with your dad, like at speeches and stuff."

"That's not really her." Nathaniel sounded wistful. "I mean, that's her—her body. But her mind is different. Like she's not even there. Sometimes she doesn't know who I am, or where she is. During the day she sits in a chair, not speaking. Not doing anything."

This was horrible. I'd had no idea. As much as I'd imagined what had happened to my ma, it had never crossed my mind that having her come back might be worse.

"I'm sorry," I said, inadequately.

"Yeah," he said. "Me, too."

"My pa's still alive," I surprised myself by saying.

Nathaniel glanced at me. "I know."

"They don't think...they don't think he'll last much longer." Why was I telling him this? I'd never even spoken to Steph about it.

"I'm sorry," he said.

I let out a breath, looking at my feet to avoid tripping on rocks and old roots. "I go see him, in the hospital. As often as I can. I tell him what I'm doing, just like it was normal and we were waiting for dinner."

"Can he hear you?" Nathaniel's voice was gentle.

I shrugged. "I don't know. He never...reacts. But I still talk to him. Tell him to get better." I shook my head. "It's stupid, I guess."

"He's your pa," Nate said. "It's not stupid." Then he stopped and squinted into the distance. Wordlessly he pointed, and far away, way down the boundary road, I saw it.

My truck.

45

WHEN I'D MENTIONED TONIGHT'S LITTLE excursion, I hadn't expected
Nathaniel to want to tag along. But he'd pointed out, to my annoy-
ance, that he had much more experience exploring the Boundary.

Now, as we skirted the trees and made our way through the
brush parallel to the boundary road, I was thankful I wasn't out
here alone.

When we got close to the truck, Nathaniel motioned for me to
crouch down next to him.

"What are we waiting for?" I whispered.

"To see if it's a trap," he murmured matter-of-factly.

Again, a thought that hadn't occurred to me. It was like I'd
been living half asleep, and was now waking up to see how things
really were.

"Come on," he said at last, and we scurried over to my beloved truck. Which was totaled. As I took in all the damage, I had to keep swallowing so I wouldn't cry. The passenger side was crunched in, and three of the four tires were shredded. The driver's side door hung open, and the interior was already covered with a thick coating of red dust.

I gestured to the windshield. It was broken, and the point of impact was where the driver's head would have been. Gingerly I brushed sand off the seat and eased myself in. The keys were in the ignition.

This was where Becca had sat, just a few days ago. I pictured her in my mind, speeding down this road, hair flying, whooping as she broke curfew, took my truck without permission, and pretended, just for a few minutes, that Ma and Pa were both sleeping safely back at home.

My throat closed up and my eyes got hot. Slowly I traced the steering wheel with my fingers, knowing I would give anything to meet Becca's hand on the other side. Then I was crying silently, salty tears sliding down my face, my throat aching, my breaths coming in painful jerks.

Nathaniel reached in and took my arm, pulling me out gently. I stood against my ruined truck and sobbed as quietly as I could. My former enemy folded me into his arms and patted my back, one hand smoothing down my hair, not saying anything.

I'd been strong for so long. For years. Out here in the cool night air in the middle of forbidden territory, I let it go. Nathaniel's shirt was damp by the time I hiccupped to a halt. Without speaking we turned to head back through the brush, and from there we made our way across the barren land, down into the gully, through the woods, and then through the barbed wire fence.

Kneeling, Nathaniel quickly wired the pieces of fence back together. "So it won't be noticed in a quick inspection," he said.

I got my moped and wheeled it onto the ring road.

"I'm so sorry about Becca," he said.

I pushed the ignition on my moped, but kept its headlight off.

"Now what?" Nathaniel asked, one hand on my handlebar.

"I really don't know," I said politely, and headed for the empty house that would never feel like home again.

46

AT SCHOOL, STEPH, MY BEST friend, was waiting at my locker.

"I heard that Mr. Harrison had a heart attack," she murmured. "But now they say someone shot him!" She looked up and down the hallway. "I bet it was some girl's dad."

I looked at her. "Some girl's dad?"

Steph wrinkled her nose. "You know how he was. All handsy. Wouldn't surprise me if someone's dad decided to put a stop to it."

I'd known about Mr. Harrison molesting me and Becca. I hadn't heard about anyone else. I wondered if Steph was right.

"Cassandra Greenfield, please report to the principal's office."

Steph raised her eyebrows. "What have you done now?" she teased, because of course I never broke rules or did anything wrong, and all the teachers loved me. Good thing they didn't know about my sneaking past the Boundary. Or did they?

I rolled my eyes. "Must have been that fire I set."

In Ms. Ashworth's office I sat in a hard chair in front of her desk, as I had done—was it only last week? This time we were joined by Mr. Lewis, the guidance counselor, who usually picked vocations for the students. Was he going to change my vocation? Should I remind him that I'd wanted to be a teacher?

"Cassie," Ms. Ashworth said abruptly, "this isn't going to work."

"What?" I asked, surprised.

"You speak when we tell you!" Mr. Lewis almost shouted, and I jumped in my seat.

Eyes wide, I turned back to Ms. Ashworth, whose face was stern.

"We tried to make an exception for you," she said, and my eyes widened further. "But there was your mother, who never did fit in. Your father, and his shameful action a few months ago."

My face started to burn.

"Didn't have the decency to die!" Mr. Lewis said. "That's what the SAS is for! But no—Greenfields always have to do it their own way."

"And Becca. An Outsider," Ms. Ashworth said.

"You Greenfields think you're above everybody else!" Mr. Lewis snapped. "Like the rules of the United don't apply to you!"

My jaw dropped open.

"You're setting a bad example for the other kids," Ms. Ashworth went on. "You lied about Becca being sick, didn't you? You know this isn't tolerated in the system. I have no choice but to expel you."

"Wh—*expel?* What do you mean?"

"It means you leave here and don't come back," Ms. Ashworth

said in a voice like steel. "We won't take the risk of you infecting the other kids—good kids—with the Greenfield attitude."

"Leave school?" I was dumbfounded. Sure, kids had been kicked out before, but they'd done extremely bad citizen–type stuff. What had I done?

"As for your vocation, forget it!" said Mr. Lewis, a vein in his neck starting to throb. "No one will hire a Greenfield anyway! You can kiss that good-bye!"

I stared at them both, back and forth. In our cell, almost everyone graduated high school. And almost everyone had a vocation. Without a vocation, you couldn't do much. You ended up like the losers that Becca had played chicken with.

"I've done nothing wrong!" I exclaimed. "You can't expel me, or take away my vocation!"

"It's not only our decision," said Ms. Ashworth. "Though of course we support it. But you've been stirring up trouble. You've gotten a bad name for yourself. That kind of thing gets noticed."

The idea was so unbelievable that it was hard to take in. "But... what will I do?" I asked, wanting to argue but too shocked to put coherent thoughts together.

"You should have thought of that before!" Mr. Lewis said.

"Before what?" I asked. "Before I was a Greenfield?"

"You're dismissed, Cassie," Ms. Ashworth said as Mr. Lewis began to gather steam for another attack. "Go home. And don't come back."

47

PEOPLE IN THE HALLWAY LOOKED at me and whispered as I slammed open my locker. I grabbed whatever was mine, stuffed it into my backpack, and slammed the locker door shut. *They can't do this!* I fumed. *This has to be illegal!*

But who would I turn to? The Provost's office? Ha!

In the parking lot I strapped my backpack to my moped. Glancing up, I saw Steph staring at me through a window. She mouthed, "What happened?" but all I could do was shrug, get on the moped, and putt-putt furiously away.

What had just happened to me? My world was turned on its head. Even without Ma, even without Pa, and yes, even without Becca, I'd still had *me*. I'd still had school. I'd still had my vocation. I'd had a future, a life. Now what did I have?

This mother-lovin' moped and an old, broken-down farmhouse. A dying farm that was too much for me to keep up. I couldn't harvest what little crops we had all by myself. Did I even have friends? Would Steph's parents forbid her to see me—one of the disgraced Greenfields? Everything was crazy!

As I drove by our nearest neighbors' house, my eye caught something black and shiny. The System-Assisted Suicide van. Mr. Preston had retired recently—the system always contacted retirees about making their retirement permanent.

You know who else they contacted? *People who had no vocation.* Maybe not today, but soon I would be getting a visit from a facilitator, someone who would pat my hand sympathetically and listen to all my woes. And then, at a lull in the conversation, their eyes full of understanding, they would murmur something about *other options.* About making way so a new life could be born.

Our house seemed twice as shabby as it had this morning, and I gritted my teeth as I slammed the door so hard I almost broke the glass. In the kitchen I stared into the almost empty fridge—I hadn't been to work at the All-Ways in days and there was damn little to eat. I was probably fired.

What had happened to me? I was Cassie Greenfield, candidate for a President's Star! I'd been my class representative three times!

Upstairs I stomped past Pa's closed door and Becca's closed door. Then I threw myself on my bed, waiting for the major tears to come, knowing that they wouldn't end for a long while.

But they didn't come. Not even my tears knew what to do anymore.

On my bed, I closed my eyes in case this was all a bad dream. Maybe even Ma and Pa had been just a bad dream. Maybe I would wake up and hear Ma making breakfast downstairs, hear Pa getting ready to head out to the fields. Hear Becca's horrible singing in the shower.

I popped my eyes open hopefully and listened.

All I heard was the wind making branches scrape against my window. My fingers gripped my quilt. This couldn't be real. This couldn't be my life.

I watched the sky outside turn gray, then red, then black. My stomach rumbled but it didn't matter. While I'd been lying there, it had come to me: What I should do. What I had to do. What was my only option, at this point.

Downstairs, I got Pa's rifle and loaded it.

48

BECCA

"ROBIN WELLFLEET," I WHISPERED. "SHE was the best."

"She helped us," Merry whispered.

"She was good to everyone," Diego added.

"We will never forget her," Vijay finished, and we all bumped fists. As long as I was alive, Robin Wellfleet would not be forgotten.

"Becca Greenfield!"

"What is it now?" I asked the guards as they cuffed my wrists. "More tests? More workouts?"

"Fight," one of the guards grunted, and poked me in the back with her billy club. I hadn't fought anyone since Tim. My innards were nowhere near healed from my miscarriage, but that didn't matter to anyone except me.

"Prisoners, report to the stadium!" Ms. Strepp's voice crackled through the ancient comm system, making everyone wince. "Report to the stadium!"

Inside the now-familiar halls, I glanced up: no Hope. Get it? No Hope? Ha!

When we got to the stadium the guards pushed me toward the ring. As soon as the helpers approached with my armor, I quickly shimmied out of my jumpsuit. I was learning.

Then my armor was on, the crowd filed in, and I slowly climbed the steps to the outside ropes.

If my opponent was Tim again, I was gonna lose another tooth, or have bones broken. But all I had to do was get through this. An hour from now this would just be a sucky memory.

When I saw my opponent, my heart sank. *Oh, no.*

It was Little Bit, one of the smallest, youngest kids here. I didn't know her real name—maybe no one did. I had a good eight inches on her, and maybe thirty pounds. She was wearing her jumpsuit under her armor.

This was going to be a bloodbath.

The hateful Strepp climbed through the ropes and motioned us to meet in the center of the ring.

"You know what you have to do," she said.

Little Bit nodded, fear in her dark eyes.

Strepp's eyes lingered on me. "Do not disappoint me, Becca." Her tone was soft, but her meaning was icy. I gave a brief nod. If I didn't make this good, my time was up.

Then she left the ring, and Little Bit and I went to our corners. *Ding!*

Little Bit didn't have a chance. She was brand-new and her inner rage had not yet ignited. She was well behind me in the roiling, seething resentment department. My very first punch clocked her, but she got up after the six-count. Ten seconds later she almost managed to hit my side, but I snapped my foot out and cracked her knee, making it buckle. She was down again.

This time when she got up, there was fire in her eyes. She came at me like a tumbleweed, bouncing and spinning across the canvas. She got in a not-shabby jab to my kidney, but I whirled and slammed my glove against her head. Her eyebrow split open, and within moments blood streamed down her face.

I circled and grabbed her jumpsuit, yanking on it the way Tim had done to me. Little Bit let out a whimper as the seams dug into her skin beneath her armor.

Between the blood and the pain, Little Bit's swings became wilder, made contact less. It was easy to skip away from her poorly aimed kicks.

Leaping in back of her, I smashed the same knee. It buckled again, she went down again. This time my fist followed her down, the blow landing solidly on her shoulder. She cried out in pain.

All of *my* pain was gone. My insides didn't hurt, my empty tooth socket didn't ache. All I felt was victory, reaching out to fold me into its embrace.

Little Bit staggered to her feet.

"I'm really sorry about this," I murmured, and put everything I had into my uppercut. It slammed her head back, her eyes fluttered, and then she dropped like a sack of wheat.

The crowd didn't clap. I would have been pissed if they had. Instead I stood panting as Strepp climbed through the ropes again. I started to think about being in the pen with Little Bit, how I would apologize.

Ms. Strepp picked up one of Little Bit's limp hands. "I declare this girl the winner!" she said.

For a moment I was stunned, speechless. But just for a moment. "Are you nuts?" I screamed. "Did you not see that fight? Are you a complete *idiot?*"

An awed silence swept the stadium, but I was too far gone to recognize it as a warning. Instead I hauled back my bloodied glove and aimed a powerhouse punch right at the woman I hated more than anyone.

Strepp was quicker than she looked, and she bobbed to the side. I missed, my glove whistling past her ear. The crowd gasped.

Two high spots of color appeared on Strepp's cheeks. Looking at her, I saw the knowledge in her eyes. I had just signed my death warrant.

End of game.

End of Becca.

49

CASSIE

THE NIGHT AIR WAS STILL and chilly. My moped was almost silent as I took the route out to the ring road. From here, the boundary road was six miles away. It would have been faster to cut across the cell, but there were fewer people on the ring road, and it was darker.

When I got to the gateposts, I barely hesitated—just putt-putted through as if I'd been coming and going my whole life. I could have cut the fence farther away and walked through, like I had with Nathaniel, but didn't want to take the time. Right now it didn't matter if anyone spotted me. It was too late for them to do anything.

Nathaniel. I hadn't talked to him—hadn't seen him at school during the eight minutes I was there this morning. By now he must know that I'd been expelled and had no vocation, no future. If he was the old Nathaniel, he would sneer at me in the street. What would the new Nathaniel do? I might never know.

Last night I hadn't noticed how far out the truck was on the road. It seemed like I should have reached it by now, and I started to worry that my last link to Becca had been taken. Five more minutes, I told myself. If I don't see it by then, well, I guess I'll just stop anyway.

Then it was there, a shape in the darkness. You could hardly tell that it was red.

I pulled up next to it and opened the driver's side door for the last time. I would never see this truck again. I would never be out here again. Hot tears, the tears that hadn't come before, streaked through the dust on my cheeks.

I loved this truck so much. For a moment I let myself drift back in time, seeing Pa behind the steering wheel, the sunlight flashing across his suntanned skin. When we were little, when Ma was happy, we'd gone on picnics in this truck. If the ground was too wet or muddy, we sat in the truck bed, our picnic blanket spread there instead.

I'd had a family once. I'd been happy. It felt like a very long time ago. Now I was seventeen and my life was over. No family, no high school diploma, no vocation. My other option—to find someone to marry me—had just taken a nosedive. Who would get involved with the last of the notorious Greenfields?

The sky above me was a deep, deep navy and sprinkled with so many stars that I and my problems suddenly seemed tiny. Maybe when we die, we become stars. Maybe Ma was a star up there, winking down at me. Maybe Becca was.

Maybe it was time to join them.

I had Pa's rifle, after all. But I couldn't flub the job, like Pa had. I couldn't end up like him. I'd have to do a better job of aiming, is all.

The wind began to kick up then, blowing fine, silty sand against me. I had no idea wind could make so much noise—was there a storm coming? The sky was clear.

With my very next blink, the world around me exploded into light so bright that I couldn't see a thing.

"Cassie Greenfield!" a voice thundered. "Put down the rifle and put your hands up!"

Oh, hell no, I thought, and leaped for the moped, throwing my leg over the saddle and grabbing the handlebars. By touch alone I jammed it into life, gunned its tiny motor, and raced away.

50

BECCA

"PRISONERS! REPORT TO THE RING! Report to the ring!"

Diego, Merry, and Vijay all looked at me with sympathy. Half an hour ago, I'd actually taken a swing at Strepp. I'd screamed at her in public, had called her an idiot. We all knew what was coming.

"Been great knowing you," I said, trying to sound normalish.

"Oh, Becca!" Merry said, starting to cry.

I attempted a brave smile, but inside I was shrieking. "It was only a matter of time," I said. "There was no way I could keep my mouth shut much longer."

Both Diego and Vijay had tears in their eyes.

"I can tell you one thing I won't miss," I said. "I know damn well Diego won't be stinking up heaven!"

My roommates did smile a tiny bit then.

"Or hell, whatever," I went on. "Either one. Actually, if it's hell, then I'm sure there'll only be the one john, and that Diego will be with me."

That reaped a few small chuckles.

"That will be my eternity. Me, Diego, and a toilet." I was almost laughing myself now, and my roommates looked much better.

The jail block alarm sounded, and all of our barred doors slid open at the same time. Prisoners streamed out of their rooms and headed toward the stairway. Guards stood around, clubs and Tasers at the ready.

"Weird," I muttered as we filed out into the crowd. "Usually they would have come for me first. I guess they'll just pull me out when we get to the ring."

Merry linked her arm in mine.

My throat closed then, and my eyes got hot. My one regret? Cassie. I would never see Careful Cassie again. I'd never steal her clothes or her truck again. I'd never sneak so much sugar into her coffee that she spit it out into the sink. I'd never belt out songs in the shower, extra loud because I knew it made her crazy.

I was about to die. I was glad I knew why—because I'd mouthed off to my jailer. I'd taken a swing at an enemy. It was so much better than not ever knowing, like Robin.

Ma, I miss you. I've always missed you.

Pa, I wish I'd said good-bye. Even if you couldn't hear me.

Cassie, I'm sorry. You know I love you. I'll miss you forever. You were always my favorite sister.

In the stadium I headed toward a guard, expecting him to grab me and haul me up onto the canvas, where a gurney was waiting.

"Sit down!" he yelled at me, and pointed to the bleachers with his club.

Diego, Merry, Vijay, and I exchanged puzzled looks, but I sat with them on the bench.

The lights dimmed and Strepp ducked through the ropes of the ring. Two assistants were there, checking the monitors and the IV machine. I sat on the edge of my bench, heart pounding and mouth dry, waiting to be called. I hoped I could die without crying. I would try hard.

Then...a guard brought Little Bit up to the ring! They'd wiped most of the blood off her brow, and the split was held together with a butterfly bandage. Even from here I could see the bruises I'd given her, could see how she limped from where I'd smashed her knee.

Until the assistant helped her up on the gurney and started to lock her in, I had no idea what was going on. No idea if she was there just to watch me die. But there was only one gurney on the canvas, and Little Bit was on it.

She was being executed.

I was going to live. At least for now.

Little Bit started crying when they hooked up the IV.

When the bright green blips on the monitor slowed and then flattened out, when Little Bit's bruised face went slack, her eyes still open a slit, that was when it felt like someone had buried an axe in my chest.

It had been bad—really goddamn bad—when Robin died.

But I hadn't killed her. She hadn't died because I'd beaten her in a fight.

I didn't look away, forced myself to acknowledge the small, hard life that I'd helped to take. And damn if it didn't seem like Strepp was searching the crowd until her gaze caught mine. And damn if she didn't smile at me, just a tiny bit.

51

CASSIE

ONCE THE LIGHT WASN'T IN my eyes, I could see where I was going. I had no idea who was after me, or how many of them there were. Taking a gamble that my moped was nimbler than whatever they had, I suddenly veered off road and headed out into the hard-packed wasteland that lay behind the trees.

It was dark out here, and I kept my headlight off. Motors revved behind me and then bright, arcing lights swept the scene. A sudden, shallow gully caught me off guard: the moped skidded, I braced myself with one foot, and then tore down the gully. It was too narrow for a car, too narrow for a truck. No idea where it led. Didn't care much.

Of course, even gunned, the moped went—say it with me—twelve miles an hour. It took barely moments before a dark, non-electric car was roaring along on one side of the gully and a jacked-up all-wheeler was spewing dirt on the other side. Their headlights bounced as the vehicles crossed the rough terrain. I crouched over my handlebars, trying to stay out of the raking searchlights.

I just barely saw the fork to the left and wrenched my handlebars over without thinking. This wasn't a gully; it was a deep, rough ditch, ridged with old roots from the trees that had reached this far. Time seemed to slow as the car, still heading straight, hovered right over my head. I saw the axle and the transmission column, and then there was a loud, metallic crunch as it plowed head-on into the far side of the ditch.

That was lucky, I thought, and winced as I hit another big root.

The all-wheeler had been on the other side of the gully, but it must have nosed down one side and up the other because it soon took the car's place, easily pacing me despite hitting tumbleweeds and having to avoid big rocks.

Praying for another unexpected fork, I gripped the handlebars as hard as I could. Roots twisted my front wheel left and right, and more than once I almost ran into the high, dirt sides.

"Cassie Greenfield! Stop your vehicle!"

I ignored them, tensely trying to see what lay ahead of me. They knew exactly where I was—might as well use the headlight. With my thumb I hit the switch, and the anemic, diffused beam told me my battery was getting low. Crap.

Then it was there ahead of me, only feet away. There was no time to stop, nowhere to turn, and I slammed tire-first into the old, gnarled tree trunk. My moped crumpled against it like tinfoil, and I watched almost calmly as my body flew slowly through the air and hit the ground so hard the wind was knocked out of me. Pa's rifle was beneath me and my spine cracked against it as I slid in the dirt.

The world lit up again: the all-wheeler was right on top of me. Its driver saw me at the last second and stood on the brakes, making the vehicle skew sideways and missing me by less than three inches. I heard swearing and tried to suck in air, tried to stagger to my feet, prepared to run.

"Stop right there!" a voice shouted.

I raised Pa's rifle and found my voice. "I have a gun!" I wheezed.

Several figures passed through the high beams. They were circling me.

"I have a gun!" I yelled again, more strongly, and set the rifle to my shoulder.

In one short day I had gone from a President's Star hopeful to...what? A murderer? Was I really threatening to shoot another person?

I tipped the front sight up a bit and fired into the air, knowing the bullet would whistle over their heads.

Crack!

Something plowed into my chest, sending a starburst of pain radiating through me. After a moment of wavering I fell backward, the night sky losing its stars as my consciousness melted away.

I couldn't breathe. Lying on the ground, I blinked, the world narrowing to a pinpoint above me. The last few stars twinkled, seeming to move, almost seeming alive. Just as the final black curtain was drawn over my face, I saw the stars align...into a dragonfly. A diamond dragonfly in the sky.

52

BECCA

"EXPECTATIONS." STREPP LOOKED DOWN AT us from the steps leading to the chapel's altar. "'When one's expectations are reduced to zero, one really does appreciate everything one does have.'"

Jesus, here we go again. I was still trying to suck up my crying over poor Little Bit. I'd seen three executions now, and they'd been so much worse than getting beat up by Tim. Some kids here had seen ten. Twenty. More. It was a wonder they were still mostly human.

"A man named Stephen Hawking said that," Strepp told us. "And it's the key to everything. If your expectations are zero, then anything you have is gravy." She paced back and forth, sometimes putting her fist to her mouth as if it helped her think. "You may believe," she said, facing us, "that you have nothing right now. You may believe that everything you had has been taken from you."

Pretty much, yep.

"You would be wrong!" she said, jabbing her finger at us. Her eyes seemed to pick me out from the hundreds of prisoners. "You still have food. You have a roof over your head. You have companions. You have clothes and indoor plumbing." Her eyes narrowed. "Picture what your life would be like if you had *none* of that!"

Oh, my God—was that the next stage of this horror show? I tried not to show fear, kept my face blank. Knowing Strepp, if she thought I was afraid of something, you could bet that I would end up with it.

"Expectations," she repeated, continuing her pacing. "Expectations and discipline. A man named George Washington said, 'Discipline is the soul of an army. It makes small numbers formidable; procures success to the weak, and esteem to all.'"

Where this woman got all these dumb quotes was a mystery. She seemed to have a million of them tucked up her sleeve.

"What did Mr. Washington mean by those words?"

It was weird, but her pacing and droning voice were helping me calm down. I'd been so upset about Little Bit, but ten minutes of pointless yapping and my brain waves were smoothing right out.

"He meant—" she began but was interrupted by the comm system crackling to life.

"Guards, prepare for incoming!" a voice said, and everyone looked surprised except Strepp. Instead she seemed—almost victorious. Again she met my eyes, or maybe I was imagining it. But she seemed to look at me with that weird, triumphant expression. As if she knew something I didn't.

Which of course she did.

53

CASSIE

I WAS SURPRISED WHEN I realized I wasn't dead.

Turns out, getting shot with a plastic bullet hurts so, so bad, and can definitely make your consciousness yell uncle for a while. Afterward, you have a bruise that goes from your front straight through to your back, and then continues down the road for a while. Right now it hurt so bad that I was sure in five years if someone touched me there, I would scream.

I'd drifted back into consciousness some time ago—maybe half an hour? Maybe ten minutes? It was hard to tell. I was in a vehicle, but not the all-wheeler, because this had a roof and doors. My hands were tied painfully behind my back and I had a black cloth hood over my head. At first I'd asked a bunch of questions, but they'd slapped a piece of duct tape over my mouth, so that was that.

Now that I wasn't talking, no one else was, either. I'd made out two different voices at first, and I thought the hands that had pushed up my hood just enough for the tape were maybe a woman's hands. Or a boy's. I could be surrounded by twenty armed guards, or I could be in the back of someone's ma's car with a couple of assholes who didn't know there's no one to pay ransom for me.

Not that there had ever been a kidnapping in the cell. Of course, I had left the cell.

Finally the vehicle slowed and I heard a rusty, metallic scraping sound: gates opening. Someone yelled for us to go through. We took a bunch of turns, lefts and rights, before we came to a stop.

My heart was pounding so loud I knew they could hear it. People outside this car or truck or whatever could probably hear it.

I tried to inhale calmly through my nose. When they'd first taped my mouth I'd panicked, trying to breathe so fast that I almost passed out. Now all I was trying to do was stay upright, stay conscious, and not wet my pants from terror.

The vehicle stopped. The door opened. Rough hands grabbed my arms and hauled me out. My legs were wobbly but they held. Someone shoved me forward, so I almost fell, then shoved me again. I started walking, hesitantly, blind, hoping they weren't sending me straight into a brick wall for laughs.

Another door opened. I stumbled across the threshold. It smelled different in here, like stale air and the industrial cleaner we used at the All-Ways. Someone yanked off my hood and I squeezed my eyes almost shut—the bright light was painful.

I was in a... prison. Not like the little jail we had downtown that hardly ever got used. This was a prison, like I'd seen in books. So they hadn't taken me back to the cell. Which meant I'd disappeared.

Just like Becca. And the other kids.

And no one would know where I was. Not Steph. Not Nathaniel.

A woman was there, big and broad with odd yellow hair and a very red face. She came up and pulled the duct tape off me—not fast, but not nearly slowly enough.

As soon as I could breathe I gulped in air, my chest rising and falling and my bullet-bruise hurting with each movement.

"Where am I?" I gasped.

A guy in a uniform stepped forward and gave me a smart rap on my arm with a billy club.

"Ow!" I said, then shut up quickly as he raised it again.

I was led down a cement-block hallway with peeling vomit-green paint. Bare lightbulbs flickered overhead, and several times we had to walk through puddles.

Oh, God, where am I? What's happening?

In a small room, two guards took my clothes, cutting the zip ties on my wrists so they could get my hoodie off. I was shaking with cold as well as hysterical, razor-wire fear, but all they did was throw a yellow jumpsuit at me. I leaped into it as fast as I could.

Down another hall. Through a heavy metal door. Its tiny glass window had wire fused into it. This door opened into a wide hallway with a tall ceiling four stories high. Each story had a walkway around the outside, bordered with a line of barred cages, little jail rooms, one after another.

Each room held kids. Kids who looked like Outsiders, all colors, all types.

The guards shoved me up concrete steps and down one of the walkways. They put me into an empty, barred room, and just then a horrible alarm sounded. The din of hundreds of marching feet filled my ears. Pressing my face against the bars, I saw more kids, all in yellow jumpsuits, filing in and heading to their cages.

Then... one head out of the entire crowd. One face that was like looking into a mirror.

"Becca!" I screamed as loudly as I could. *"Becca!"*

54

BECCA'S HEAD SNAPPED UP AT my voice, and she met my eyes
instantly. In a flash she put a finger against her lips, telling me to be
quiet. I was shocked at how different she looked; she was thinner
and moved stiffly and slowly. Her hair was a rat's nest, and any skin
I could see was either dirty or discolored with bruises or scrapes.

Kids in jumpsuits began to file past my barred door. No one
seemed surprised or curious about my being there. A hulking, uniformed guard stopped in front of me to unlock the door. The bars
slid open, and he pushed in a small girl with mouse-colored hair, a
light-tan boy, a taller, dark-tan boy... and Becca.

"Get inside!" he shouted as Becca lingered, looking at me like I
was an icy soda on a haying day.

The guard pushed her in roughly, then slammed the door shut

and locked it. Becca suddenly spun and looked at him in shock. "Tim?"

The guard didn't answer—just marched away.

"Oh, God, Becca!" I exclaimed, and grabbed her in a hug. After a moment, she brought her arms up and hugged me back. She felt bony, and it was like hugging a stranger. "I missed you so much!" I said. "I looked for you everywhere! I never stopped looking."

When we pulled back, the other kids were staring at us.

"There's two of you," the small girl whispered.

"Yeah. The before and the after," one of the guys said wryly.

"This is my twin sister, Cassie," Becca said quietly. "Cass, this is Merry. And this is Vijay, and this is Diego."

I didn't know what to say. We were just kids, locked in a prison together. This was a nightmare I could never have predicted, and I had no idea how to act. But I nodded at them, and they nodded back.

"Why are we here?" I asked Becca. "What happened to you?"

She shrugged and sat down on a narrow bunk. "Got taken," she said. "Like everyone else."

This is Becca, I told myself. *This really is Becca. It's just . . . a completely different Becca.* I didn't know what she'd been through to make her like this; she was serious, calmer, and just so . . . not Ridiculous.

"You've been here since you disappeared?" I asked.

She nodded. "What about you? Where did they get you? At home?"

"No." I had to gather my thoughts for a minute. "You disappeared, so I went all over looking for you. I talked to Taylor, that guy you played chicken with, out on the boundary road."

Becca looked surprised.

"Then Nathaniel showed me the Outsider hangout. I didn't know you were an Outsider," I said wryly. "And then one night he cut the wire on the boundary fence and we went down the road till we found the truck—my truck." I couldn't seem to work up any anger about that now. "Then someone killed Mr. Harrison. I mean, first I hit him with my backpack and knocked him out, and then someone shot him."

Becca's eyebrows rose farther on her forehead. "You...hit him..."

I nodded and took a breath. "Yeah. Then today—today?— maybe today I got kicked out of school. I'm expelled. Plus they took away my vocation. So I got the moped and Pa's rifle, and drove through the gates down the boundary road to the truck—to where you had been last."

Becca's mouth was hanging open and her eyes were wide.

"Suddenly I was surrounded, don't know by who. I took off across the brush and drove down into a gully. Then I was in a ditch, and one of the cars crashed right over me, and then the second one was chasing me, and it was dark, and I hit a tree trunk head-on. 'Fraid the moped is totaled," I admitted. "I flew up out of the ditch and almost got run over by an all-wheeler. Anyway, I still had Pa's rifle, so I aimed at them, but then in the end I couldn't shoot 'em, so I fired over their heads. But then *they* shot *me* with a plastic bullet and knocked me out. And *that's* gonna hurt until I die. When

I woke up I had a black hood over my head, and they brought me here, and now here I am."

Four pairs of eyes stared at me like I was a two-headed calf.

"You..." Becca began, shaking her head in wonder. "You hit Harrison, and you found Taylor, cut the fence, and met the Outsiders, and you got expelled, and you *left the cell* and got chased and *fired* at them..."

"Over their heads," I pointed out.

"I thought you said she was the good one," the guy named Diego said.

55

BECCA

"SHE IS," I SAID, STARING at my sister. "She's the good one, the careful one. Careful Cassie."

Cassie looked surprised. "Well, you're the ridiculous one!" she said. "Ridiculous Rebecca! Only now, you're..."

"Sounds like you're not so careful anymore," I told her. "Like, rob any banks while you were at it?"

"No! Of course not." Cassie looked embarrassed.

"Someone shot Harrison?"

She nodded, her expression darkening. "Yeah."

"Do they know who?" I asked. I couldn't believe that he was dead. That I never had to dread him again.

Cassie shook her head.

I had to tell her. As if sensing it, Merry came and sat next to me on the bunk. "Uh…you know, Harrison…anyway. I got pregnant."

My sister looked appropriately horrified, then did the sweetest thing. She came and knelt before me and took my hands. "Oh, honey. I'm so sorry. That…that asshole."

I'd never heard her use bad language before, even at her maddest. "Yeah. But a couple days ago I had a miscarriage. I got kicked really hard. And they operated on me to make sure it was all gone."

"Someone *kicked* you?" My sister looked outraged.

I sighed. While that had been really, really bad, it was barely registering on my current list of awful life events.

"Cass. I'm really glad to see you, but trust me when I say that I would give anything for you not to be here."

"I want to be where you are," she said stubbornly.

"This is a prison," I said carefully. "Full of kids from hundreds of different cells, including ours. Kathy Hobhouse is here, and I guess Livvie Clayhill used to be. But in here there are tests and training and fights."

Cassie frowned. "What? Why?"

"How well you do at any of them decides how long you'll stay," I said, still pussyfooting around.

"So people get out?"

I hated seeing the spark of hope in her eyes. Slowly I shook my head. "No. This is…death row. The only way out is…to get executed."

Cassie cocked her head to one side like a retriever. "What are you talking about?"

"Welcome to the crazy house," I said.

56

CASSIE

BECCA HAS ALWAYS BEEN A big exaggerator. If we had a strong breeze, it was a tornado. If we caught a little trout, it gained ten pounds by the time Becca told someone about it. If Pa spoke to her sternly, then he had "taken her head off" or "skinned her alive."

So at first I thought "executed" was an extreme description of something yucky, like having to mop these halls or whatever. Then Diego, Vijay, and Merry started backing her up, all of them speaking in low voices.

I still wasn't convinced. Fighting until someone was knocked out? That was crazy. Push-ups over a board of nails? Who would come up with such an insane idea? Then Becca unzipped her jumpsuit and I gasped: her chest was covered with rows of unhealed dots of blood. She pulled her lip to one side and showed me the gap where her tooth had been. I stared at her, stunned.

They told me about their friend Robin. And a boy named Tomás. A girl named Little Bit. Becca blamed herself for that one.

By the time they were finished, tears were streaming down my cheeks. They were telling the truth. My sister had actually endured all this, and worse. Horror filled me—all this time I'd been searching desperately for Becca. Now that I'd found her, I'd never been so afraid in my whole life. I sat down on the cold concrete, unable to move, terrifying images spinning through my brain.

The lights went out at 10:00, just like back home. I curled up on the floor next to Becca's bunk. She gave me her thin, ratty blanket. I pulled it over me and shut my eyes, then lay there shaking from cold and fear.

But I must have finally slept because a few hours later, the barred door slid open with a scraping sound.

"Cassandra Greenfield!" They were different guards than last night. "Get up!"

I saw Diego and Vijay were in their bunks, but Becca and Merry were already gone.

The guards handcuffed me and prodded me with their billy clubs. I tried to memorize the route, but soon gave up. All these hallways looked—and smelled—alike. When they undid my hands and shoved me through a doorway, I was only a little surprised to see a classroom. And the woman inside, staring at me with narrowed eyes, must be the legendary Ms. Strepp.

57

HOW WELL WE DID DETERMINED how long we lived. Becca told me that.

"Take a seat. I'm Ms. Strepp. I'm glad to finally meet you, Cassandra Greenfield."

I sat down at a desk. Why would she care about meeting me?

Written on the whiteboard at the front of the room was: "Appearances are often deceiving" - Aesop. I'd heard of Aesop—we'd read some of his stories in school. His morals were always good lessons for the cell.

"First you'll be tested on the basics," Ms. Strepp went on briskly.

"Okay," I said, and she strode over and whacked my desk with her wooden ruler.

"You speak when I tell you!" she snapped, and I pressed my

lips together because I'd heard that same expression just...maybe yesterday?

It began. I was hungry and cold and exhausted, but I concentrated, thinking each question through carefully. It was all stuff I'd seen before, so if I didn't make any sloppy mistakes, I would be all right.

Ms. Strepp paced back and forth all night and all day long, staring at me, glancing at her watch. A couple of times she left the room, but a guard immediately came in each time.

In the middle of an essay about the history of our cell (a cinch because we were all required to memorize it anyway) a few hot tears filled my eyes. I brushed them away.

This was ridiculous. Surreal. I'd only wanted to find my sister. I hadn't been a bad citizen. I hadn't even been an Outsider.

It was dark again when Ms. Strepp finished looking at all my test results. I was so hungry I felt almost sick—that horrible, hollow feeling you get when you've gone too long without refueling.

Finally Ms. Strepp looked up. "You did extremely well. I guess you're used to being a star pupil, eh?"

I nodded cautiously.

Ms. Strepp threw my tests into the trash can. "I'm not impressed, star pupil!" she snarled. "Every kid in here gets scores like this!"

The words came out of my mouth before I could stop them. "Not Becca."

Ms. Strepp stopped in mid-pace and turned to me. "Yes, Becca," she said. "Becca aces these tests. *She's* a star pupil."

"Becca?" I couldn't help asking. "Becca Greenfield?"

"Yes, Becca Greenfield," Ms. Strepp repeated snidely. "She now gets almost perfect scores. Like you."

Well. All I could think was: *What the hell happened to Becca?*

"In fact, I think you'll find your sister very changed from when you last saw her," Ms. Strepp went on.

No kidding, I thought. *She's a* different person.

"And you're about to find that out in a very visceral way," Ms. Strepp said.

I raised my eyebrows as she motioned for the guards to come in.

"Take her to the ring," she said.

58

NATHANIEL

"HERE." NATHANIEL'S FATHER THREW ANOTHER photograph down. Like the others, it was grainy and obviously taken from a distance. Like the others, it was a picture of Nate. Nate and Cassie Green-field. His father had photos of him talking to Cassie in the school parking lot, outside by the town square, in the hallway at school by her locker, and then, from very far away, Cassie and him on their mopeds, heading for the ring road, the day he'd taken her to meet the Outsiders. To his relief, there were no photos of the abandoned farm or its barn.

Rage began to heat in Nate's chest but he knew not to show it. Instead he put an innocent, puzzled look on his face. "Gosh, Dad. Why do you have pictures of me and Cassie?"

"Because you're my son and you can't be too careful," his father said. "You're the son of the Provost. You're going to be Provost yourself someday. There can't be any hint of a scandal in your past."

"Provosts are chosen by the system," Nate said, legitimately confused this time. "It's not inherited."

His father looked smug. "We'll just see about that, my boy. Your dad has some plans in place."

"Dad. I'm not going to be Provost. I don't want to be."

A familiar coldness came into his father's eyes. "You'll do what I tell you, son. I've done a lot to increase the position of the Provost here. You're going to do even more. Your son will do even more. And the next thing you know, they'll be talking about the reign of the Allens. They'll be talking about Overseer Allen or President Allen."

Nate felt the blood drain out of his face. He'd had no idea his father's delusions of power ran this deep. Automatically he glanced into the living room, where his mother sat as still as a statue in her chair. She was dressed and tidy, all matching, hair done, but her face was blank. Had she seen this side of his father? Had she objected to it? Is that why he'd sent her away for a mood-adjust?

It was one thing for his father to be power-hungry. It was another thing for him to expect the same of Nate.

"I've been slated for higher schooling," Nate said stiffly. "We can talk about it after that." Because he would be long gone by then and would never see him again. He hoped.

His father's icy green eyes bored holes in Nate's skull. "There's nothing to talk about, Nathaniel. This is the right path for you, and you will follow it! And when you're my age you'll thank me for it!"

Highly unlikely, Dad, Nate thought, but said nothing. Saying nothing had served him pretty well so far in his messed-up life.

The Provost tapped the photos on the table. "You know this girl, this Cassandra. You know she's been expelled from school? That she's had her vocation taken away?"

Nate frowned. "Yeah, I heard that, but I was sure it was a mistake. Cassie's a Goody Two-shoes."

"It was no mistake, son. We've determined that the Greenfields are weeds, and they must be uprooted!"

"What?" Nate blurted. "Who determined that?"

"Never you mind. Lucky for you, I've taken steps to avoid having you tainted by the Greenfield independence. This girl, Cassandra, is salt! And she will ruin every acre she touches!" His face was turning red: Nate's signal to disappear.

This was just craziness. He had to find Cassie immediately. He needed to help her plan her escape.

"Okay, gotta go, Dad."

"You wait a minute, young man! We're not done talking!"

"Yes. We are." Nate grabbed his moped key and headed for the door. "You've gotten it all wrong, Dad," he yelled over his shoulder. "You always get it all wrong!"

59

CASSIE'S HOUSE WAS DARK. HER moped was gone. Shit. Nate headed to where there might be people hanging out, some of whom might have news of Cassie: school.

Actually, he was still freaking about what his dad had just revealed: That he'd been overreaching his position as Provost. That he expected Nate to continue in his power-mongering ways.

It was hard to admit—this was his dad, after all—but Nate had just realized that he wasn't simply an egomaniac who should be avoided or circumvented as much as possible. That last conversation had revealed that his father needed to be stopped. He needed to be taken out. For the good of the people.

Nate would just have to figure out how.

At school, the only kids still around were the soccer teams.

He had no idea if Cassie was friends with any of them. Probably. She was pretty popular. He parked his moped, grinning slightly as he moved the chain holding his new radio in place. The look on Cassie's face when she'd seen that…

"Nate." Eddie Carter, still sweaty and in uniform, nodded at him. His mom was waiting in their beat-up van.

"Yo, Eddie," Nate said casually. "Hey, you seen Cassie Green-field around?"

Eddie's friendly face immediately shut down. "Naw, man," he said, and headed to his mom's car.

The Provost's influence. The blanket of fear that had crept over the cell in the last couple of years with hardly anyone noticing.

A girl named Stephanie Morrow came out next. She'd changed out of her soccer uniform and into her waitress uniform—Nate had seen her at Mrs. Kelly's Kitchen, when he and his parents had gone to the diner after church.

"Stephanie?"

She looked surprised. "Yeah?"

"Um, you're friends with Cassie, right?" he asked. "I've seen you hanging out."

Just like Eddie, Stephanie's face went from friendly to wary.

"Yeah?" she said. "So?"

"I'm looking for her."

"Why?" Distinctly unfriendly.

"I'm worried about her," Nate said. "She got kicked out of school. I want to make sure she's okay."

"Uh-huh," Stephanie said. "So you can rat on her to your dad?"

Because of his carefully cultivated public face. "Cassie and I are friends, actually," he said mildly.

"I don't know where she is," Stephanie said tightly. "She's not at home, she's not at the All-Ways."

A cold feeling curled up in the pit of his stomach.

The sound of tires squealing caught his attention. Two police cars pulled into the school parking lot and jerked to a stop by the front doors. Nate stayed very still—maybe his dad had sent them to get him. Maybe he should quietly get on his moped and split.

"So no one knows where Cassie is?" he asked out of the corner of his mouth.

"No. It's like she disappeared. Like Becca." Stephanie gave him a withering look, then unlocked her bicycle from the rack. She didn't glance at the cops.

"You!"

Nate turned at the cop's voice, but he wasn't speaking to him.

His friend Jake was heading toward him, his face intent, like he had to get to Nate before the cop did.

"You!" the cop shouted again. "Stop!"

Jake picked up the pace, keeping his eyes on Nate's.

"Jake?" Nate said, heading over to meet him.

"You!" The cop shouted, and then two other cops ran up and seized Jake.

"Hey!" Nate yelled. "That's my friend!" Usually the cops would give him a respectful nod—one time, someone had even called him sir.

Now, however, they ignored him. Jake was struggling in their grasp, and Nate grabbed one of the cops' shoulders to pull him off. The cop elbowed him hard, and then there was a sharp buzzing sound and Jake went down like a sack of potatoes. They'd tased him.

"That's my friend!" Nate shouted again as they started to haul him off. Jake's eyes had rolled back into his head, and his mouth hung open. The cops ignored Nate, except to shove him out of the way as they stuffed Jake into the backseat of their cruiser.

Then the two cars peeled away, their tires spitting tiny rocks. Jake had slumped down in the car, and Nate couldn't see him.

The cops had just arrested his friend. And a fellow Outsider.

60

CASSIE

BECCA HAD TOLD ME ABOUT the ring. She and her friends had tried to give me as much advice as they could in case I was picked to fight. A tiny part of me hadn't accepted that this might really happen.

As the guards shoved me toward the boxing ring in the middle of this huge auditorium, I tried to remember what Becca had told me. Something about my jumpsuit—that I'd be better off without it. How? Why?

Two kids were waiting for me. One of them grabbed my shoulders, spun me, and quickly twisted my hair into a tight braid that he shoved up under a rough metal helmet.

"Jumpsuit on or off?" the other kid demanded. I couldn't see stripping down in front of these two guys, much less a whole audience, so I said, "On." He shrugged, as if it were my funeral.

The rest of the armor was heavy and looked like it had been made from old car parts. It didn't fit me at all, pressing painfully into my spine and collarbones, and pinching my waist every time I moved. I couldn't believe this was happening. The image of Becca's gaping tooth socket kept crashing into my brain, and I was so scared I could barely stand.

One of the guys laced gloves onto my hands. There was lead shot sewn into them to make my punches hit harder. Where was I? What in the world was happening to me?

The other guy rapped his knuckles against my helmet. Terrified, I looked at him. "Keep your tongue in your mouth!" he said, which made no sense. "You don't want to lose it!"

My eyes flared wide, and he gave me a crooked grin. I saw that half of his face didn't move—it was paralyzed. He grinned wider—halfway—when he saw my shock, and pointed to the other guy. The other guy grinned also—evenly—but then opened his mouth.

My knees buckled, and they had to quickly grab my arms to keep me upright. The other kid had no tongue—just a healed nub where it had once been. He was also missing most of his front teeth.

I almost barfed. But then they were pushing me up the wooden steps and shoving me through the ropes. Bright lights made the ring almost glow; the rest of the auditorium was relatively dark. I'd heard hundreds of kids coming in and climbing up the squeaky wooden bleachers. This time two weeks ago I was stocking rolls of paper towels at the All-Ways.

Was Becca one of the kids watching? *Becca, help me.*

There was an excited roar from the audience, and several

shadowy figures climbed the steps opposite me. Squinting into the lights, I tried to control my shaking. Becca had said, *Just get through it. You will be broken down. Go ahead and be broken down. Do what you have to to survive. In an hour it will only be a bad memory.*

What would happen if I turned and ran out of here? How far would I get before I was caught and dragged back? How would I be punished? Was it too early to start crying and pleading for mercy?

My opponent climbed through the ropes. I was so frantic with terror that I could barely focus. But when I did...

I blinked several times, wondering if I was hallucinating.

It was Becca.

61

I'D NEVER BEEN SO GLAD to see my sister in my whole life. But a split-second later, that feeling faded. This Becca was gazing at me coldly. She wore armor, like me, but had taken off her jumpsuit. She turned her head and spit onto the canvas. I saw the bruises on her arms and legs, saw her grim expression and clenched jaw. Her heavy, gloved hands were swinging by her sides, as if she was eager to get started.

To get started fighting me.

Well, she knew more than I did. She would know how to make this look good without really hurting me. I would go through the motions of hitting back, and then I would just fall down and pretend to pass out.

It was a plan.

The bell dinged. Becca motioned for me to join her in the center of the ring. I met her with a slight, hidden smile: we were in this together.

Then my sister drew back her right arm and walloped my chin so hard I staggered, my arms flailing, and then fell to my knees, scraping them painfully on the hard canvas. My mouth filled with blood from where I'd bitten my tongue, and after a few seconds of stunned numbness, an unbelievable pain made me feel like I'd been hit by a truck.

"What are you do—" I tried to say, but my tongue was swelling and I was gagging on blood.

"Get up."

I stared at her. *Was this even my sister?*

"Get up!" she ordered.

Stupidly, still somehow trusting her, I got to my feet and put my arms up like I'd seen boxers do. One of her feet snapped out against my knee, making me buckle, and then she punched me in the stomach so hard I lost my breath.

Doubled over, wheezing, I wobbled clumsily to the side ropes and grabbed one to keep from falling. I was trying to suck in breath, blood dripping out of my open mouth, but as soon as I stood up slightly, Becca was there.

She slammed her glove into my lower back, sending an electric, radiating pain through me, and then spun on her heel and punched me in the stomach again.

"Wh-why?" I gasped, and turned just in time to see an enormous, blood-spattered glove aiming right for my eyes. Instinctively

I jerked back so instead of barreling into my forehead, she hit my left eye. I felt my eyelid split, felt the sudden heat of blood running down my face.

Then, in about two seconds, every single thing that Becca had ever done to piss me off came flooding back to me. New anger rose up in me, and I swung fiercely in a kind of punch I'd never thrown in my whole life.

Right before my weighted glove connected with her head, whipping it sideways, I saw…her smile, just a tiny bit.

Then she used the force of my blow to continue a spin, and came at me with an arm that felt like it was made of steel. That punch made me see stars. I wasn't aware of falling, but I realized I was looking up at lights. A big dark shadow loomed over me.

My sister.

"Becca?" I said, my words garbled and full of blood. "Why?"

62

BEATEN AND BLOODY, I'D EXPECTED to limp back to my jail room, where I intended to smother Becca to death with her blanket. Instead, after they bandaged my split eyebrow, two guards pushed me into a tiny room—four walls of cinder blocks with a steel door that had one weensy window in it.

"Oh, no way!" I said, as my waiting sister gave me a tiny smile. "Why the hell are *you* in here? And by the way—you're a goddamn bitch!"

My one working eye widened as Becca smiled a bit more. She gave a quick glance at the door's window, then came closer to me.

"I'm gonna kill you," I warned her, holding up a finger. "You better get back."

"They always put fighters together in this pen after a bout,"

Becca whispered, her back to the door. "And as far as I know, this is the only place that isn't bugged."

"The second we get out of here, I'm going to run you over with the tiller," I promised her, conveniently forgetting we were on death row.

"Cass—listen to me!" my sister said. "I don't know how long we're going to be in here!"

"It's already been too long!" I snapped, lisping slightly because I'd bit my tongue during the fight.

Becca got the mulish expression I knew all too well, and I tried to angrily clench my jaw, but couldn't because it hurt too much.

"I can't believe I wasted so much time looking for you!" I said.

"Shut. The. Hell. Up!" Becca said, grabbing my shoulder. She pressed her forehead against mine, the way we used to when we were little. I glared into her eyes, and she glared back into mine.

Then we had a prolonged shout-whispered argument, going back and forth, until we heard the lock of the door click open. Becca drew back and gave me a hard-eyed stare.

I spit on the ground by her feet. "I don't accept your apology!" I hissed as one guard grabbed my wrist to shackle.

"Well, you can go screw yourself!" Becca yelled back. She jerked her hand away from the guard. "I'm not sharing a room with her! You put her somewhere else! I never want to see her again!"

Ten minutes later I was in a new jail room, on a different hall, far away from my sister. This one had only three kids in it, so I got my own bunk. I lay down on it gingerly and put tentative fingers up to my puffy eye. *Oh, Ridiculous,* I thought. *What are we doing?*

63

NATHANIEL

CASSIE WAS GONE. NATHANIEL KNEW that, but he looked for her anyway until it was close to curfew. Crap. Both Greenfield sisters gone. Goddamnit. It was all happening too fast. He'd hoped to have more time. Worse, he couldn't help feeling that it was all his fault. Had Becca been taken because he'd recruited her to be an Outsider? Yeah. Had Cassie been taken because she was poking around too much? Yeah. Probably. This was on him. Squarely on his shoulders.

At Healthcare United, Nathaniel parked his moped and glanced up at the modest building. He'd only been inside once, eight years ago, to see his mother. He'd run to the bed and thrown himself against her. She had opened her eyes and looked at him, giving him a slight, quizzical smile, and Nathaniel's heart had turned to ice. His mother wasn't there anymore. They were a stranger's eyes.

"I'm here for Mr. Greenfield," Nate told the receptionist. She looked puzzled, but gave him the room number. Nate wondered how long it would take before she called his father. Well, he would make this quick.

Though he knew Mr. Greenfield couldn't see him, Nate still tried to keep the shock off his face as he looked down at the frail man hooked up to machines. He knew what had happened—everyone did—but he hadn't imagined the ruined face, the shattered shoulder, the slow, rasping breath.

"Mister," Nate began, then cleared his throat. He went closer to the bed, drawing up the plastic chair from beside the bed table. What the hell should he say? Sorry I got your daughters disappeared? Here's hoping they come back before you die?

Or...

What had Cassie called him? Dad? Pa?

"Pa," Nate said, keeping his voice light. "It's Cassie." He reached out and patted Mr. Greenfield's hand, trying not to flinch at the paper-thin skin. "I just wanted to let you know that everything's okay. School is fine. The All-Ways is fine. The farm is fine."

What else? What else could he say to this man who had been disgraced because he'd wanted to die by his own hand?

"Pa. It's Becca." Nate thought—what would Becca say? "I got a sixty-seven on a math test. The teacher says I can retake it."

Nate patted Mr. Greenfield's other hand. "But everything is fine. Um, a window accidentally got broken, but Cassie can fix it. Don't worry. You just get better, okay?"

Mr. Greenfield would never get better. His labored breathing told Nate that the end he'd sought months ago was at last drawing near.

God, this was all a mess. His own mother, Cassie's dad—the twins. How many more people would his father ruin?

"Okay, Pa," Nate said. "I gotta go. My shift is starting at the All-Ways. I'll see you soon, okay?"

Feeling overwhelmed by a sudden grief, Nate stood and stumbled past the nurse coming in. The ride home had never been so long.

64

MS. STREPP

"SHE'S FITTING IN SURPRISINGLY WELL." Warden Bell's dry observation echoed what Helen Strepp had been thinking.

"Look here," Ms. Strepp said, pointing at one of the screens from a bank that almost covered the wall. It was focused on the inmates' recreation yard—an outdoor, chain-linked rectangle as gray and grim as the rest of the prison. Cassie Greenfield was sitting cross-legged on the cement, surrounded by fellow prisoners. She had the nerve to be playing one of those patty-cake hand games that Ms. Strepp had never gotten the hang of. Prisoners were gathered around, watching and raising their hands to be next. Some of them were actually smiling. In the past several weeks, Cassie Greenfield had become unusually influential.

"She's . . . quite dangerous," Ms. Strepp said.

"Yes," Warden Bell agreed. "Just as we hoped. Don't get attached to this one, either, Strepp. You know the one-way path she's on."

"I know." Ms. Strepp was irritated at the Warden's suggestion that she was getting soft, sentimental. It was nothing like that.

"How are the experiments going?" The Warden's shrewd gaze seemed to look right inside Ms. Strepp's head.

"They are...ongoing," Ms. Strepp said shortly. In fact, she was concerned. The video feed showed Rebecca Greenfield standing by the chain-link fence, sullenly watching her sister. Ms. Strepp had expected the twins to immediately join forces, combining their strengths. Instead, the opposite had happened, against all her expectations.

"Okay, now watch this." Ms. Strepp pointed at a screen showing the same scene from a different angle. The two women watched as a hulking behavior problem strode up to Cassie and kicked her none too gently in the back.

Cassie stood slowly, her once-animated face turning expressionless.

"Her sister beat her easily in the ring," Warden Bell murmured.

"Yes. But that was weeks ago. She's made progress."

"Let's hope this lunk doesn't cripple her." The Warden's voice held a note of warning, telling Ms. Strepp not to push things too far.

Ms. Strepp was too tense to answer as the action unfolded on the screen. The guy outweighed Cassie by at least fifty pounds, and was six inches taller. Some inmates backed up to give them space, while others came to watch.

The guy made a fist and drew it back to give himself maximum power, but before he could even swing, Cassie launched herself at him as if she were a windmill in a hurricane. He was much more powerful, but she was lithe, hard, and fast. She flitted around like a mosquito, getting in multitudes of sharp, angry, well-placed jabs. It seemed only seconds before both of his eyes were swelling, his lip was split, his nose broken and bleeding. He limped from where she stomped on his instep, and was grimacing in pain from the killer kidney punch she had nailed him with—twice.

It was over quickly. The bully limped off to the jeers of the prisoners, his fists still clenched as he spit blood on the ground.

Cassie had a welt swelling on her jaw, a knot forming on her forehead, and her knuckles were bruised and scraped. She sat down again, somewhat stiffly—he'd landed one or two rib punches—and managed a smile.

Her devotees quickly sat down next to her, and as Strepp and Warden Bell watched, Cassie held up her hands again to start the game.

"Amazing," Warden Bell said.

"Yes," Ms. Strepp said, somewhat breathless. "I wish—"

"You know what's going to happen," Warden Bell said sharply. "There's a bigger plan in play here."

"I know."

The women turned away from the screen, and so they didn't see Becca Greenfield scowling at her sister, then hurrying after the guy her sister had just beaten.

65

BECCA

AFTER CASSIE'S SHOW-OFFY DISPLAY IN the prison yard, I was twice as glad that she wasn't bunking with me, Merry, Diego, and Vijay. They fell in beside me when the alarm sounded for us to go back to our rooms.

"Is your cell, like, really hostile?" Vijay asked. "You and Cassie have both kind of...taken to fighting super quick."

"Nah," I said, but I'd noticed the same thing. "Maybe just 'cause we're used to hard work? So we're strong?"

"You!" a voice boomed. "You quit talking!"

I clenched my teeth as I recognized the voice of our crazy-house traitor: Tim the Guard. I'd felt for him after our fight, when we were in the pen and he was yapping about being forced to fight, blah, blah, blah. But now, as he stood a head taller than anyone, important in his guard uniform, all I could muster up was loathing. He strode toward me and Vijay, tapping his billy club against one open palm.

"Shut up and hustle, people!" he said, pointing his billy club at me.

I narrowed my eyes and gave him a quiet sneer.

In seconds, he had yanked me out of line, slammed me against a wall, and pressed one forearm against me, right under my neck.

"You shut your trap!" he snarled, then grabbed my jumpsuit and practically hurled me back into line. Facing forward, I seethed and started swearing in my head, and then I realized my pocket felt weird—heavy. I put my hand in...and managed to keep my face blank for the rest of our march to our room. I didn't dare look at Tim as he slammed our door open and waited for us to file inside, then slammed it shut. He marched off, locking in other prisoners, and I moved slowly to the back wall, trying to get as much out of the view of the hall camera as possible.

Then I turned my back and carefully took my hand out of my pocket. The hand that was holding an apple that Tim had sneaked to me.

A real apple. It felt like forever since I'd seen one. The tasteless mush they fed us had no recognizable real food ingredients, and here I was with a whole real apple.

"Guys," I whispered almost soundlessly. "Circle round."

My roommates' eyes fastened onto the apple as if it were a unicorn.

"Where did you—" Diego began, then held up a hand. "Never mind. Don't want to know."

Slowly I brought it to my mouth and bit into it, feeling the skin break and tasting the sweet burst of juice. I almost moaned out loud. Then I passed it to Merry, whose startled, ravenous look gave me all the thanks I needed. She took a bite, closing her eyes and chewing slowly, and passed the apple to Diego. Diego made the sign of the cross and muttered a prayer, and then took his bite. He did moan out loud, but squelched it pretty quickly, handing the apple to Vijay.

Vijay almost inhaled it, and I remembered that they had all been here longer than me. It had been even longer ago since they'd seen an apple.

We took turns passing it around, and each managed to have at least five bites. We ate everything, even the core, and afterward I was as happy and full as if I'd just gotten up from Thanksgiving dinner.

Then I lay on my bed, savoring each bite over and over, reimagining it, running my fingers against my lips, still tasting the apple in my mouth.

The apple that Traitor Guard Tim had given me.

What was he doing?

Was this a trap?

If so, I had just jumped right into it, headfirst.

66

CASSIE

MY ROOMMATES WERE ALL RIGHT. I was the only girl, but Hayden, Mikaelus, and Rayray didn't treat me any different. Now that I was in another hall, I hardly ever saw Becca—maybe sometimes at meals or out in the yard. Mostly we just scowled at each other, like we were two other people instead of Cassie and Becca Greenfield, twins.

Back home in our cell, there had been lots of people, but lots of space. There had been room to be alone, where you could just sit under a tree listening to the breeze. Here, I was never alone, ever. There was approximately zero privacy, from the bare, stainless steel toilet in our cell to the coed showers, and coed everything else. Share an open toilet with three guys? It went from being an unthinkable impossibility to just business as usual in about four hours.

Same with the coed showers. At first you think you'd rather just stay dirty. But after a day or two of caked blood, mud, dank water, random dust, and the possible slime mold you sat on in the mess hall, you were completely and totally eager to strip down in front of thirty other kids. Completely and totally eager to bully a smaller kid out of the very rare soap. You didn't even mind the obnoxious WHAT'S GOOD FOR THE CELL IS WHAT'S GOOD FOR THE CITIZEN sign rusting on the wall.

"That's a good look for you."

Becca's dry voice made me turn quickly, brushing suds out of my eyes.

"What, clean?" I asked.

She shook her head and stood under the next ancient metal shower where sometimes rusty water flowed out in a tepid trickle. "Bruised. Banged up. Makes you look tough."

I gave a tense, fake laugh. "Yeah, that's me. Tough Cassie."

Becca snorted and tried vainly to work up a lather from the hard sliver of soap.

"Listen, Beck," I said in a low voice. My sister gave me a chilly, uninterested glance. "I think I know what's going on."

Becca ignored me.

"Listen, you little ass," I said, "who I somehow still happen to love. I think we're being drugged."

That got her attention; she shot me a startled look.

"I think they're drugging our food," I whispered. "I haven't eaten the last two meals. Please quit eating the stuff they give us, okay?"

My sister's eyebrows climbed.

"Just for a while," I pleaded. "We're going to get out of here—I know we are. But they're drugging us. Please, try skipping the food—for a short while, at least. We can escape—have you seen the dragonflies?"

Becca's face turned cold. "Guard!" she yelled.

I stared at Becca in disbelief, aware of all the eyes turning our way.

A guard, the big woman with bright yellow hair, strode toward us, billy club raised.

"Make this bitch leave me alone," Becca said, pointing at me.

"You're so stupid!" I shouted at Becca as the guard began pulling me away. "Listen to what I'm telling you! It's the truth! Just think about it!"

My sister said nothing. As I scrambled, still wet, into my jumpsuit, I wondered if the seed had taken. Time would tell.

67

NATHANIEL

HE'D BEEN LYING LOW FOR a couple of weeks, trying to figure out a plan, trying to put all the pieces together. Trying to get his dad off his back. Now he knew he had to act, had to do something.

The night air was cool and quiet, and this time Nathaniel drove right through the gates on his moped. When he got to Cassie's old truck, he could tell that something had happened here. There were the thin tire marks of a moped, and then the bigger, deeper treads of an all-wheeler and another vehicle leading off the boundary road. Nathaniel turned off road and followed the tracks as far as he could, which wasn't far—the wind blowing over the hard, dusty ground had scoured any sign of Cassie out of existence.

In the end Nathaniel went back to the boundary road and continued driving down it, going farther than he'd ever been before.

He had no idea if he would eventually fall over the edge of the world, or if he would come to a fairy-tale city or what. Probably he would go for a while and then get captured. Possibly disappeared. It wasn't like he had any other plans—life in Cell B-97-4275 was over for him. He knew that.

It was peaceful in the quiet evening air, with just the low electric hum of his moped barely audible over the wind, the occasional bird cry, the even more occasional sound of an animal.

He saw other vehicles abandoned by the side of the road. He knew why they hadn't been reclaimed for scrap—they were warnings. Signs that people had been here and had come to a bad end. Maybe tomorrow his moped would be found lying in the dirt, its radio gone, its chains cut. He would be the warning.

At first he thought the dark shapes ahead were low hills, or maybe shadows thrown by the moonlight. When he was much closer he saw the fence, the gate, the signs: this was a cell. A cell he'd never seen or known about, despite being only fifteen miles away from home. They might as well be on another planet.

Cautiously he drove through the gate. There wasn't much here—some buildings, a few houses. The whole place looked abandoned, except for the few weak lights that swayed in the wind.

Thunk! A stone came out of nowhere and hit Nathaniel right above his ear. He jerked to a stop, his hand on the sting, and looked around.

Ping! Another small rock hit the body of his moped.

Whirling, Nate peered into the darkness. The main thing he could see was a typical sign that said STRONGER UNITED, showing people holding hands and smiling. But this one had been graffitied—the O had been crossed out and replaced with an A, so it read STRANGER UNITED. And someone had drawn fangs on a woman's smile, and horns on a man's head.

"Who's there?" Nate called, just as another stone plunked against his foot. He saw the tiniest movement beneath the sign, which he raced toward after dropping his moped. A small boy jumped up and darted away, but Nate was taller and faster. He tackled him, and they both went down in a patch of scraggly grass.

"Oof!" The boy's breath left his lungs in a *whoosh,* and they started wriggling like fish on a bank.

Nate expertly pinned the kid to the ground, twisting one small arm up behind his back and sitting on his legs.

"Get off me, you stupid ape!"

Nate pulled the arm higher, causing the boy to squeal in pain and kick his feet against the grass.

"Let go of me, asshole!"

"Not till you tell me where I am," Nate said.

The figure stilled, though Nate could still feel the boy's quick breathing.

"What do you mean?" the boy said. "You're in Cell B-97-4280, duh!"

Nate eased up a little, and the boy turned to look at him.

"Hey, you're not from here, are ya? Huh! Lemme up, schmuck."

Slowly Nate eased up, and the boy scrambled to a sitting position, rubbing the shoulder joint Nate had stretched. He stared at Nate like he wasn't sure Nate was human, but was fascinating anyway.

"Where you from?" the kid asked. He looked about ten or eleven years old.

"Another cell," Nate said.

"No shit," the kid said, frowning. "There's only maybe two hun-nert folks here—I thought you was someone else, at first. If you was from here, I'd know it."

"What does this cell do?"

"Mining," the boy said. "Mining coal. Then we ship it off."

That explained why this place looked so dead—at home they were switching over to wind or water power, according to Cell News.

"Okay." Nate let out a breath, wondering what the hell to do now. This place was no help—he didn't know any Outsiders from here.

"Yep, mining now," said the boy. "'Course, we used to have the prison, too."

Nate frowned, looking at the boy intently. *"Prison?"*

68

"YEAH, PRISON," THE BOY SAID. "Hey, you got anything to eat?"

Nate patted his jacket pockets and found a candy bar. He handed it over and the boy fell on it with joy.

"Real chocklit!" he exclaimed, tearing off the wrapper.

"What's your name?" Nate asked him. "How old are you? How come you're out by yourself so late?"

The boy spoke through a mouthful of candy bar, counting off on his fingers. "None a yer business. None a yer business. None a yer freakin' business."

"Tell me about the prison," Nate said.

"What else you got?" the boy demanded, still chewing.

Nate felt his other pockets. He waved a five-dollar bill, but kept it out of the boy's reach. "Name?"

The boy frowned, licking his fingers. "They call me the Kid."

"Uh-huh. Age?"

"Thirteen."

"You're ten if you're a day," Nate scoffed.

"Eleven. And a half," the Kid said, scowling. "And I'm out this late by myself because who cares? Why wouldn't I be?" He gave a little jump and snatched the five-dollar bill, looking at it happily before stuffing it in the pocket of his grubby jeans.

"Now tell me about the prison," Nate said.

The Kid shrugged. "The bucks was for my name," he said. "What else you got?"

Sighing, Nate searched his other pockets and came up empty. Except—he unzipped his inside jacket pocket and felt around—it was still there.

"Here. This is all I have." Nate held the wrapped condom out to the Kid.

"Now we're talkin'," said the Kid, peering at the condom, reading the front and back of the foil package. "This is cool! This says I got a future, you know?"

"The prison?" Nate pressed.

"Heh," said the Kid. "Even better. I'll show ya."

The prison turned out to be a bunch of abandoned buildings surrounded by hills and sloping cliffs, a couple miles out of the cell. Nate lay his moped down, and he and the Kid dropped to their stomachs on a cliff.

There were no lights, no signs of life.

"How long ago was it abandoned?" Nate asked.

"That's the thing," the Kid said knowingly. "We don't do the prison no more—they closed it 'cause there ain't much crime in the United. But just you wait."

"It's dark," Nate pointed out. "No one's there."

"Nah, hang on," said the Kid, his bright black eyes shining like a beetle's. "There! Looka there!"

It was over in an instant—but Nate had seen it. At least, he was pretty sure he had: a black cloth twitching aside, revealing a stripe of bright light at one of the windows. Just for a second. As Nate looked closer, he saw that instead of moonlit emptiness behind the glass windows, there was a matte blackness. The windows were all covered.

"So who's in there?" Nate asked.

"Heh," said the Kid. "Who knows? But just watch. Ya gotta wait."

Waiting gave Nate all too much time to think—about his father, his mother, Becca, Cassie, the cell…

He was practically dozing off when the Kid gave him a sharp jab to the ribs.

"Lookit!" the Kid whispered, dropping lower into the dirt.

Two big trucks were approaching, sounding unnaturally loud in the dark night. Their headlights were dimmed, and they had no names or logos painted anywhere.

As Nate watched, the trucks paused in front of tall metal gates topped with razor wire. The gates screeched open and the trucks drove through.

"Was they construction trucks?" the Kid asked archly. "Didn't look like it. Was they food trucks? Who they feedin' in there? Mices? Rats?"

"You've seen this before?" Nate asked. "And then the trucks leave?"

The Kid nodded: he was the source of all knowledge. "They'll leave in a couple hours."

"Have you ever seen anything else?"

Shrugging, the Kid said, "Seen a van once, with tinted windas. Once I seen a black funeral car, like what the SAS uses."

Nate sat back, thinking. A secret prison in the middle of nowhere? Trucks bringing supplies? Call him crazy, but this seemed like an excellent spot to bring...disappeared kids.

Now he just needed a plan to get in.

69

BECCA

"OH, HELL, NO," I SAID.

Tim crossed his arms over his chest and glared at me. "Wasn't my idea."

The click-click of the Strepp's heels immediately put me on edge. Or, further on edge, I should say.

"It was my idea, Rebecca," she said coolly. "You've become one of our strongest fighters. Therefore you warrant more specialized training. As our *best* fighter, Tim is most suited to training you."

Nine snide retorts popped into my brain, but since I didn't want to get slammed with a billy club, I kept my mouth shut.

"You will do well, Rebecca," said Ms. Strepp. It wasn't a prediction or an encouragement. She didn't need to say, "Or else." It was understood. Giving us each a last look, she left us in the small, dank room.

Last time I'd seen Tim, he'd mashed me against a wall for talking in line. And then given me an apple. I had no idea what to expect now.

"Drop and give me thirty," he said.

For a second I considered dropping and giving him thirty one-fingered salutes, but again, not eager for a beating. Gritting my teeth, I got down on the ground and did thirty push-ups without a word.

And that was how it went. Tim was as much of a slave driver as Strepp was, but he never used the nail board, and he hardly ever whacked me with the billy club. We did weights, cardio, sparring, kickboxing—you name it. If it was heinous and sweaty, we did it. And of course once I was exhausted and as limp as corn silk, I had regular classes with Strepp. This week we were focusing on astrophysics, like how to determine the phase of the moon by only knowing the time of its setting or rising on a certain date. It was so much less fun than it sounds.

I was assigned a fight, as usual, and dreaded it, as usual. When I saw Tim was my opponent, my heart sank. I knew he wouldn't show me any mercy, and I knew if I didn't give it my all, I might be executed. Rock = hard place = death.

The bell dinged and Tim and I circled each other, our gloves raised. What was Cassie thinking, watching me? Were they really drugging our food? It would make sense. If *I* were an evil overlord, *I* would—

Wham! Tim's first punch slammed into my shoulder and spun me backward. I caught my balance, jumped in the air, and barreled my fist down into his face. He made a gagging sound, and then blood rushed from his nose. I smiled. And Tim…kind of smiled back. Was he proud of his student?

The first time I'd fought Tim it had been over within minutes and he'd annihilated me. This time was much worse because I was a much better fighter. The fight went on for a long, long time, and we damaged each other more—I actually heard one of his ribs crack at one point. He nearly dislocated my shoulder and fractured my instep.

Finally I was so whipped that I didn't jump out of the way quite fast enough when he landed a powerhouse punch to my head, and I went down. Out for the count and for several minutes afterward. I came to when someone waved ammonia under my nose, and as soon as I could stand they brought me to the pen.

Because that's what Strepp did. She made you fight, and then she locked you up together in a room barely big enough to sit down in.

They opened the door and shoved me in. Tim was waiting, one eye swollen shut, bloody and sweaty with bruises and scrapes all over. I'd done a good job of beating the crap out of him.

The guard slammed the door shut behind me, and I heard the lock click.

Tim and I looked at each other.

"You okay?" he asked.

I nodded. "You?"

Tim nodded. Then, without saying anything else, he grabbed me. As I looked up at him, startled, he angled his head and leaned down. When his mouth closed over mine I was too surprised to react, but within seconds my body was saying, *Oh, yes.*

Rising on tiptoe, I wrapped my arms around him and kissed him back, harder. I felt his lip split again, tasted his blood. When his shoulder pressed against the goose egg on my head, I made a sound. When I squeezed his fractured rib too tightly, he made a sound. But other than that, Tim and I were very, very quiet, kissing each other as wildly and as hungrily as if we were food, real food.

70

CASSIE

WATCHING MY SISTER FIGHT TIM had been horrible. As hard as it was to see her get hurt, it was even harder for me to see the deadly intent behind her eyes. I'd seen Becca happy, sleepy, sick, devious, defiant, and afraid, but I'd never seen her look like she wanted to actually kill someone. She truly was a different person now.

Of course, I couldn't point fingers. I was a different person, too. Since I'd gotten here, I'd discovered that being threatened all the time with beatings and torture was a surefire way of getting me to do my absolute best in anything—taking tests, working out, fighting other kids. I felt like Careful Cassie was dead, and would never come back.

"Cassie?" It was one of the younger inmates, shyly tugging on my jumpsuit.

"Yeah?"

"Can you show me that sticks game?" she asked. "The one I saw you playing before?"

"Yeah, okay." I started gathering up as many small straight twigs as I could. I mean, I was still *Cassie*. In some form.

But even after a few weeks, it was still a surprise to see how different these kids were, not only from me, but from each other. Other cells had different childhood games, different schooling systems, and vocations I'd never heard of. At first all I'd wanted was to escape and go home. I still wanted to escape, but would I go back home? Pa was still there...as far as I knew.

"Geez, you haven't changed much since grade two, have you?" Becca's cool voice made me look up.

"I'm teaching Peanut how to play Pick-Up Sticks," I said stiffly.

"You do love to impart your wisdom."

"Look who's talking, Queen Bee," I said, "with your little gang of followers." I glanced at a couple of the tough inmates Becca was hanging out with. "Does she have you fetching things for her yet? You like being a lapdog?"

The girl's face flushed angrily, and Becca's eyes narrowed. "Don't you talk to her like that!" she snapped.

I stood up. "Did I hurt your dog's feelings?"

The other kid lunged for me but Becca shoved her away. "You think you're so great 'cause everyone likes you!"

My eyebrows rose. "You want to think that last sentence through?"

That was all it took. Becca's lip curled in a snarl, and in the next second her fist came up and smashed me in the eye. But I'd learned a few things by now, and not only could I take it, but I could dish it out. I hooked my foot around her ankle and yanked, making Becca fall to the ground amid puffs of dust. Kids gathered around us, quickly dividing into two teams as Becca and I rolled on the ground, punching each other furiously.

I was barely aware of guards arriving, but the first whack of a billy club against my leg made me pause, blood running from my nose.

"You want to get tased?" a guard bellowed, and then the crowd parted for the Strepp, who was running toward us. Her face was white with anger and a strand of hair had escaped from her usually perfect bun.

"Animals!" she yelled at us when she was close enough. Four guards had pulled us apart, but Becca and I were still trying to kick each other. Our jumpsuits were filthy, we were both bloody and bruised, and I could barely see out of my left eye.

"You're supposed to be sisters!" Strepp screamed. "How can you turn on each other like this?" Looking at a guard, she said, "Put them in the pen!" Glaring at us with disgust, she added, "Maybe that will teach you to get along!"

71

BECCA AND I STRUGGLED AGAINST being shoved into the tiny concrete room, but the guard managed to get us in and slam the door. We stood there panting and glaring at each other until the guard's heavy footsteps pounded away down the hall.

Then Becca gave me a slow, wide smile.

I smiled back.

We smacked our hands together in high fives, and then hugged.

"It worked!" Becca said into my ear.

"Yep!"

That had been our plan, the one we'd thought out during our first time in the pen. This was the only place we could talk to each other without being spied on. At first we assumed we'd be signed up to fight each other again, but when that didn't work, we'd moved on to phase two: fighting each other anyway.

Quickly, in hushed whispers, we got each other caught up on what we'd been doing when we weren't together. I'd been trying to track any kind of schedule, in case there was a time that we could possibly try to escape. Becca had been tracking guards and teachers, in case any of them seemed more sympathetic.

The total sum of our knowledge was thin and depressing, and felt pointless.

"Did you tell your roommates what we were doing?" I asked.

Becca shook her head. "I'm being careful. You're the only person I can really trust."

"Back atcha," I said.

"Oh, guess what!" Becca's face was alight beneath the dirt and blood. "I made out with Tim!"

"Wha...? Tim-the-Guard Tim?" I asked, amazed. "The one who knocked your tooth out? The one you just fought again?"

My sister nodded, her eyes shining. "I don't know what it meant, if anything," she admitted. "But it was so hot."

"Might have been hotter if you hadn't been covered with sweat and blood," I mused, trying to wrap my head around this.

"Did not stop us," Becca said, grinning.

"Ew. Well, I wish I had made out with Nate before I got kidnapped," I said.

Becca looked surprised. "Nate Allen, the Provost's son?"

I nodded. "Yeah. He helped me look for you a couple times. Took me to the Outsider hangout," I reminded her. "I don't know. I miss him."

"Huh," Becca said. "You and the Provost's son."

"You and the prison guard," I countered.

"Did you tell Nate how you felt?" she asked.

"No. I mean, I shot his radio with Pa's gun."

"You flirty vixen, you," Becca said drily. "If that didn't win him over, then he's unwinnable. Anyway—enough about them. Let's talk about us. You've seen the dragonflies around here?"

"Yeah," I said. "A couple times. Why?"

"It occurred to me," Becca said. "If dragonflies can get into this place..."

"Then we can get out," I finished. "That's what we need to focus on next: figuring out how they got in."

And we put our heads together and started to plan.

72

NATHANIEL

NATE DIDN'T KNOW IF THIS prison was where they took the disappeared kids. But with no other leads, he had to take a chance. The Kid had been right; last night, after a couple of hours, the trucks had driven away. Nate had slept on the hill, but there had been no other activity at the abandoned-looking buildings.

"Do the trucks come every night?" he asked the Kid.

The Kid positioned a blade of grass against his thumbs and tried to whistle with it, unsuccessfully. "Don't know, do I? Ya think I'm out here every night? I gotta sleep sometimes."

"How come you're not in school?"

The Kid shot him a look of irritation. "'Cause it's a holiday, duh! Geez, you're a moron, ain't cha?"

Nate thought back, adding days to his mental calendar. "There's no holiday right now," he said.

Now the Kid openly sneered at him. "Oh, yeah? When do *you guys* get off for Bauxite Day?"

"We don't," Nate told him. "We don't celebrate Bauxite Day. Our cell is mostly farming. So we get, like, the Harvest Festival in the fall."

For a second, the Kid's armor of toughness fell away, and he was just a regular kid, amazed by something he hadn't known before. "Huh," he said, looking much younger than his eleven years. Then he came back to himself, and the small, pinched face hardened.

"It'll be dark again soon," Nate said. "I'm going to try to get inside the prison tonight."

The Kid laughed. "Sure you are! You can just mosey on up—"

"I'm gonna get closer, and when the trucks stop at the gates, I'll climb underneath one. I saw last night—they just got waved through. No one checked anything."

The Kid's black eyes narrowed. "You magnetic? How you gonna stick up under a truck?"

"There's pipes and axles and big bolts and stuff to hold on to," Nate explained patiently. "We used to do it for fun under big dump trucks at home."

The Kid looked unconvinced, but said, "I'm goin' with ya."

"No." Nate shook his head firmly. "This is my deal—I think they have my friends. You can't get mixed up in this."

"Well, screw you!" the Kid shouted, jumping to his feet. "I showed you everythin'! And this is how you treat me! You go jump down a mine shaft, asshole!" He raced down the hill, not looking back. Nate sighed, rubbed his eyes, and started scouting a place closer to the prison road where he could hide.

73

THE DEEP, SLOW RUMBLE OF the trucks made Nate blink, then quickly sit up. He'd almost fallen asleep! The trucks were hours later than they'd been last night. But they were coming, their headlights showing dust, insects, and the broken, potholed road that led to the chain-link fence.

With his stomach grazing the ground, Nate crawled closer as fast as he could. A large rock stuck up about twenty yards from the gates; by angling himself exactly, Nate couldn't be seen if the guard glanced over.

At least, he hoped he couldn't. This time two days ago, he'd been taking out the trash. Now he was about to break into a mysterious prison. When had his life gone sideways?

The trucks lumbered to a squeaking stop at the gates, and like before, it was a few minutes until a light clicked on and an armed guard came out.

Now! While the driver was showing his papers to the guard, Nate sprang forward, running hunched over and staying in the deepest shadows. He flung himself between the big wheels and immediately grabbed the truck's chassis. Wedging his feet against an indentation, Nate clung tightly, sweat breaking out on his forehead.

A slight scuffle to his right electrified his muscles and he stared wildly into the darkness—just in time to see the Kid scramble beneath the truck.

The truck's engine revved as the Kid peered upward, searching for something to hold on to. Nate wanted to yell at him, or at least hiss instructions, but he couldn't make a sound. Instead he jerked his head quickly toward another bar of the frame.

The Kid frowned, reaching up one hesitant hand as the truck rolled forward.

Nate's eyes almost popped out of his head—this weird little guy was about to be crushed beneath the wheels! The Kid hesitated another second, and Nate let go of one hand to point with frantic silence toward the bar.

The Kid's face cleared, he grabbed the bar, and at the last second he swung himself up. One leg dangled and the big wheel glanced off his shoe before he snatched his foot out of the way. But at last he was clinging like Nate was, bracing his feet up and holding on to the bar with all his might.

Nate sent him a furious, tight-lipped glare.

The Kid grinned back at him, even taking one hand off the bar to give Nate a thumbs-up.

The truck drove through the gates and rumbled down a narrow alley. A bit of grimy oil dripped onto Nate's face, and he shook his head so it wouldn't roll into his eye. When the truck squealed to a stop the Kid started to get down, but Nate shook his head urgently. Booted feet passed them and opened up the truck's cargo area. Voices shouted about unloading.

The Kid looked anxious. Nate's muscles were starting to shake and burn. He tried to send the Kid a mental message—hang on just another minute—but the Kid was looking distinctly uncomfortable.

This was an awesome plan, Nate congratulated himself bitterly. What now? Just hang on until the freaking truck drove right back out the gates and into the darkness? Why did the stupid Kid have to follow him here, anyway?

The vehicle jolted as the rear doors were slammed and bolted. The Kid looked over at Nate with wide eyes.

The driver climbed back into the cab and started the engine.

Nate made a quick decision: when the truck rolled forward he dropped down, staying carefully between the sets of wheels. The Kid didn't wait for instruction but dropped down, too, lying on his stomach and covering his head with his hands as the heavy truck rolled over them.

If they could just run and find cover...

"Hey! You there!"

The Kid's head jerked up as Nate scrambled to his feet. He

grabbed the Kid's arm, half dragging him toward the open door of the building. They hadn't gotten five yards before they were surrounded by guards holding rifles.

"You!" one of the guards said unnecessarily. "Who are you, and what are you doing here?"

Nathaniel looked around wildly, weighing his options. Which were zero, and zilch.

"His name is Nathaniel Allen," a woman's voice called.

The guards parted respectfully as a pale woman in an olive-green suit, her brown hair coiled up into a bun, strode toward them. She gave Nate and the Kid a chilly, serpentlike smile.

"Welcome, Nathaniel," she said. "We've had our eye on you for some time. Now you've saved us the trouble of fetching you. And you brought a little friend."

The Kid started to speak angrily, but the woman held up her hand.

"Save it," she advised. "My name is Ms. Strepp. I'm in charge here."

"Where is *here*?" Nate asked bravely.

Ms. Strepp smiled again. "You just broke into prison. Welcome to death row."

74

CASSIE

BECCA AND I CAME UP with the next steps in our plan, agreeing to keep it to just the two of us.

"What about Hot Tim?" I asked.

She made a rueful face. "Hot Tim will be merely decorative until I know him better. I mean, it *seems* like I can trust him, but—"

"Yeah," I said.

The sound of the door lock opening made us jump apart and immediately put scowls on our faces.

"It's about time!" Becca snapped as the guard stood aside to let us out. "How long were you gonna make me breathe the same air as her?"

"At least I shower sometimes!" I snarled, shoving her shoulder.

She wheeled on me, face contorted with amazingly convincing rage, and the guards pulled us apart.

"I see your time in the pen didn't have the desired effect." The Strepp's voice was dry and brittle, like a tin can rolling down a street. "It looks like I'll have to take further measures." She gave the guards a crisp nod, and they hustled Becca and me down the hall.

I expected us to be separated into our usual rooms, but instead we were taken to a hall that was new to both of us. It was smaller than the others, lower ceilinged and darker, as if it never saw fresh air or light.

I tried not to look at Becca as the guards shoved us toward the end of the hall. As we approached, rats scattered with angry squeaks, and I felt a chill penetrate down to my bone marrow. I'd been beaten up, seen *executions* of innocent *kids,* been tested to within an inch of my life—and here I was, finding that Strepp had found an even lower level to sink us to.

Glancing around, I saw that most of these rooms were empty. The few kids that were here looked more neglected: skinnier, more ragged, their eyes more hopeless, if that was possible.

The guard had trouble sliding open the rusty barred door, but finally it was barely wide enough for us to get through, and we were pushed inside. This cell had no bunks and no open toilet—just a bare concrete floor and a plastic pail. I was shaking but trying not to show my fear. On the wall across from us, a rusted sign hung by one screw. I could barely make out the words ORDER + DISCIPLINE = A HAPPY, HEALTHY CELL.

With effort the guard closed our door and made a show of locking it. She sneered at us, showing cracked, yellowing teeth, and then marched down the hall. For a minute Becca and I stood silently, seeing the rats start to cautiously come closer.

"Shit," Becca breathed, barely loud enough for me to hear.

I nodded in agreement. Shit, indeed.

The one bare bulb halfway down the hall flickered out, leaving us in almost total darkness. I reached out and felt for Becca's hand. Her grubby fingers interlaced with mine.

We were facing something even worse than we'd had so far, but at least we were together again. Too scared to keep up the pretense of being enemies, we simply stood in the darkness and waited, listening to the scurrying rats and the slow drip of water somewhere.

Then a voice floated across the hallway to us: "Cassie? Becca?"

75

BECCA

CASSIE AND I IMMEDIATELY PRESSED our faces to the peeling, decrepit bars, peering into the darkness. Across the hallway a figure stepped closer to the bars of the opposite cell.

"Nate!" Cassie gasped.

"Nate?" I echoed in surprise.

"Who're those chicks?" said a voice next to him, and then a smaller figure appeared. I couldn't make out what he looked like, but he was just a kid, one of the youngest I'd seen in this hellhole.

"Nate, what are you doing here?" Cassie asked. I remembered her saying she'd wanted to make out with him.

Nate shrugged, though his face was tense. "Skipping out of a hybrid corn test."

My sister smiled, her teeth almost luminous in the dimness.

"So what is this joint?" the little kid asked.

"The crazy house. It's—" I started to answer him but was interrupted by the harsh buzzing of the alarm. Cassie and I knew what to expect, stepping back fast so our fingers wouldn't get pinched by our door opening automatically. But Nate and the kid looked startled, snatching back their hands at the last second.

"What's happening?" Nate asked.

All down the hallway, doors opened with grinding creaks. Cassie and I had to push against ours, but finally got out and filed down the dank hall with the other kids.

"Well..." Cassie began reluctantly.

"It's...actually, it's an execution," I said quietly. "This is a prison just for kids. It's death row for everyone. And...kids get executed pretty often."

Nate looked horrified and the little kid's pale, pinched face grew whiter, if possible.

"Whaddaya mean, *executed?*" the kid asked.

"I mean...killed," I said. "Put to death. Usually for no reason at all." No sense in prettying it up—they'd have to get used to the idea, and the sooner the better.

"Wait," Nate said, shaking his head as we streamed upstairs and down another hall, heading to the ring. "What are you talking about?"

Cassie looked at him with pity. "It's true," she murmured, since we were now surrounded by guards. I was scouring the place for Tim, but stealthily.

"First you'll get tested," Cassie explained in a low voice. "Try to do your best. How well you do determines how long you last in here."

Nathaniel looked a bit green.

"Okay, when you says, 'killed,'" the kid said, "ya mean, like—"

"What's your name, kid?" I asked.

He frowned and nodded. "Yeah."

"Yeah what?"

"Yeah, that's my name," he said. "They call me the Kid."

"Geez," I said. "That's original."

"You there!" barked a familiar voice.

I narrowed my eyes and turned to see Tim in his guard suit, brandishing his billy club. "Shut up and keep moving!"

"Eff you," the Kid began angrily, but I clapped my hand over his mouth and dragged him along.

There had been a glitter in Tim's eyes. My face ached with wanting to smile, but of course I didn't, just shuffled up into the bleachers with the others to await some fresh horror.

My life sucked more every day.

76

IT WAS MERRY.

Today's victim was Merry.

My heart seized and I sucked in a shocked breath when I saw my roommate getting hauled onto the canvas floor of the ring. As usual, there was a gurney and two "nurses," who were checking the equipment, filling syringes, getting ready to kill a kid.

Merry's small face peered into the bleachers, but I knew she couldn't see anyone past the lights. I wanted to shout out to her, which would be fine if I didn't mind getting dragged out of the bleachers, beaten, and possibly tossed up on the stage next to her for a double feature.

All I could do was send her thoughts—pointless, I know. But it was all I had.

It's okay, Merry. It won't hurt. It will all be over soon. I didn't know if I was trying to comfort her or me.

"What the hell they doin'?" the Kid whispered next to me.

"Shut up!" I hissed between clenched teeth. "Unless you want the crap kicked out of you."

They put Merry on the gurney and hooked her up to the machines. I remembered how young she was, how hard prison was for her. I wondered where Diego and Vijay were. I thought about Robin, how she and Merry had helped me. Glancing over the Kid's head, I saw Cassie staring somberly at the ring. Her face was still, her eyes heavy with unshed tears.

Merry was scared, her eyes wide with fear. Her fine, mouse-colored hair hung limply over the side of the gurney. She had parents. They didn't know what had happened to her. Now she was about to die, and they would never know.

"Jesus H. Christ," the Kid muttered next to me. When his wiry little hand gripped my arm, I took pity on him and let it stay there.

It was the usual, the machines, the injections. I'd seen it several times before, but I wasn't getting used to it. It was still terrifying. It still made me feel frantic, sick, enraged, and helpless. My throat closed when I saw Merry's eyes go blank, and I forgot to breathe as her heartbeat flattened out and stopped. I tried to ignore what was happening, tried to think about anything else instead, but found tears spilling out of my eyes and my nose stuffing up. Angrily I wiped my sleeve over my face.

"Every ending is a beginning," Strepp announced, standing in the center of the ring. "Remember that."

I'd never hated her more, never wanted to kill her more than right then.

As we got up to file out, Nate suddenly doubled over and threw up. Inmates shrieked and jumped away from him. Cassie patted his back.

"People die in here," she told him, and the angry, hard tone in her voice didn't sound like Cassie at all. "People get beaten and tased and broken. Better get used to it—you don't know how long you have left."

Nate was heaving and gasping, but managed to straighten up and get back in line just as two guards came over.

"One more thing," Cassie muttered as we joined the hundreds of other somber kids. "Don't eat the food. I think it's drugged. It's another way for them to control us."

Next to me, the Kid looked like he was about to pass out. I jabbed him in the ribs and he blinked.

"Wise up, Kid," I said, not unkindly. "Let's see how long you last."

He nodded and looked straight ahead, as did I. We didn't speak again, and when they locked us back in our room, Cassie and I sat down on the damp concrete and didn't look at each other. In the darkness I let my tears come again, but kept perfectly silent as the sobs wracked me.

Merry. Merry, like Merry Christmas. Dead.

77

I'D SWORN TO REMEMBER ROBIN forever, and now Merry. How many names would I have to memorize before I either got out of here or got killed myself?

Our new room was so oppressive and horrible that being let into the cheerless "exercise yard" actually seemed like a treat. Bare dirt, chain-link fence topped with electrified razor wire—I was glad to see it.

Of course, it was hard avoiding the Cassie Fan Club when we were outside. As always, people were drawn to her and wanted to be near her. It used to irritate the living daylights out of me. Come to think of it, it still did.

"Jesus, we need two seconds of privacy here," I muttered as another kid came up to us in the yard.

Cassie looked at me solemnly. "I'm sorry I'm popular."

I made a face at her and turned away as she dealt with the latest suck-up.

"I'll come play with you in a couple minutes," I heard my sister promise, and rolled my eyes.

When she was free we went back to planning.

"I've seen the dragonflies in two different halls," Cassie murmured.

"I saw them in the hall leading to the ring, and in the hall toward the infirmary," I whispered, then immediately tried not to think about the infirmary. Every so often, when I least expected it, I suddenly flashed on the pain, the terror, the despair of that day. The day when I'd lost the baby I hadn't wanted and had refused to acknowledge. It had scarred my soul, and that scar would be there till I died.

"But in the actual buildings, I haven't seen any holes or broken windows," Cassie went on. "Nowhere they could get in or out."

"Nowhere *who* could get in?"

I jumped slightly—hadn't heard Nathaniel come up behind me. As the Provost's son and an Outsider, he had finely honed sneaking skills.

"Not who—what," said Cassie. "Dragonflies. We've seen dragonflies in some of the hallways. And if they can get in—"

"Then we can get out," Nate said, catching on immediately.

"We need to get organized about remembering where we've seen them," I said. "And try to search as many halls as possible."

"That won't be easy," Cassie said. "It's not like we get a lot of unsupervised wandering time."

"No," Nate agreed. "Though this morning I got a tour of the classroom." He grimaced and I looked at him with sympathy. We'd heard them come for him this morning. More than almost anything, it was being powerless to help others that was making me nuts.

"Once we find a crack in a window somewhere, then what?" I asked impatiently. "Did everyone remember to bring their magic spell so we can just fly out of here?"

"I brought mine," Nate said seriously.

I gave him a look. "Nate, the last place someone would find a magic spell is Cell B-97-4275."

"I know a way out," said the Kid, but of course we all ignored him.

"Okay, everyone scout around as much as possible," Cassie said. "Tomorrow we'll meet back here and compare notes."

"I know a way out," the Kid said more insistently.

"Did you ever see them in the mess hall?" Cassie asked me.

"I know a way out!" The Kid's small, pointy chin stuck out aggressively, and he wedged himself between me and Cassie. "'Cause I know how them bugs got in!"

78

CASSIE

I HAD NO IDEA WHERE Nate had found this boy, but he was a character. I'd barely paid attention to him before now—my senses were still all squirrelly over seeing Nate again. On the one hand, I was so, so glad to see him. On the other hand, I was so, so, so bummed that he was in here, and was praying that I wouldn't have to watch him die.

Now I looked down at the Kid in his heinous yellow jumpsuit—way too big for him, rolled up at the sleeves and ankles.

"Yes?" I said politely, figuring we'd humor him for a minute so we could get back to business.

"Yeah," he said, sticking his chin higher in the air.

"Okay, I'll bite," Becca said, crossing her arms over her chest. "How did the dragonflies get in?"

"There's a tunnel," the Kid said.

"A tunnel," Becca repeated, obviously not believing him.

"Yeah. I live around here, see? And when I was little, this is where they put crazy people."

I didn't point out that in fact he was still little. At least comparatively.

"Crazy people?" Cassie asked.

"Yeah. Nowadays they do them mood-adjusts," the Kid said, not knowing that the three of us all had firsthand knowledge of that. "But back then they just locked crazy people up. People who talked bad about the cell and all. There was a guy who was crazy, and they put him in here, and he dug his way out."

"Wait...what?" I asked. Guess I was right—it really is a crazy house.

"He dug hisself a tunnel," the Kid said, glancing over his shoulder to make sure no one was around. "From in here to out there." The Kid pointed to the scrubby pines about fifty yards outside the prison fence.

"You're...almost making sense," Nate said, frowning.

"So what happened?" I asked.

"He got out, didn't he?" said the Kid, shrugging.

"He *escaped?*" Cassie said.

"Well, nah, not really," the Kid amended. "Like, he got out, but they caught him. And then the tunnel sort of fell in, at least partly."

"What happened to the guy?" I couldn't help asking.

"Oh, they shot 'im," the Kid said, and snapped his fingers. "Just like that."

"How do you even know this?" Nate asked.

"'Cause it was my dad," the Kid said.

79

SO WE DECIDED TO FIND this tunnel, and to make sure the four of us got out. As a plan it wasn't exactly a three-season, cell-wide, crop-rotation schematic, but it was all we had.

From memory we drew lines in the dirt to represent various halls, the ring, the mess hall, the classrooms. Of course, we each remembered things differently, and in the end our drawing looked like a chicken had been trying to scratch a worm out of the ground. We smudged it with our feet and tried to come up with ways to explore.

After about fourteen seconds we felt crushed by how hard that would be and how long it might take us. We might not have that much time. I wanted to cry.

"Look," Becca said urgently. "This could take forever. I say we just commit! Let's say we're going to bust out of this hellhole tonight, no matter what!"

"Tonight? How are we going to do that?" I demanded.

My sister smacked her hand against the dirt. "We're just going to break out! The bars on our cell are about rusted through. We'll break them! Or we'll knock our guard out, steal his keys!"

I gritted my teeth. This was sounding a whole lot like Ridiculous Rebecca, Queen of Fantasyland.

"It's not that easy," I said tightly. "There are other guards, other doors, alarms. And clearly we have no idea of how the hell to get out of here!" I pointed to the rubbed-out failure of a map.

Becca's eyes narrowed. "Okay, Careful Cassie. How do you think we should do it? Or should we just stay in here like good kids until they kill us?"

"Of course not!" I snapped. "We need to get out of here as soon as possible, but—" A sudden burst of static made me wince as the loudspeakers in the yard crackled to life.

"'The best-laid plans of mice and men...'" said Strepp, and as the words sank in I looked at Becca and Nate in surprise.

"Is the yard bugged?" Nate asked in an almost silent whisper. Eyes wide and heart starting to pound, I raised my shoulders in a "don't know" gesture.

"Prisoners!" said Strepp. "Report to the ring!"

"Man!" said the Kid as we started to move toward the doors like a herd of milkers at sundown. "We better not be seein' some other kid get offed. I hate this shit."

"Me, too," I said fervently as we passed beneath the hated

PHYSICAL HEALTH LEADS TO MENTAL HEALTH AT THE UNITED! sign. "I do indeed hate this shit."

Usually I paid attention to faces, low conversations, the discomfort of my jumpsuit, my hunger. This time I scanned every ceiling, every door, every crack everywhere, searching for a hint of the tunnel's location.

At the door to the ring, a guard stepped forward and grabbed Nate's arm.

"You!" he said. "Come with me!"

I grabbed at his jumpsuit, but he was hauled away. Nate gave me a last, freaked-out look, but I was helpless as he was dragged to the edge of the ring.

Becca and I stared at each other in horror.

"What's happenin'?" the Kid demanded. "They gonna off 'im?"

"No," I said in dismay as we filed into a row of the bleachers. "They're going to make him fight."

80

"HE CAN TAKE CARE OF hisself," the Kid said confidently.

I let out a deep breath. "Not like this." Nate hadn't had time to be trained. He'd never seen a fight, to pick up tricks and moves. I remembered how bad my fight had been, and what Becca had told me of her first fight, and felt kind of sick.

I met Becca's eyes over the Kid's head. "Will it be better or worse if it's Tim?" I asked her, and she shook her head, looking upset.

They clapped armor on Nate; he'd chosen not to wear his jumpsuit, which was good. His farmer's tan showed beneath the armor, his arms and legs browned by the sun, and the rest of him milk-white.

It was all so surreal, so unbelievable. I closed my eyes, pointlessly praying that I could open them and it would be 6:00 a.m. and I would hear the hiss of the coffeemaker brewing downstairs. But when I opened them, Nate was standing on the canvas floor of the ring and someone I'd never seen before was climbing through the ropes.

He was huge. He wasn't a kid—he must be one of the grown-up guards. Nate was tall; his opponent was at least six eight. Nate wasn't skinny; he had the muscles of a kid from a farming cell, despite his father's job—but this guy outweighed him by at least sixty pounds.

"Why would they do this?" I whispered to Becca. "Why not just let him fight another prisoner?"

Her eyes were full of sympathy, and she reached behind the Kid to pat my shoulder.

"Oh, no," the Kid murmured, his black eyes wide. He reached up and covered his face with his hands, not wanting to watch.

"Kid?" I murmured unhappily. "You should watch. And learn. You'll need to know how to win when it's your turn to fight."

Slowly the Kid uncovered his eyes. He was such a tough little guy, but prison was starting to break him down in a way that even a hard life in a mining cell hadn't. Becca was right. We needed to leave—tonight.

Nate's face was pale beneath the bright lights. He clenched his jaw as the huge guy started to circle him.

Suddenly Nate shot forward with a harsh cry of rage and walloped the guy in the jaw. If it had been anyone else, they'd have been out cold. As it was, the giant staggered but rallied immediately. He was enormous and powerful, but Nate was nimbler. The big guy had a longer reach, but Nate was faster.

But his opponent had more experience, and it wasn't long before his glove exploded against Nate's metal helmet. Nate's head spun as the punch lifted him a couple inches in the air, and then his arms flailed as he crashed to the ground.

"Okay, not too bad," I muttered to myself. "If he doesn't have a concussion, he should be—"

Nate rolled onto his hands and knees, shaking his head. I wanted to scream, "Stay down, you moron!" but didn't dare.

After that it was bad. Nate's nose was bleeding, so every time he got hit, a thin stream of blood whipped against his opponent. He got in a couple of good hits, but the other guy just destroyed him, his punches seeming like the unstoppable motion of a robot. Nate went down twice more and twice more got up, because he was a *stupid freaking goddamn idiot.*

We heard his ribs crack even from where we were sitting. I covered my mouth, hoping I wouldn't throw up. His lip got split. His metal helmet smashed against his forehead and opened a gash three inches long. Deep, ugly bruises—the kind that continue to worsen over days—were blooming all over him.

But it was the last thing that made me gasp, made me feel like I really would hurl. It was that last kick, the one the giant aimed right at Nate's knee. The one that shattered the bone, bent his leg nauseatingly sideways, and made Nate topple onto the canvas like a stork. That was the one that got me.

Strepp came into the ring. Nate, his face white, his eyes glazed and unseeing as incomprehensible pain wracked his body, lay at her feet. Strepp grabbed the mic and said, "'It is our choices...that show what we really are, far more than our abilities.' A woman named J. K. Rowling said that. Think about that." Then she left the ring with the hulking guard following her.

Rage boiled inside me and threatened to erupt as a shrieking howl. Nate's leg was broken, his knee destroyed. He wouldn't be escaping from here any time soon.

What kind of *choice* did that leave me now?

81

BECCA

GODDAMNIT. BY THE TIME WE got back to the cell, Cassie was shaking with fury.

"Tonight was the night!" she hissed at me after we'd been locked back in our room. The Kid, all by himself, was across from us. Nate was in the infirmary, of course—that last kick had been brutal. He'd be lucky if he ever walked again.

"We were supposed to try to escape tonight! Now what?"

What do you mean, Now what? I thought, but said, "What are you thinking?"

She paced our small room, her fists clenched. "I think we still have to go," she said, sounding tortured. "But how? Nate *came here* for *me*—for us! And now we're supposed to leave him here to be killed? I can't stand it!" She crumpled to her knees, her hands over her face, trying not to cry. I knelt next to her, putting my arm around her shoulders. This was my twin: we'd been comforting each other our whole lives.

"What do you want to do?" I asked, carefully. "I hate leaving Nate, too. But the longer we stay..."

"The more likely we'll be killed," Cassie said. "I know. But... shit!"

"Psst!" Startled, I jerked my head toward the sound. A familiar silhouette stood by our barred door. I jumped up.

"Why are you here?" I asked Tim, and he put his finger to his lips. Then he unlocked our door as quietly as possible, opening it just enough to let me through.

"What are you doing?" I whispered. "I won't leave my sister!"

"You'll be back in a minute," Tim promised, and led me down the hall. Most of the rooms here weren't occupied, and about halfway down the hall Tim ducked into one, pulling me in after him. We went to the far corner where it was completely dark and we were hidden.

"Listen," Tim began softly, but I launched myself at him, slamming my mouth against his, holding him as tightly as I could. This, *this* was the only comfort I'd had in this hellhole, just this human touch, the warmth of his arms around me. I wanted to feel like a teenage girl with a crush on a boy, instead of a prisoner or a fighter or a rebel. I knew if we were caught we might both be killed; at any second an alarm might sound that meant the death of one of my friends, or some nameless kid, or my sister, or me. I didn't care.

Minutes later, when I felt human again, I rested my head in the shallow of Tim's shoulder, hearing the quick-paced *thumpthump-thump* of his heart beneath my cheek. He was warm and solid—maybe the only thing in my life that was. It felt like heaven.

"Listen," he murmured again, his lips against my hair.

"Mm?" I said, my eyes closed.

"Later tonight there's going to be an execution," he said softly. "So everyone will be in the auditorium."

"Uh-huh," I said, wondering why he was telling me this. Unless he knew who it was going to be. Maybe me?

"Here," he whispered, and pressed something into my hand. My fingers closed around it and I looked up at him, startled.

"What's this?" I asked.

He told me.

"Huh," I said as ideas started to tumble through my brain. We talked very quietly for another minute, and then he said, "Babe, I gotta take you back." He gave me an apologetic look. "I'll see you later."

He locked me back in our room. I pressed my face hard against the bars so I could watch him walk down the hall. He'd said he'd see me later. Had that been a promise?

82

CASSIE HAD FINALLY FALLEN ASLEEP, curled up on the damp, decaying concrete floor. I let her rest as long as possible, but had to wake her a little after 1:00 in the morning.

"Wha?" she said sleepily.

"It's time to go," I whispered into her ear. "We're going to grab the Kid and start looking for the tunnel."

She blinked owlishly in the dim light. "Don't be dumb. That plan is nowhere."

I dangled a ring of keys over her head, and her eyes widened. "Tim gave them to me. Keys to the crazy house. If we can get out of here, he's going to steal a truck and get us back to our cell."

Cassie's mouth opened in an O of surprise.

"'Course—we still need a master key, and only Strepp has that," I told her. "We'll have to cross that bridge when we get to it."

Cassie was on her feet, rubbing sleep out of her eyes.

"In a minute the execution alarm is going to sound." I had no sooner finished saying the words than it did sound, loudly and harshly, a horrible Klaxon of death.

We waited for the barred door to slide open, and as soon as it did, I nipped across the hall and got the Kid.

"Ain't we supposed to go?" he asked in confusion.

"Not this time," I said, and drew him back into our cell to wait for the sound of shuffling feet to fade. We were so conditioned to follow the crowd when the alarm rang that *not* following made us all jumpy and tense, like rats that weren't being allowed to run the maze.

At last it was silent—our hall was empty.

"Let's go," I breathed, trying to sound like I knew what I was doing. In truth, I was so tense and keyed up that it took all my concentration to not start babbling at any second. I was quivering with cold and fear—was I leading Cassie and this kid into certain death? Or was I seizing our only chance?

"And the plan is…?" Cassie asked.

"We've got the keys to get us through most of the hall doors," I explained. "Everyone's in the auditorium. So we're going to search for this tunnel like our lives depended on it." I gave a sardonic smile. "Because they do."

Cassie looked at me. I was pretty sure she was remembering the time I dared her to jump off the rope swing into the river. She'd broken her collarbone. Or the time I'd convinced her to take the long way home so we could watch the last of the geese streaking southward as winter approached. We'd been late for dinner and had gotten our hides tanned by Pa.

If she was smart, she'd back away from me and sit down in our cell. And I wouldn't blame her.

Instead she gave a glimmer of a smile and nodded. "I'm with you."

And damn if that didn't practically make me cry.

Nodding, I eased out of our cell. And of course we'd only gone as far as the *very next* prison room when Strepp sprang out at us, her face aglow with triumph.

"Not so fast," she crowed.

83

CASSIE

I'M THE LEVELHEADED, SENSIBLE, RULE-FOLLOWING one. I had doubts
that this tissue-paper-thin plan would work, and was pretty sure
we'd all end up *even more* on death row. The smart thing to do was
leap back into my cell and insist I knew nothing about any of it,
they were making me, etc.

Instead I balled my hand into a fist, jumped forward, and
slammed it into Strepp's face as hard as I could. To tell you the
truth, it probably hurt me more than her; I heard a snap and my
hand exploded in pain.

Strepp went down like a shock of wheat in a windstorm. Her
eyes fluttered closed and an angry red blotch appeared on her tem-
ple where my knuckles had left imprints. I dropped to my knees,
staring at my hand in amazement: I hadn't known anything that

small could hurt that much. It dangled in front of me like a dead thing, radiating ungodly pain.

Becca gave the Kid a brisk order. "Search her. We need any kind of key she has on her."

Hesitantly at first, the Kid started rifling through Strepp's pockets. I got to my feet with difficulty. When the Kid pulled out a handkerchief, I took it and bound it gingerly around my throbbing fingers.

"Here!" The Kid held up a key ring and shook it excitedly.

"None of them are marked—that would be too easy," Becca muttered, examining them. "We'll have to try them all." She gave me a grin. "Excellent work, Killer."

I gave a tight-lipped smile.

"Kid, help me out here," Becca instructed. They each grabbed a foot and dragged Strepp into our room, stepping out quickly and hauling the barred door closed behind them.

"You just signed your death warrant!" Strepp's voice, angry but weak, floated out to us. Becca hurriedly began jamming key after key into the lock, trying to find the right one.

"More of a death warrant than being on *death row?*" Becca countered, working fast. She snapped a key sharply to the left, locking Strepp in, and stepped back triumphantly.

Getting unsteadily to her feet, Strepp put her hand in her pocket. "You forgot I have a panic alarm." A slight frown creased her forehead as she tried another pocket.

"You forgot you was out like a light, lady," said the Kid, and pointed to the contents of her pockets, piled on the hallway floor.

For the first time, Strepp looked scared. "You don't understand," she said, licking her thin lips.

"I understand that you're lost in the weeds without a hoe," said Becca, starting to stuff Strepp's belongings into the pockets of her jumpsuit.

"No," said Ms. Strepp. "Girls—be careful."

That made Becca snap her gaze to the older woman. "Be careful? A bit late for that, isn't it?"

Ms. Strepp pressed her face against the rusty bars, like we always did. "Think about this, girls—we aren't drugging you. We've been getting you *off* drugs—the drugs they put in every cell's drinking water."

We stared at her. She looked oddly sincere.

"You're only seeing part of the picture," Ms. Strepp went on. "I promise that if you saw the whole picture, you would understand."

"Mostly I sees *you,* stuck in that jail," the Kid said.

"Really," Becca said, crossing her arms over her chest.

I couldn't listen to another minute. I didn't want to stand here and yap with our enemy, I didn't care what the big picture was. While they were still arguing, I faded off down the hall.

84

BECCA

WAS THIS WOMAN BATSHIT CRAZY or was she telling the truth? Was this a trap or was she possibly trying to help us? Jesus. *Of course it was a trap!* What was I doing, standing here?

"Come on, guys!" I said, and that was when I noticed that Cassie wasn't right next to me.

I strained to see up and down the dark hall. "Cassie?" I hissed as loudly as I dared. To my shock, she didn't immediately pop out of an empty room, didn't appear out of the shadows.

"Shit," the Kid said, looking left and right. "She's gone!"

This was so totally un-Cassie-like that I froze for a second, thinking it through. Cassie was a girl who, even when she was at her most furious at me, would still care enough to shout at me to take the shortcut home so I wouldn't get in trouble. There's no way she would have left me. No way at all.

I looked at the Kid, who seemed small and very young. He was relying on me. I nodded at him.

"Let's go."

As we ran almost silently down the hall, Strepp didn't say a word.

85

CASSIE

THE LAST TIME I'D BEEN to the infirmary—the only time—had been after Becca had wiped the floor with me in the ring. I wasn't totally sure of the way there; I'd been unconscious going in, and then a mess coming back.

The halls were empty. Everyone was in the auditorium. I thought about what was happening right now, some kid getting hooked up to a machine, and it sent a cold chill down my back.

I turned into one hall and crept most of the way down before I saw it was a dead end. Swearing under my breath, I darted from doorway to doorway, listening for footsteps, the sounds of doors opening, anything that would force me to abandon my mission.

After I'd retraced my path, I went down the second hall I found, and my heart leaped when I saw the broken, unlit sign: INFIRMARY.

Keeping below the windows of these doors, I made my way along the hall, sticking my tongue out as I passed the HEALTHIER TOGETHER AT THE UNITED! sign. Just as I heard footsteps coming, I ducked through into the infirmary. Unfortunately, instead of turning, the footsteps grew louder: they were coming here!

Scanning the room frantically, I saw a cupboard beneath a sink and sprang over to it. It held only a few bottles of cleaner, and I crammed myself inside as fast as I could. The infirmary door opened and voices became loud.

"We'll need to order more of the knockout drug," someone was saying. "Warden Bell has upped the executions faster than we expected."

The other person laughed and said, "Put it on the list. We need more paper towels, too."

Inside the dark cupboard, folded up like an origami crane, my face burned. Ordering more of the drug to kill innocent kids was right up there with paper goods! These people were soulless monsters!

Steps came very close to me, and right above my head someone turned on the sink. I scowled as a cold drip, drip of water started leaking from the pipe jammed against my neck. The icy water ran down inside my jumpsuit and puddled at the small of my back. This was the stupidest thing I'd ever done.

After several long minutes, the water was turned off, the footsteps left, and the tiny crack of light at the cupboard door went dark. I waited a while longer, then cautiously opened the cupboard door, groaning at my stiff muscles from the cramped position.

Slowly I unfurled myself, and then crept toward the back of the infirmary.

There he was. Lying on the bare plastic of a hospital bed, one leg encased in a plaster cast from thigh to ankle, Nate was looking up at the ceiling. The muscles in his jaw were clenching and unclenching, and his face was bruised and battered. Black sutures held together the three-inch gash on his forehead.

I came up silently, so silently that he jumped when he realized I was standing there. Then he winced, suppressing a groan at how his startled movement had made everything hurt all over again.

"Hey," I said softly. "Come with me now, or die."

86

BECCA

THE KID AND I STRUCK out, tunnel-wise, in our quadrant of the jail, and we moved to the next block. My mind was racing, worried sick about Cassie and wondering what the hell had happened to her. I hadn't heard her get dragged off—she must have left me voluntarily. Which made *no sense,* just *no sense.*

"Was your dad able to tell you anything at all about the tunnel?" I asked the Kid as we started down another hall. Time was running out—executions rarely took more than five minutes. Any moment now the alarm would sound and inmates would start filing back into their rooms, accompanied by guards. Lots of guards.

The Kid thought for a moment. "He said...he said it was behind a wall. In a room, behind a wall."

I stopped and stared at him. "Why didn't you tell me this before? I've been looking for a doorway, or something blocked off!"

The Kid's small face took on a familiar pinched look. "Why ain't you aks me before now? This ain't my fault!"

"No, no, you're right," I said, shaking my head. "Come on, let's try in here." We were in the mess hall, and at the back of it was a storage room that had other doors opening off it. Shrugging my shoulders, I chose one randomly and unlocked it.

Nothing could have prepared me for what waited behind that door.

It was my sister, who jerked up her head in alarm when we opened the door. She was panting, her eyes wild, and she was holding a large can of sliced peaches in heavy syrup.

At her feet lay a cafeteria worker, knocked out, with a can-shaped lump on the back of his head.

Next to Cassie, Nate was clinging to a door frame, looking like he was about to be sick. Everything clicked into place.

"You left me to go get Nate," I said.

Cassie nodded a bit sheepishly. "I couldn't leave him."

"Uh-huh. Who's Ridiculous now?" I said.

87

I'D HAD HOPES FOR THIS hallway, maybe just because it was a hall-way I hadn't known existed. After the Kid and I stepped over the unconscious cafeteria worker, I urgently began unlocking doors, using the keys on Strepp's key ring. It took us way too long to figure out which keys opened which doors. And all we found was store-room after storeroom, most of them full of crates marked FOOD stacked haphazardly on top of each other. Some crates were coated with a thick layer of dust, like they were left over from another time. It wouldn't surprise me if that was the stuff we'd been eating.

Door after door, we struck out. As we reached the end of the hallway, an alarm sounded: the execution was over. It was time for the prisoners to be locked up again.

"People will be here any second," Cassie said, her voice tight.

"One more door," I said, trying another of Strepp's keys. Would it have killed her to label one of them "master"? We felt the vibrations of feet moving before we heard them, and a moment later heard the dim, indistinct voices of guards as they let the other cafeteria workers back into the mess hall.

"They gonna open that door, see that schmuck lyin' there," the Kid said nervously.

"Yeah," I said, jamming in a key, trying to turn it, not succeeding.

The voices grew louder. I was aware of Nate's labored breathing; glanced back to see that his face was tinged with green and clammy sweat had broken out on his forehead.

I pushed another key in. It didn't turn. I had two keys left. Maybe Strepp didn't have a master key after all? She was the *deputy* warden. Or maybe this room was never used. Maybe this was the end—for all of us.

The voices were right outside this hallway. Even from down here, we heard the scrape of a key being fitted into its lock. My hands shaking, I quickly tried the second-to-last key, turning it hard—too hard.

Snap!

I stared in horror at the broken head of the key in my hand. "Cassie!"

Her horror mirrored mine as she saw what had happened.

The door at the end of the hallway opened. There was no light down here, but it would only take about ten seconds for them to see us in the shadows.

"Check those storerooms!" someone ordered.

"They gonna off us," the Kid breathed almost silently.

In desperation, Cassie reached out and savagely turned the doorknob, her arm muscles flexing with the effort.

And...it turned! The door swung inward, leading into another lightless room. I grabbed the Kid and practically threw him in, then helped Cassie drag Nate and his clunky cast through the doorway. Of course the sound alerted the guards that they had company, and one of them shouted.

Boots pounded down the hallway as we slammed the door.

"There's no way to lock it!" Cassie cried.

"Push some crates against it!" I ordered.

We all leaned against a stack of crates and pushed against them, our bare feet sliding on the cold, dusty floor, Nate grunting with the effort of keeping his cast out of the way. We managed to shove them up against the door just as someone outside grabbed the doorknob.

The door rattled but couldn't move against the heavy crates.

"Do some more!" I said, feeling my way around. With great effort we managed to shift another stack of crates against the first, but there were multiple voices outside and someone was slamming something heavy against the door. It had already opened a crack. We were two strong girls, one little kid, and one messed-up guy who wasn't much help. Outside that door were a bunch of beefy grown-ups.

A flame flickered into existence.

"Wha?" I whispered in amazement, and then my gaze focused on the Kid, holding a small lighter.

"How did you—" Cassie began, but I stopped her with a wave of my hand.

"Ask him later!" I said. "Kid, let's see what we have to work with in here!"

The Kid lifted his lighter and moved around. We were in a room of crates, just like every other room on this hallway. The only way in or out was the door that the guards were about to break in. We could push more crates against the door, but at most we'd be buying ourselves a minute or two. In the end, they would come in, we would be captured, and then we would be put to death.

88

CASSIE

BECCA AND I REACHED THE same conclusion at the same time: we were trapped, this was a dead end, and it was really, really the *dead end*, if you know what I'm saying.

As the sounds of the guards trying to smash the door open surrounded us, we stared at each other, each thinking furiously. Then Nate's quiet, pained voice said, "Well, we tried."

The Kid let his lighter flicker out, and we were again in almost complete darkness—the only faint light coming from the tiny crack around the door as the guards pushed it inward.

Looking down, I realized I was somehow still holding the stupid can of peaches. Overcome with tiredness, rage, desperation, and frustration, I drew my arm back and hurled the can against the wall with every bit of strength that I had, almost howling with anguish.

There was a dull, hollow thud and the sound of plaster chipping and falling to the ground.

"What the hell was that?" Becca asked.

"The can of peaches," I said wearily.

"Oh. Well, we could use it to club the first person in," Becca said. "If nothing else."

She was right. From the pounding at the door, that would be soon.

"When did you become the practical one?" I asked. "Kid? Light?"

The small lighter clicked into existence and I peered at the floor, looking for the can. The light went out.

"Kid, I can't see in the dark," I said crossly. "Can you keep it on?"

"I ain't flicked it off," the Kid said, just as crossly. "It got blew out."

"I feel cold air," Nate said. I heard him shuffling a bit. "Here. Maybe it's a vent or something. You guys, at least, might be able to get through it."

The lighter clicked and again cast its small circle of light.

There wasn't a vent. What there was, was a tiny hole in the wall, where I'd thrown the peaches. I put my hand up to it and felt chilly air whistling through.

Looking quickly, I found the dented, bloodstained can and grabbed it. Holding one end, I slammed it against the hole. More plaster crumbled away, making the hole big enough to put my fist through.

"That would be awesome, if we were rats," Becca said drily.

In the dim glow of the lighter, I saw despair on her face. The Kid looked just as crushed. Nate was white-faced and leaning against the wall, his eyes closed. Outside, the guards had gotten organized, at least three of them pounding against the door.

Then…the tiny light flickered on something. Something iridescent.

"Oh, my God," I breathed. The light was glittering on the wings of a dragonfly, fluttering into the room from the hole in the wall.

We'd found the tunnel.

89

"OH, JESUS," NATE SAID, AND hobbled toward it, his face contorted in pain. He reached out and grabbed a hunk of wall in his bare hands and pulled, breaking off another piece.

"See?" the Kid said. "It's behind a wall, in a room, like I said!"

"We need to get through that hole. Start working!" Becca said.

Then we were all scrabbling at the hole, pulling away chunks of plaster that broke into powdery shards.

"Becca! Kid!" I said. "You guys pull some crates over here! We'll get into the tunnel and then hide the hole!"

They immediately did what I said, which might be the very first time in our lives that Becca hadn't argued first. Nate leaned on his good leg, his arms moving like pistons as he pulled away chunk after chunk of plaster. Our hands were bleeding but it didn't matter. Nothing mattered except getting out.

With just the two of them it was harder for Becca and the Kid to move the crates, but we were all seized with a sort of superhuman fury that seemed to make us stronger than we'd ever been. Finally the hole was wide enough for Nate to slip through—he was the biggest of us—and we stood there panting as we tried to figure out how we would get his leg, stiff with a cast, through it.

He shook his head grimly. We had to move fast—the guards had gotten the door open almost an inch and were shouting at us.

"No way else," Nate muttered, and before I knew what he was doing, he put his arms over his head as if about to dive into a pond...and he dove through the hole headfirst.

His cast slammed against the side of the hole. He didn't even try to swallow the shriek of pain from that or from his heavy landing on the other side. He'd had no way to break his fall, no way to temper the shock to his ruptured knee. I heard him start sobbing in the darkness, and I quickly scrambled through, trying not to land on him. Becca boosted the Kid through, and he knelt by Nate with his lighter casting a small flame as Becca crawled through herself.

She and I put our arms through the hole, grabbed the brace of a crate, and yanked as hard as we could. It didn't move. We heard the sound of the other crates scraping across the floor as the outer door pushed open, and we grabbed it again. My fingers locked onto the brace like claws, and with every ounce of strength I had, I pulled toward us.

It moved. It moved a bit. Biting our lips, tears welling in our eyes, Becca and I grabbed and pulled again, moving it another inch closer. Again. And again. My fingers were slippery with blood, a long splinter had shot through my index finger, and Nate was try-ing to stifle his sobs in the background.

"One more time, babe," Becca muttered, sweat making her hair stick to her forehead in lank strands. I nodded and fastened onto the crate again.

Somehow we pulled the crate another four inches until it was smack-dab up against the wall. Instantly the tunnel's darkness deepened. We heard the roar of the guards as they finally man-aged to slip through the doorway, heard their feet as they swarmed into the room ... and heard their cries of confusion as they looked around a completely empty room, with no visible means of escape.

90

BECCA

WE HAD MAYBE A COUPLE minutes before the guards started moving crates around to find out where we'd gone. I hoped they would first open all the crates to see if we had magically sealed ourselves up inside.

In the meantime, we had to put as much space as possible between us and them.

All this time I'd been thinking of the tunnel like a sewer tunnel, with yucky water and rats and slime and whatever. Now I was like, I wish. This tunnel had been *hand-dug* by one crazy person a little at a time. After the initial hole, we couldn't stand up. We couldn't even stoop. The four of us crawled, single file, on our hands and knees, and there were plenty of times when it was hard for me to get my shoulders through.

And poor Nate. It's possible to crawl with a full-length cast on your leg, but it isn't easy, it isn't fast, and it hurts like a son of a bitch, given the language that was floating up to me from his position in the rear.

I was going first, with the Kid's lighter. I flicked it on every so often to reveal the disheartening view of more seemingly endless, tiny tunnel. I thought uncomfortably about how we had only the Kid's story to go on, that he thought it had *caved in* at one point, and how in the end, his dad had gotten captured anyway.

But I kept crawling. Small rocks embedded in the dirt bruised my knees almost unbearably. Every so often there was a large boulder that the Kid's dad had been forced to tunnel around. At the first one I flicked on the lighter and saw words scratched into the rock: "Gimli, son of Gloin, ha ha ha," and a date from six years ago.

The Kid was right behind me, and I shone the flame on it.

"Was your dad's name Gimli?" I asked.

The Kid frowned. "No! You think my dad had some weird-ass name? His name was Ebenezer!"

I shrugged and kept crawling. On another boulder, the Kid's dad had carved, "Screw the United!" and we all cheered quietly. To save the lighter fuel, we mostly crawled in the utter, complete, intense blackness, using it only when we seemed to hit a dead end or a rock, and the first time I almost brained myself on a heavy tree root that had grown down into the tunnel.

There was no sense of time. I couldn't tell if we were burrowing deeper underground or going in circles or heading right back to the prison. After it felt like we'd been crawling for an hour, my nerves started fraying. Like, what if a truck rolled over us? We would be crushed. What if the tunnel just collapsed? The idea of dying down here buried under a ton of dirt was possibly more terrifying than the first time facing Tim in the ring.

"How much longer we gotta go?" the Kid asked. He was panting, as all of us were. "I cain't breathe."

My eyes opened wide in the darkness. Oh, God, was there enough oxygen down here? My heart seized as I suddenly remembered folks digging wells, back home. More than one man had passed out from hitting a pocket of gas—natural methane, which you can't see or smell. If he didn't get hauled out fast, he'd die.

Well, gas was *flammable*—one way to get rid of it was to throw a lit match in the well and stand back. Way back.

I'd been using the lighter. If I used it again, I could blow us all into fish bait. Shit. The idea of not being able to at least check where we were going—

The Kid couldn't breathe—

I couldn't use the lighter—

Cassie had whispered that Nate was about to pass out—

I had to get out of here.

I had to get out of here.

I had to—

91

CASSIE

MY HEAD BUMPED INTO THE KID'S backside, which was how I knew that he'd stopped.

"What's going on?" I asked.

"Becca's stopped," he said, sounding close to tears.

"Beck?" I called.

"Yeah?"

It was just one word, but it made the hairs on the back of my neck stand up. I knew Becca's voice, and her voice now told me she was close to hysteria. The last time I'd heard it was when she'd come across a big copperhead in one of Pa's cornfields. Fearless, Ridiculous Rebecca had been frozen in terror, her eyes locked on the snake as it rose up, swaying slowly.

I'd screamed, *Becca, run!* And she'd said, *I can't,* in this tiny voice. The snake was uncoiling and moving slowly toward her—into striking range.

I had circled around to her, cutting a wide swath around the snake, and came up behind her. The snake looked at me.

"Let's run," I whispered.

"I can't," she whispered back, tortured. "My feet can't move."

"Okay. I'm going to grab your arm and pull as hard as I can," I told her. "Then I'm going to run. You can either get your feet moving or be dragged."

"It's going to come after us," she whispered.

"We can outrun it."

It had worked. I don't know if the snake tried to strike at us when we turned tail, but I know we ran like jackrabbits for a long, long time.

I couldn't grab her arm this time. I couldn't drag her.

"Keep crawling, Beck," I said. Nate had caught up to me by that point. I knew he was close to giving up. He'd been dragging that cast all this time, and twice I'd heard him barfing from the pain.

"Flick dat lighter," the Kid said.

"I can't," she said in a small, tense voice. "Well gas."

My heart dropped down into my stomach. Of course. Oh, my God. No wonder she was frozen. I felt myself start to panic, the darkness starting to smother me. What could I say to get her moving again? Like, "I don't wanna die down here?" Or, "What's the matter, is your ass too big to fit?" Anything, I had to say *anything!*

"Beck?" I said.

"Yeah?" Her voice trembled.

"I'd like to see Pa again," I said softly. "Just once. You know?"

She was silent.

A minute later I heard a sound like Becca was swallowing a sob, then she started crawling, her knees scraping the damp earth, her head and shoulders hitting the sides and top of the tunnel. Ahead of me, the Kid followed her.

"Cassie?" Nate whispered just as I was starting to move. "I don't think I'm going to make it. You guys head on without me. If they get this far I'll try to stall them."

Oh, not him, too.

Somehow I kept a grip on my temper and my panic, and took a firm, no-nonsense tone.

"Nate, if we get out of here, I'm going to totally, totally make out with you," I said briskly. "I've been wanting to, and if you give up or die and not let me, I will kick your ass."

There were a few moments of silence.

"You're in my way," he said.

"I thought so," I said, and began crawling as fast as I could.

92

SO WE HAD PRETTY MUCH decided to crawl until we died, no matter what. A tree root gouged my face, but what was more dripping blood? I was used to it. The hand I'd punched Strepp with was so swollen I couldn't make a fist, and hurt worse with every passing minute. I crawled one-handed with it cradled up against my chest, throbbing with pain.

Then I ran into the Kid's bony backside again.

"Now what?" I asked, because I was fresh out of motivational speeches.

"This is where it caved in," Becca said wearily. "Apparently. I can't feel any opening anywhere around me."

All I wanted to do was curl up somewhere and pass out. I almost didn't care if they caught us again. A nice, quick, painless execution didn't sound so bad right now, and I suspected the other three felt the same way. And of course there was no way to go back. I didn't think any of us was up for that.

That was when a mole accidentally tunneled into our tunnel, dropped down onto Becca's neck, and turned her into a human tiller. She shrieked, flailing her arms and kicking her feet, and the poor mole jumped off her and trundled right into the Kid, who also shrieked and flailed. Then the mole ran past me, making me squeal like a baby pig, then ran into Nate, who went, "Ugh!" and was prevented from flailing because he was too big to move almost anything.

The mole scuttled away down the tunnel as we all twitched uncontrollably, remembering the feel of its dry little paws scrabbling at us.

"Hey," the Kid said finally. "Lookit."

As stupid as it was to turn my head and peer into the infinite darkness of an underground tunnel, I did.

And I saw the barest, dimmest bit of light.

"What is it?" Nate asked.

"I...I think I see something," I said in wonder. "Like, actually see something."

"You do," Becca said, a tremulous joy in her voice. "I kicked a hole in the cave-in, and this is where the tunnel ends."

"Oh, God, really?" I breathed.

"There's light," she confirmed. "Like, starlight. But I have to get this dirt out of the way."

After spending a *lifetime* in the tunnel, it was *agonizing* to wait as Becca dug, to help push the dirt back into the tunnel, first from Becca to the Kid, from the Kid to me, from me to Nate, and Nate finally pushing it behind him. But we had to, or there'd be no room to get out.

"Okay, let me try it," Becca said, crawling forward. I saw most of her disappear, and then I was looking at just her filthy, bare feet because she was standing up.

"Okay," she said a moment later, ducking back down. "We're actually really far away from the prison! I can't even see it! Your dad did good," she told the Kid, and his proud smile was visible even in the frail moonlight.

"That's the good news," she said. "The bad news is we're in the middle of the woods, and I have zero clue where. We were supposed to meet Tim on the road outside the prison, but there's no way to tell where that is."

"Get me out of this goddamn hole," Nate said hoarsely. "I don't give a shit where we are."

Becca nodded. "Right." And her feet disappeared as she jumped up, out of the tunnel and into the world.

93

BECCA

THE SUN WAS JUST BARELY spreading a pale-pink mist over the horizon. We must have been crawling for hours—I'd been sure we were going to die in that freaking tunnel. If I'd had any idea what it would really be like, I don't think I would have done it. Not to mention that goddamn mole dropping down on me...

But now we were out, not behind bars, not behind fences, not shuffling along as guards whacked us with billy clubs. For *this second*, at least, I didn't have to dread alarms and calls to the ring for fights or executions. It was an amazing feeling, and tears streaked through the dirt and blood on my face.

I flopped down on the grass, hearing the Kid scramble up after me, then Cassie, and finally, with Cassie's help, Nate. I was exhausted, filthy, starving, cold, and afraid. But as I looked up at the wide-open sky just starting to lighten with the promise of a new day, I knew I'd never been so happy. A couple of dragonflies zipped by overhead, as if relieved to be free also. "Thanks," I whispered to them.

We lay there, the four of us, as the clammy sweat dried on our skin. I had no idea if I would ever feel clean again.

"Not to be a wet blanket," Cassie said finally. "But this doesn't count as an escape until we're actually somewhere better than the woods outside a prison."

"I know," I said, sitting up and looking around.

Immediately I dropped back to the ground and hissed at everyone to be quiet. "Lights," I whispered. "I see lights."

Slowly I raised my head and looked again. There they were—lights in the distance. Were they guards with flashlights? Was Strepp out here searching for us? How long had we been underground?

"Thems is headlights," the Kid said after a minute of watching.

"How can you tell?" I asked him, and earned a sneer.

"'Cause I seen headlights before. Jesus," he said.

"Is that Tim?" Cassie asked.

"I don't know," I said.

Another light popped into existence, this one wavering, sweeping back and forth. A flashlight. Far in the distance, I heard dogs barking.

"Shit," Cassie whispered.

I met my sister's eyes, knowing we were thinking the same thing: only three of us had the slightest hope of outrunning dogs. And probably not even us three. As tired as we were...

"I'll go see." I didn't want to risk standing, hiding behind trees, so I gritted my teeth and freaking crawled again. My knees were so bruised that every movement brought new tears to my eyes. My wrists ached from being bent for so long, and my palms were scraped and bloody. I had knots on my head from hitting roots in the tunnel.

But I crawled, sticking to the undergrowth, being as quiet as possible, no doubt leaving a trail as obvious as a rainbow to anyone tracking us. At least I was making another path for the guards to follow—maybe leading them away from the others.

A few minutes on, I heard the faint idling of an engine. Then I heard it shut off, heard the truck door open and close softly. I didn't hear guards talking to each other, and the dog barking grew slightly dimmer, not louder. Above my head, the flashlight beam bounced from tree to tree. If there was only one guard, could I take him? With my fighting skills? I just didn't know.

I was crouched down, thinking through my next move, when my ears caught the barest glimmer of a birdcall. I sat up slightly, straining to hear.

There it was—a whip-poor-will! It called again, and my heart leaped. Standing carefully, I whistled back. It returned the whistle, and a moment later the truck door opened and the headlights flashed. It *was* Tim! Somehow he had found us!

Still I kept to the shadows, moving cautiously. I took slow steps, making sure he was alone. He called again like a whip-poor-will, and seemed startled when I returned the call from so close.

Then I stepped out of the woods, he saw me, and he dropped

the flashlight and took long strides toward me. He caught me up in a tight embrace, and I threw my arms around him.

"I was so afraid you wouldn't make it," he murmured against my hair. "I've been waiting for hours."

I smiled tremulously. "Thanks for not giving up. Now can we get the hell away from here?"

He nodded. "Definitely. Where's Cassie?"

Tim came with me through the woods and was surprised to see we had the Kid and Nate with us. I was so thankful for Tim's hulking strength as he put his arm under Nate's shoulder and practically carried him to the truck.

Five minutes later Nate and Cassie were in the backseat of the United truck, and the Kid was next to me as Tim sped down the road away from the crazy house, toward freedom. Toward home.

94

"NO," THE KID SAID, HIS small, pinched face set in an all-too-familiar stubborn look.

"You'll like it in our cell," I said.

"No," the Kid said. "I'm goin' home. You cain't stop me."

I didn't point out that we could *totally* stop him, since there were four of us and we were all bigger and, oh yeah, we were in a speeding truck. Instead I said, "Is it safe for you to go home?"

He sneered. "Safer'n comin' with you guys!" he said. "You got *taken* from yer cells, didn't cha? Me, I jest *wandered off!* I'm goin' back. Ain't no way I'm comin' with youse." He crossed his thin arms over his chest and stuck his jaw out. His black eyes were narrowed.

Tim looked at me. I shrugged: the Kid had a point. "I can take him to his cell," Tim said. "I know where it is. My dad drove a semi for the United, picking up wheat here, delivering stoves there. I used to go with him."

"Now yer talkin'," the Kid said.

His cell wasn't far away. Only twenty minutes later we pulled up to the gates of a run-down cell. When we got close to the entrance gate, Tim stopped the truck and cut the headlights.

I got out to let the Kid jump down from the front seat. It was barely daybreak and only a few of the houses showed lights on.

"Take care, Kid," I said.

"Yeah. Hope I never sees you again!" He turned to run off, but I grabbed his wiry little arm. He glanced back at me, startled, as I pulled him to me in a fierce hug. His too-thin body told the tale of how hard life was in a mining cell, and yet it was home, and he wanted to go back.

"Thanks for everything, Kid," I whispered into his ear. "We would have been lost without your dad's tunnel."

For one second he softened into me, becoming just a scared little boy who had gone through a horrible experience. Then he stiffened and pulled back.

"Yeah. My dad did good." Without another word he turned and ran off. He didn't look back.

"Geez, I hope he's okay," Cassie murmured, and I nodded.

Feeling suddenly older than dirt, I climbed back into the truck. Now that the Kid wasn't in between us, I moved over and leaned my head on Tim's shoulder.

"What about the rest of us?" Tim asked.

"We gotta go back, too," I murmured, trying not to fall asleep.

"You can't come with me to my cell?" he asked, trying not to sound hopeful.

I sat up and looked at him. "I don't want to leave you. But our Pa is still back home. And we have scores to settle. Can you come with us?"

Regretfully, he shook his head. "My mom and my little brother—I need to go check on them. Who knows if Strepp is going to track us, or whatever."

"Yeah. I get it."

At Tim's cell, Nate contacted someone in the Outsiders, and then we waited by the side of the road for them to fetch us. It was now broad daylight and I felt super vulnerable, missing the cover of night. My throat was tight: I didn't know if I'd ever see Tim again. I leaned against a tree, out of sight of Nate and Cassie, and kissed Tim for what might be the last time. He'd almost killed me, and he'd saved my life. Both of them more than once.

He pushed a piece of paper into the ripped pocket of my jump-suit. "This is my cell, my last name, and my phone number. Don't forget me."

"I don't need your phone number," I said, trying not to cry. "I couldn't call from my cell anyway. No outside lines."

"Just in case," he insisted, and I nodded, tears spilling down my cheeks. "Hey, hey," he said softly, wiping away my tears. "It's okay. If you don't come find me, I'll find you."

"You broke my ribs, and now you're breaking my heart," I said, trying to joke. It came out much more seriously than I'd intended, and Tim looked like someone had just punched him in the gut.

"I'll find you," he promised. "Soon."

The sound of engines coming closer made us look up. It was the Outsiders, three of them, on three motorcycles.

"You head on," Tim said. "I gotta go drive this truck into the lake."

Taking a shuddering breath, I nodded, then hugged Tim as tightly as our injuries would allow. We kissed again and again, until Cassie said, "Guys, come on! Let's go!"

I went over and nodded hi to Cecily, who was waiting on her motorcycle. Cassie was behind a guy named Jefferson, who I also recognized, and poor Nate was propped uncomfortably behind Tara Nightwing.

Climbing onto Cecily's bike, I felt again the muscle stiffness, injuries, and general pain involved with being an inmate. I held on to Cecily as she kicked the bike into gear, my lip trembling as I felt how small and un-Tim-like she was.

Then we were tearing down the road, away from prison, away from Tim. Heading home. Heading back to Pa. At last.

The big question? What the hell do we do now?

95

CASSIE

ALL ALONG, THIS HAD BEEN the plan—to get back to the cell to see Pa. I admitted (only to myself) that I had absolutely no idea what else we would do. Go someplace else? Now that we knew there were thousands of other cells, it still didn't seem possible to go anywhere, live somewhere else. Could we live out in the woods somehow? Not be part of any cell at all? That didn't seem better.

But first we had to go back to our cell. We didn't know if there would be cops waiting for us at the gates, or whether the gates would be closed and locked against us or what. But we simply drove through them, and no one seemed to notice.

I didn't know how long we'd been gone. In prison I'd lost all sense of time. But the cell looked different somehow, as if the seasons had changed or it was a new year.

"Where to?" Cecily yelled back at me, and I yelled, "Healthcare United!"

In the broad daylight three motorcycles drew attention, especially as we roared up to the hospital. But we made it there without being stopped or accosted. Once we'd parked it took all of us to drag Nate off of Tara's motorcycle.

"Thanks so much," I said to Jefferson and the others. They didn't smile, but nodded as they revved their engines.

"See you soon," Cecily said, and they tore off down Main Street, drawing surprised stares from passersby.

Becca took one of Nate's arms and I took the other. Together we supported him as he limped into the Healthcare United emergency room, dragging his battered, casted leg behind him. The triage nurse did a double take when she saw the two of us with the Provost's son—especially since we all looked like we'd been shot through a blender of dirt and blood.

"I got it from here," Nate told us tightly, his face white with exhaustion and pain.

"Are you sure?" I asked. I was dying to go see Pa, but everything in me told me to stay with Nate.

"Yeah," he said. "Pretty sure my dad will be here soon." He grimaced, but I didn't know if it was from that thought or because of pain. A nurse tried to get him to lie down on a gurney, but he became even paler, if possible, and shook his head. Becca and I couldn't look at the gurney, either. I don't think we ever would be able to again.

I held his hand tightly as he sank awkwardly into a hard chair.

He had come to prison looking for me—like I'd gone looking for Becca. He'd risked his life for me, and had just gone through a nightmare of danger and pain in order to stay with me as we escaped. How could I leave him?

"Go see your Pa," he said wearily. "I'll talk to you later." He gave me a meaningful glance—I still owed him some serious making out. I think he also meant: Watch your back. It was dangerous for us to be here again. At last I reluctantly let go of his hand as another nurse came over, talking to Nate about getting X-rays. I looked back at him as long as I could, feeling like I was leaving something important behind.

96

OUT IN THE HALLWAY BECCA and I immediately turned left and headed up the stairs to the second floor. Pa was in his same room—he hadn't died while we were gone, and I was so thankful. I dropped into the chair by his bedside and took one of his pale, frail hands in my bloody, dirt-encrusted ones.

"Pa," I whispered. I was so happy to see him, had *kept living* just to see him again. But of course no miracle had happened while we were gone. He was still dying, would still never be the Pa I'd grown up with.

Becca pulled the other chair over. In the bright light of day, she looked like shit on a stick. I assumed that, as usual, I looked identical. She took Pa's other hand, and I saw her lip tremble. She didn't have to say anything. I knew what she was feeling.

I was bent wearily over Pa's hand, trying to summon the strength to get up and walk home, when suddenly his fingers twitched in mine. That had happened a lot in the early days, but not at all lately. My eyes flew open and I almost jumped to see his calm blue eyes, looking at me.

"Pa?"

Becca sat up and looked at him, too. We hadn't seen his eyes in *months*.

"My...girls." It was a withered, dry rasp of a voice.

"Yes, Pa!" Becca said. "We're here!"

His eyes drifted closed again as Becca and I stared at each other. Could he be getting better? I glanced at the machine, and my hopes fell. His numbers were lower than ever, his breaths fewer, his heartbeat more erratic. His blood oxygen level had never been lower; his lungs were almost nonfunctional.

"A boy...came here." His wasted chest wheezed with the effort of speaking.

Becca and I frowned at each other. A boy? Maybe it was a new male nurse, or lab tech?

"Okay," I said, not knowing what else to say.

"Provost's...son."

I sat back and exchanged another puzzled glance with my sister. Nate had been here? When? Pa would recognize him—I'd gone to school with Nate for twelve years. But I knew he hadn't seen Nate this morning—we'd just dropped him off.

"Said...you were okay." Pa's words were barely audible, but his pale lips turned up just a tiny bit, at the corners. His eyes stayed shut, but his fingers moved in my hand again. "My girls...are okay."

"Yes, Pa, we're fine," I assured him. "And you are, too. They say you're getting better every day."

"Yeah," Becca agreed, looking deflated. "Listen, Pa—I've got a history test. I need to go home and learn everything there is to know about the cotton gin. But I'll see you tomorrow, okay?"

Pa didn't say anything or react. It was like he'd had a burst of energy and then slipped back into his comalike state. It was so disappointing.

"I'll see you tomorrow, Pa," I said, standing up. I leaned down to kiss his cheek and whispered, "You get better immediately, if not sooner, you hear me?"

97

BECCA

"I JUST DON'T KNOW WHAT we're doing here." Cassie had waited till we were on the road going home before she shoved more reality at me.

"We saw Pa. We're going home," I said shortly. "Tomorrow's another day."

"No—I mean, we've seen a whole other existence!" she said, waving her arms. "There are other cells. There are other people. Other vocations. We now know all that. And we know that we left a bunch of innocent kids behind to get tortured and killed."

I looked at her. "We couldn't take everyone with us. It was risky enough."

"I know. But can we leave them there?" Her voice was exhausted, anguished.

"What do you mean?" I asked. "We left them. They're there."

"Becca." Cassie turned and faced me. "There's nothing for us here, except Pa, and his sun is setting. And we left all those kids there. Don't you think we need to go back and get them?"

My mouth dropped open. "Get them? How? We don't even have a vehicle! Not to mention all the guards, guns, Tasers, billy clubs, handcuffs, and Strepp!"

She frowned at me. "What if we had a whole army?" she asked.

I didn't even turn around. "A whole army of what? Corncobs? Where are you going to get your army?"

"School?"

Now I did stop to look at her. I leaned over and put my hand on her forehead, feeling its dirt and blood. "You are raving with fever," I told her, and strode ahead.

"We could talk to our friends!" she cried behind me.

I whirled. "Yeah? Like all the friends who couldn't even help you find me?" Her face fell, and I felt a little bad. But just a little. "You're going to get a bunch of *sheep* to go against the Provost? Against the whole United? Really?" Again I turned and hurried on, this time so I wouldn't see her start to cry.

98

I SAW THE SIGN FIRST. Cassie was still dragging her feet behind me, looking dejected. But when we got to our gate she saw it. We looked at each other, confused.

FOR SALE.

Our house had a FOR SALE sign on it. It said, CONTACT THE PROPERTY OFFICE AT THE MANAGEMENT BUILDING.

Pa wasn't in any shape to put our house up for sale.

"Oh, my God," Cassie said, opening our gate.

"What's going on?" I asked. There was another sign on our front door: PUBLIC AUCTION. It gave the date and a list: house, land, tractor, tiller, irrigation pump (wind-powered), household items, clothes. "What the hell?"

Cassie tried the front door. It was locked. I fetched the spare key hidden inside a drainpipe on the side of the house, and we let ourselves in.

Inside, our house had been searched. Not like torn apart or destroyed, just messed with. Furniture had been moved, some pictures taken off the walls, kitchen cupboards opened. All our dishes were stacked on the kitchen table, like someone had been counting them.

"What the hell is going on?" I said, feeling anger ignite. "Who did this?"

"Oh, Becca," Cassie said, looking around. "Oh, my God. They didn't think we were coming back."

"What?"

"Ma's gone. Pa's not going to last much longer. We were the only two kids, and we *disappeared*. So there was no one left to take over the farm. So they're selling it. And everything in it."

"No freaking way!" I said, my hands clenching. "Those signs are coming down now! This place is ours!" I headed back to the living room, but Cassie grabbed my arm.

"You're not getting it," she said. "Beck, they didn't think we were coming back. Other kids have disappeared. *None of them have ever come back.*"

I stopped and looked at her, thinking about the other kids we knew who were missing. It was true. Those kids were gone—the few we'd seen at the prison had been left there.

"But they know we're back now," I said. "The folks at the hospital saw us. Nate will tell his dad we helped him. Right?"

"Yeah," Cassie said, her voice trailing off as she thought. "They must know by now. So...what are they going to think about us? What are they going to do with us?"

I grimaced. "Maybe arrest us, for daring to leave?"

"Do they know we left on purpose?" Cassie asked. "There's no one watching the gates, right? Not all the time, anyway."

"Probably because no one ever leaves," I said.

"Yeah," Cassie agreed. "So it's like the cell doesn't actually know how or why kids are disappearing—the Provost acts mad, like people are sneaking out for the fun of it. Does he really not know what's going on?"

"If he did," I said, "then he wouldn't call them traitors. He might just be quiet about it, since he couldn't fix it."

"So, think," Cassie said. "Kids disappear, no one knows why, they never come back, it's a big mystery. Then...three come back. What's the Provost gonna do?"

"He's going to come get us, maybe question us?" I said.

Cassie nodded. "Maybe. On the other hand, we saved his son. We brought Nate back. Maybe he should be thanking us."

"You're crazy," I said, grinning. "I like it."

"I bet you anything that they're gonna be knocking at our door soon," Cassie predicted. "And I, for one, will have showered." She leaped toward the stairs, pounding up the steps, beating me to the bathroom, slamming the door in my face.

I heard the water gush out of the pipe, imagined how hot and clean it would be, and sank down to the floor. Overcome with exhaustion I slid sideways, luxuriating in how delightfully dry and comfortable this wooden floor was. The last thought I had was of Tim's face, bruised and handsome. I wanted to see him again.

99

CASSIE WOKE ME UP, PRACTICALLY hauling me off the floor and into the bathtub. After the cold, crowded, soapless showers at the prison, this was complete bliss. Then I got to put on clean clothes—no yellow jumpsuit in sight.

Downstairs, Cassie had opened a couple of cans of non-prison food.

"No one's showed up yet?" I asked, and she shook her head. I grabbed a bowl and a spoon and ate ravenously, not caring what it was. It was hot and resembled food and had actual flavor. Neither of us could eat much—we were used to starvation rations.

Afterward we went outside to take the signs down.

Our house looked about nine times more decrepit than I remembered it. It used to make me so mad, how run-down the place was, how Cassie hopelessly tried to keep it clean. I didn't understand why she wasted her time and energy on sweeping dust off a porch that had three boards missing, or wiping down a kitchen counter so worn that you couldn't see the pattern on the formica anymore.

It had been different when we were little, of course. When Ma was here, the house was painted, screens fixed, everything clean and tidy—just how the United likes it. After Ma was taken away for her mood-adjust, things were different. Pa couldn't make the effort, I wouldn't make the effort, so it was up to Cassie.

Now, as my sister and I tore down the FOR SALE sign and the auction sign, I was filled with anger and guilt all over again. All I'd ever wanted to do was get out of this stupid cell, this broken home.

It was only now that I understood it was the most beautiful thing I'd ever seen in my life. Only now that I realized, in the time I was gone, I'd somehow lost any chance of being happy in it ever again. Cassie was right. There was nothing for us here. This was the house we'd grown up in, but it would never be home again.

100

CASSIE

BECCA AND I SAT UP and waited till after curfew, waited for the Provost or the cops or whoever to come get us.

No one came. Maybe they were planning to grab us in the middle of the night. We decided to get some sleep, and for the first time since we were five years old, we slept in the same room. We both slept in Ma and Pa's double bed, and talked the way we used to.

"We might not be able to get the kids from school behind us," I admitted. "But what about the Outsiders?"

Becca nodded in the darkness. "Tomorrow we can bike over to the hideout. But Nate was the leader, and he's out of commission. His leg was a mess."

"Okay, we'll go to the hideout tomorrow," I said. "Then what?"

"Then I'm going to go to Mrs. Kelly's Kitchen and eat myself sick," Becca said.

I wasn't sure if she was serious or not. Probably she was.

"I can't believe we're home," I said, watching the ceiling fan turn slowly overhead. "I thought we were going to die there."

"I was sure of it," Becca said. "Being here, home, with warm, dry clothes, in a warm, comfy bed...it's like a dream. I hope I never wake up."

"Yeah," I said. But inside I was thinking about all the kids we'd left behind. They weren't in a dream. They were still in a nightmare.

"Hey, Beck?" I said, softly, but her even breathing told me she was asleep. I'd said I wanted to go back and free all the other kids, but in truth I had no idea how to do it. Those people were armed. The kids were scared and cowed by the fights and executions. We would need the Provost to go with us, or the police force.

How was I going to pull that off? And with that thought I, too, fell asleep, next to my sister in our parents' bed.

101

THERE WAS NO ONE AT the Outsider hideout, which meant we had biked for half an hour for nothing. Becca scratched a coded message next to a hay bale on the floor, basically saying *Call me*. Everyone might have decided to wait for Nate to get better, or they might be off doing other things, or they didn't want anything to do with me and Becca.

Nate. I hoped he was doing okay. I didn't dare call him. Later today, when I went to the hospital to see Pa, I would find him and say hi.

We biked home. I thought it was so weird that we had disappeared and come back, and no one was taking any notice. It left me with the uncomfortable feeling that they were just biding their time, coming up with a plan to really get us.

I gritted my teeth and pedaled harder. I was different than I had been before prison. They would be dealing with a different Cassie now.

When we rounded the Henrys' field, we saw the SAS van parked in front of our door.

"So they do know we're home," Becca said drily.

"Let's get this over with," I said.

We dropped our bikes in the yard and Becca strode up to the front porch, where the SAS agent was waiting.

"What do you want?" Becca snarled, stomping to the front door and yanking it open.

The agent looked calm and capable, like they always do. Confidence-inspiring.

"Girls," she said. "I'm afraid I have some bad news. Your father passed away this morning."

Whatever we'd been expecting, it wasn't that. I actually staggered backward and fell against a porch post. Becca clung to the door as if it was propping her up.

"What?" Becca said.

"Your father was called home to greener pastures this morning," the woman said. "May I come in?" She deftly eased past Becca and sat down on the settee Ma had refinished years ago. I followed them in, my mind spinning.

"How?" I managed to get out.

The woman looked at me with sympathy and smoothed her navy-blue uniform over her knees. "It's been a long, slow process, as you know," she said. "Anyway, this morning it became critical. The hospital informed me that they tried to call you."

I looked at the black phone sitting on the small table, as if it would still be able to tell me something. "We weren't here this morning," I said. We'd been at the Outsiders' hangout, which had done us no good at all. *Pa had died.* He'd died without us there.

"I'm so sorry, dear," the woman said. "I know it's always hard to lose a parent, even when it's a blessing."

Becca looked at her sharply. "Excuse me?"

"A blessing," the woman said, lowering her voice. "Of course you loved your father, but the way it all happened..." She let her voice trail off, as if we would acknowledge the shame of my father trying to commit suicide by himself.

"Why are you here?" I asked, my voice as cold as a winter storm. My heart felt like ice. While we'd been bicycling halfway across the cell, Pa had drawn his last breath. A deep pain grew in my chest until I thought I was going to be sick.

The SAS officer gave a delicate sigh and shook her head. "The nurse at Healthcare United asked me to tell you about your father, since I was coming here anyway."

"Coming here anyway?" I asked. "Why?"

"My dears, I've come to offer you the benefit of our complimentary service," she said, as if surprised it needed explaining. "You can't keep this farm up by yourself. Your parents are now both gone. Without schooling or a vocation—"

She was saying the same things I'd been thinking myself, but hearing them from her enraged me.

"Get out," Becca said. Her nose was pink and her jaw was quivering.

"What?" the SAS officer asked.

I stood up. "Leave *now,* and don't come back."

"We don't need your services," Becca said, advancing on her.

"We'll *never* need your services," I added, standing next to Becca.

The SAS officer drew herself up. "My dears, I don't think you realize the position you're in. Certainly the painless, complimentary gift of a gentle farewell shouldn't be sneered at."

"And yet, I am sneering," Becca said.

"Girls, please," the SAS officer said. "Your lives here simply won't work now. If you choose to accept this gift, then you can have the pride and joy of knowing that you're making way for two brand-new little babies. Isn't that nice?"

"If you want to keep your *face,* you need to get out now," Becca advised, and pointed at the open front door.

"You have no future here!" the woman cried, picking up her black bag.

"No," I said. "*You* have no future *here.*" I gave her a fast shove out the door and we slammed it after her.

For a moment Becca and I stood there, wide-eyed and breathing hard. Then, for the first time in a long time, Becca broke down. She put her fist to her mouth, tears already streaming down her cheeks. "Oh, God," she said. "Pa."

Words couldn't express everything—anything—I was feeling. I nodded, and then we stood there and hugged each other and cried about Pa.

102

BECCA

WE TALKED AND DIDN'T TALK, cried and didn't cry. Much later, Cassie looked up from the sofa, where she was lying, holding a pillow to her chest. Then she frowned and sat up a little. "What's that noise?"

I listened for a second. "Sirens? Geez, maybe a fire truck? Is there a fire around here?" Then it hit me. "Oh, shit," I said. "This is it. Where's Pa's gun?"

"I lost it the night I got taken," Cassie reminded me. "I told you."

"Crap, right," I said.

"Baseball bat," Cassie said, and ran upstairs to get her aluminum slugger. I went into the kitchen and got a couple of carving knives.

It seemed to take a long time for them to get here. My nerves were razor-sharp; all my muscles zinging with anticipation. I felt like I was going to explode.

Cassie's eyes were fixed on the long road leading to our house, at the clouds of dust the cars were stirring up around them.

"You know, Beck—I was thinking about when we were in prison. What were they training us to do? To be?"

"Uh—assholes? Fighters? Bullies? Psychopaths?"

To my surprise, Cassie smiled and looked at me, and right in that moment she looked so beautiful and angelic that I wanted to smack her.

"Nope. I've decided that they were training us to be *heroes*," she said, and hoisted her bat to her shoulder.

"What?"

They were close enough for me to count: all six of our police cars were there, the Provost had his shiny gas-powered car, the SAS van was there (of course), and there were a bunch of other vehicles like Hoppers and mopeds and the bigger family cars we all called Biscuits because they were roundish and tan.

"Yeah. We can fight now—ruthlessly, even if we don't want to," she said as the cars turned down the smaller dirt road leading to our house. "But we still care about kids, people weaker than us. We still felt bad when they died."

I was so hyped-up I could hardly think straight. "Heroes?" I repeated.

She gave me another beatific smile. "Yep."

The crowd seemed to swell and grow, getting bigger and longer like a parade.

We'd closed and locked our ancient driveway gate, and shook our heads when the Provost's car honked its horn. After it honked several times, the car backed up and rammed our gate, lifting one side right out of the ground.

"Schmuck," Cassie said.

The Provost's car drove up almost to the house. Two police cars hummed in after him. The driver got out and then opened the back door for the Provost. He was already scowling and tugged his suit jacket into place. The cops got out of their cars.

The rest of the crowd clustered around in the road outside our fence.

The Provost held up his hand for silence, and all the murmuring stopped.

Cassie stepped forward. "Is there a problem?"

"You bet there's a problem!" the Provost yelled so that everyone could hear. "The two of you are trouble! You're the definition of bad citizens!"

The crowd murmured behind him, some people looking angry.

"Can you be more specific?" Cassie asked. I was impressed—the only thing I could think of to say was a bunch of cussing. But she was holding it together.

"You're a bad influence!" the Provost said. "You're deserters! You left the cell! You made my son leave, too!"

I stepped forward, ready to tell him where to get off, but Cassie held up a hand.

"You're welcome," she said.

The Provost looked taken aback. "What?"

"First," Cassie said, "we didn't leave voluntarily. We were kidnapped."

That was stretching it, but whatever.

"You were not kidnapped!" the Provost said angrily.

"We were kidnapped," Cassie said firmly. "Just like other kids from this cell. And Nate—your son—heroically tried to save us."

Okay, okay, I thought. *This is good.*

The Provost was speechless for a moment. But only for a moment.

"You led him astray! You made him leave the cell!"

Following Cassie's lead, I said, "How could we possibly lead Nathaniel astray? You know how loyal he is to you and the cell."

Provost Allen looked trapped. Was he going to announce that his son wasn't loyal, in front of everyone?

"Becca was kidnapped," Cassie said strongly. "As her only sister, I had to try to find her. Then I got kidnapped. Nate, being a good friend and an amazing person, tried to find us. And he got taken as well."

"By who?" someone in the crowd shouted.

"There's a prison," I said. "A prison just for kids. We were all taken there."

More surprised murmuring. But Cassie wasn't finished.

"And we—all of us—have to go there right now and save those kids!" she cried.

103

CASSIE

"WHERE IS THIS PRISON?" a woman yelled. "Are any of our kids there?"

"Some," I said. "Not all of the ones who are missing. We saw Kathy Hobhouse there, and she said she'd seen Livvie Clayhill. But there's other people's kids there—hundreds of them. Kids whose parents are just as worried, just as frantic, as we are. Those kids need *saving*."

"What are you talking about?" the Provost said. This was clearly not going the way he'd thought—I could practically hear the wheels in his head spinning as he tried to turn this to his advantage.

"There are hundreds of kids who are going hungry, who are being beaten, who are facing death every day!" I said, raising my voice. "And we, as a cell, can help them!"

The crowd looked confused. Each cell takes care of its own—that's how it's always been.

"If our kids were there, and folks from another cell could help them, would you want them to?" Becca asked.

More murmuring.

"We, the people of this cell, could help those kids," Becca went on. "We might be able to return them to their own cells."

"They can't come here!" the Provost said. "It would throw everything out of balance!"

"These kids' lives are more important than balance!" I said strongly, and the Provost paled as people started to agree with me, nodding their heads.

"You know the laws!" the Provost tried again. "We're not leaving the cell unauthorized!"

"These kids' lives are more important than laws!" Becca said.

"More important than authorization!" I added.

People in the crowd were talking to each other, nodding and convincing each other.

"Who's with us?" Becca shouted, raising one hand in the air. "Who will take the risk of going to save these children's lives?"

No one said anything.

"It won't be easy," I said. "It's a scary thought for all of us. There's a lot to like about staying home, safe and sound." Nods, looks of relief. "Except we *aren't* safe!" I cried. "Our own kids have been taken with no warning! Who knows who will be next? Will it be one of your sons or daughters? Will someone you love end up in that nightmare? We're *not* safe in this cell! We won't be safe until we break up that prison!"

This was it—now or never. I waited, muscles as taut as a pulley rope. And then one person raised a hand, tentatively.

Then another person raised her hand.

And another.

And another.

"Let's go find this prison!" a woman yelled.

"Let's go find those kids!" a man agreed.

I looked at Becca, saw the disbelief in her eyes.

"Heroes," I whispered.

104

THERE WAS A CONVOY. BECCA and I had gotten everyone riled up. A line of cars, trucks, and even a few tractors swarmed toward the boundary gates. I couldn't believe it. Everything was changing. We were changing it.

Despite the Provost lecturing about the dangers of leaving the cell, only a few people turned back. It felt like everyone had been asleep, and had just woken up. It was amazing.

Becca and I jumped in the back of a pickup truck. I was feeling a sickening mixture of hope and dread, excitement and fear. I'd never wanted to go back to that prison. I'd never wanted to get anywhere near the place. But I was ready to take it by storm. Just thinking of the kids inside—setting them free...

Becca nudged my knee with hers. "Can't believe we're going back—voluntarily."

I nodded. "Yeah. But we have all these people with us—Strepp can't take us with all of them here. We have to try."

Becca nodded, but she didn't look completely convinced. She'd told the lead driver where she thought the prison was, based on our return journey. I was glad she'd been paying attention, because there was no way I'd ever find it again.

After a long time, shouts up ahead made us stand and look over the truck cab. A sudden panic gripped me: there it was. I'd recognize it anywhere—the collection of broken-down gray buildings, the tall chain-link fence with razor wire on top. I couldn't believe I was back here. Then I thought of the beaten, hungry kids inside.

The last time I'd approached this place, I'd been looking for my sister, determined to find her at any cost. Now I grabbed her hand, felt her fingers tighten around mine. We'd made it this far together. We could go farther.

My breath caught in my throat as I imagined the confrontation we'd soon face. Would Strepp be there? Would she sic the guards on us? Our cell was made up of farmers: the most extreme argument I'd ever seen had been Mr. Fenston yelling at Mrs. Parker to "move her gol' dang tractor" out of his cornfield.

"I hope this isn't a huge mistake," I muttered to Becca. "Maybe we should have thought this through more."

"Too late, Careful Cassie," she whispered. "Time to be heroes."

Within minutes we'd arrived at the gates.

It didn't take more than a couple seconds to see that my fears were justified. Something was very, very wrong.

105

BECCA

CASSIE AND I WERE STANDING in the back of the pickup, holding on to its metal frame. The closer we got to the crazy house, the more the hairs on the back of my neck stood up.

"What the hell?" I said, as our convoy came to an ungraceful stop at the gates.

I'd expected guards with machine guns. I'd expected gates shut and locked with heavy chains.

These gates were wide open. Wide open, and hanging off their hinges, as if they hadn't been used in a long, long time.

Cassie and I jumped down from the truck and ran closer.

Someone got out of a Hopper and looked at us. "Is this the place?"

"Yeah," I said. "I don't know what's going on."

"This is weird. There's no tire tracks," Cassie said, pointing to the dirt and tumbleweed-covered ground.

"What is this?" someone asked. "This place is abandoned!"

"No," I said. "It just looks that way. Let's see what's inside!" As I led the way to the main building, I noticed the Provost standing outside his car, leaning against it. He'd looked pretty panicky when the mob had insisted on coming here. Finding this seemingly abandoned building had cheered him up.

I stopped dead about ten feet away from the main door, which was also open. Bits of trash were blowing around, and dust had filtered inside. Cautiously, expecting to be set upon at any second, I peeped inside. Cassie joined me, a confused frown on her face.

"It looks completely different. Unused," she whispered, shaking her head. "But this is definitely it." She reached out and hit a light switch. Nothing happened.

We took several steps inside, still waiting for alarms to sound, guards to come running. But the place was as silent and empty as Pa's bedroom at home. The air was stale and dry, the only sounds were the wind whistling through deserted rooms and the echoes of our feet as we continued to search.

We found nothing. No prisoners, no Strepp, no classrooms, *nothing.* Just one empty room after another. The auditorium held bleachers but no canvas-floored ring, no stains of blood. The mess hall held only a few overturned chairs and tables, some broken windows, and a bird's nest above one air-conditioning duct.

"The tunnel!" Cassie cried, and we ran through the kitchen to the hallway beyond. It was just the same, with rows of doors, but when we got to the end, the very end, there was no door at all. Just a blank wall.

Scowling, I went back to the last door and opened it, in case we were remembering wrong. This room was empty. No crates and certainly no hole in the wall.

Outside in the hallway, Cassie and I just looked at each other, and then I slammed my fist against the wall where the door *should* have been. "Goddamnit!" I cried. "This is impossible! It doesn't make sense!"

"You're right," said the smooth, oily voice of the Provost as he walked down the hallway toward us. "This *is* impossible. It *doesn't* make sense."

I gave him my best slit-eyed glare, but inside, my brain was reeling with the craziness of it all. We had *just been* here. We *really did* have those experiences. I still had a lump on my head from a tree root, and Cassie's finger had been fractured from punching Strepp. *So what the hell was happening?*

106

"ADMIT IT!" PROVOST ALLEN SAID. "You are lying!"

"We aren't lying!" I snapped. "I don't know what the deal is, but we aren't lying! I have no idea why that prison seemed unused, because *believe me,* it's been used."

I glanced over at Cassie. Since we'd gotten back to town, she'd been oddly quiet. Even more than me, she seemed shocked by what we'd found. Now as we were getting yelled at in the Provost's office, it seemed like she was somewhere else.

"I don't know what you were hoping to accomplish by that stunt," the Provost said with a sneer. "But I'm glad that you were publicly shown to be liars and manipulators. In the morning the Overseer Committee and I will decide on a proper course of action. But between you and me, I'm sure a quick mood-adjust will help you both become the upstanding, productive citizens you should be. In the meantime, you'll be guests of the United—in our cozy jail, right here in the Management Building."

Cassie blinked and sat up straighter. "No."

The Provost pounced on her eagerly. "No?"

"I'm not going back to jail," Cassie said flatly. "And neither is Becca. We're going home." She stood up as the Provost's face started turning red.

"You're not going anywhere!" he said with barely controlled fury. "Except to prison, where bad citizens and traitors belong!"

I stepped closer to Cassie, rage boiling up inside me. "Listen, old man," I ground out. "Either one of us could easily beat the shit out of you—we've been trained to. Both of us together and you'll *never* find all your teeth. If my sister says we're going home, then we're going home. Got it?"

The Provost opened his mouth, and I held up a finger. "Go ahead," I said. "Call the guards. We'll take them on, too. It'll be fun."

The Provost looked like he was about to have a stroke. "Then you're under house arrest!" he hissed. "My guards will take you home and make sure you stay there until tomorrow morning's hearing!"

Cassie shrugged.

"You're the worst kind of citizen!" the Provost added. "The best kind for a mood-adjust!"

"Like your wife?" I said, meanly.

I'd never seen anyone go from purple to green in just a few seconds, and I watched his face with interest.

"Guards!" he shouted. Immediately the door burst open and two guards ran in. "Take them to their house. You and another unit will be on guard tonight. Make sure they don't leave."

"Yes, sir!" the guard said, then motioned me and Cassie out the door.

Whatever. We wanted to go home, anyway.

107

CASSIE

THE GUARDS NUDGED US OUT of their cars and up onto the porch. One of them wanted to follow us inside, but Becca stopped him with a glare.

"Forget it," she said flatly. "You're staying outside."

With a sour look, the guard motioned to the other three to surround the house. He made a big show of standing at attention, his rifle at the ready. I had no doubt he was hoping that Becca or I would try to run away.

Feeling beaten all over again, Becca and I trudged upstairs.

"How could the prison—" I started, but Becca held up her hand.

"There's no way," Becca said bitterly. "You know and I know that that prison was there, that we went through all that shit, and that we aren't crazy. But besides that? I got nothing."

"That's right," I said, feeling a weight in my chest. "We have *nothing!* No school, no vocation, no Ma, Pa...and you know the Provost is going to send us for a mood-adjust. I can't go through that. I'd rather die!" I thought about Nate, how there was no chance for us to be together, and felt even bleaker.

"They would love for us to choose that option," Becca said. "They'd get the SAS van here in five minutes. We can't give them that satisfaction."

"Then what? We have the so-called hearing in the morning!"

Becca flopped down next to me on Ma and Pa's bed. She gave me a tired smile and then yawned. "Relax," she said. "If it comes to that, we'll knock the guards out in the car, kick them out, steal the car, and then bust out of here. We'll hit the boundary road and keep going till we run out of gas or find another cell."

"Huh," I said. That sounded pretty easy, actually. "Will you try to find Tim?"

"Maybe," she said. "Depends on how much of a shit storm we have following us."

"Okay," I said, feeling a little better. My eyes were heavy and I let myself slide into an exhausted sleep. After all, I was going to knock out guards and steal a car tomorrow. I had to rest up.

108

WHEN ROUGH HANDS GRABBED ME out of a deep sleep, I thought I was just having flashbacks. Nightmares. It took a minute to react, since I expected to wake up. But then a black hood was pulled over my head and I heard Becca cry out.

"Cassie!" she screamed, then her voice was muffled.

"Becca!" I shouted back, but a heavy hand clamped over my mouth.

We hadn't gone through weeks of intensive combat training for nothing, and immediately I kicked out, connected with something hard. Someone let out a breath, and then I felt a sharp, cold pinch in my thigh. Within seconds I had collapsed to the floor, as limp as an empty flour sack. I was vaguely aware of hands picking me up, but then everything was black.

Gradually I came awake, slowly realizing that I was lying down in a truck or van, my hands cuffed behind me.

"Becca?" I said hoarsely.

"Mmm," came the answer, as if she were struggling to wake up.

The road was long and full of potholes. Apparently the driver was paid extra to hit every one. Each time he did, we bounced on the hard floor, landing painfully. Gradually I eased myself up into a sitting position. My ankles were bound together, but I managed to work my hands beneath me and then in front of me. It was much better. With my hands in front I was able to feel around for Becca.

"Get your hands in front," I told her. "Then you can untie my hood."

"'K," she said, and coughed.

After getting our hoods off, we worked on the ropes around our ankles. Our wrists were cuffed with metal rings, and though we scraped our hands raw, we couldn't get out of them.

We were being taken back to prison. Where, we didn't know. We might have to fight. We might be tortured and tested until we fell over with exhaustion. We might be executed. One of us might have to watch the other one die.

"Well," I said, panting with the effort of trying to untie my ankles, "at least we don't have to go to the goddamn hearing this morning."

Becca looked at me, surprised to hear me swear, and a slow smile lit her face. Then she was laughing, and I was laughing. Because what else could we do, facing death after everything we'd been through?

And when we finally got to our destination and the van doors were opened to forbidding darkness, that's what Strepp saw: Becca and I without our hoods, our ankles free, laughing.

109

BECCA

I WASN'T SURPRISED TO SEE Strepp waiting for us. I was, however, pretty damned pleased to see the shiner Cassie had given her. When she saw Cassie and me laughing, a weird expression crossed her face, and then she said, "Out!" and banged on the van door with a billy club.

When I stumbled out, I didn't recognize a goddamn thing. This was a new prison in some new, unknown place. We were somewhere that we'd never be able to find our way back home from. Not that we had much home to go back to.

When the van drove off, we stood there looking around uncertainly.

This prison was smaller. I'd never seen buildings that looked like this, like they were made of orange clay.

Ms. Strepp scrutinized the two of us. "Guards!" she yelled, and a new set of guards marched out, holding guns. They were your basic nondescript goons, except...

There was one...

I stared at her, my mouth open wide enough to catch flies.

For just a second she met my gaze, then looked away.

It was *Robin. Robin Wellfleet,* my first friend in jail.

I'd seen her *die.* She had *died.*

But now she was *here.*

"Robin!" I couldn't help exclaiming. I moved toward her, my arms open for a hug. I had to feel her, make sure she wasn't a ghost or a hallucination.

"Get back in line!" Strepp shouted, and another guard rapped me in the small of my back. I turned around to snarl at him, and when I turned back, Robin was gone.

Strepp ordered, "Quiet!" Then she told the guards, "Take them inside!"

We were marched into a building. I felt Cassie looking at me with questions. She'd never known Robin. But I was flipping out. *I'd seen her die.*

Inside the building it was plain old prisonlike. This one, however, was in better shape than the crazy house—newer and cleaner.

Armed guards prodded us down hallways until we reached a processing station, where we were searched. Various people were in the halls, some in prisoner jumpsuits, some dressed like guards, some just in regular clothes. I caught sight of a slight, younger-looking kid who was loading books from a cardboard box onto a shelf.

It was Little Bit.

Little Bit, who was dead because I'd beaten her in a fight. I wanted to shriek her name, but knew I'd end up with a knot on my head if I did. Again Cassie looked at me, and again I shrugged, my head spinning.

We were given jumpsuits, this time a nauseating puke-green, and hustled into a long hallway.

Strepp strode up. "You two. Come with me," she barked.

Here we go, I thought, and felt my stomach twist into a knot.

110

CASSIE

IT WAS UNUSUAL FOR US to see Strepp together. So maybe we were about to head to the ring to fight. This prison had a ring, right?

I reached out and touched Becca's hand. As outwardly calm as I'd been since we'd been recaptured, as much as I felt better prepared to face whatever was coming, I still hated the idea of having to fight my sister. We'd have to make it a good show. Have to really hurt each other. Just the thought made me feel like crying.

But we weren't led to the ring—at least, not yet. We were taken down another hall and stopped while a guard opened a door.

"Come in," Ms. Strepp said, and the guard shut the door behind us.

"What now?" Becca said belligerently. "A test? A fight?" She'd been thinking along the same lines I was.

"Sit down," Ms. Strepp said, gesturing to the two chairs in front of her desk. After giving each other a quizzical glance, Becca and I sat.

Ms. Strepp clasped her hands on her desk, not saying anything, as if thinking through what heinous exercise to make us undergo. Finally she looked at us, as if she had decided.

"Do you know the meaning of the word *cell?*" she asked, taking me by surprise.

When Becca didn't say anything, I answered, "It's a community. Like a town."

Ms. Strepp shook her head. "No. That's called a community, or a town. You came from a *cell*. Do you know why?" Not waiting for an answer this time, she went on, "The word *cell* used to mean hidden, or covered. Then it meant a small place for sleeping, like for hermits, or monks in a monastery. Its most recent meaning is as a jail cell."

A jail cell?

"Not all that long ago, bad citizens were put into jails, and the little rooms were called cells," said Ms. Strepp. "Now everyone you know lives in cells. What do you think that means?"

I had no idea, no clue as to what she was getting at, and I shook my head.

Ms. Strepp nodded and clicked a remote at a TV screen on the wall. It flickered to life. "I'll show you."

The image on the screen cleared. It was a picture of a white sand beach being gently lapped by clear turquoise water. I'd never seen anything like it, and I leaned forward slightly, my eyes wide.

The image pulled back to reveal couchlike chairs sitting right on the sand. My eyebrows raised as it showed a woman with deep-tan skin, wearing a red bikini, lying on one of the chairs. She reached a hand out and someone, a man in a suit, put a fancy drink in it. The drink was three colors—red, orange, yellow—and had fruit in it. It looked amazing.

"This is a place called Florida," said Ms. Strepp. "It's in one of the Forbidden Zones."

"I've never heard of a Forbidden Zone," Becca said.

"Most people haven't," said Ms. Strepp. "But in the United, there are at least fifteen Forbidden Zones."

"Forbidden how?" Becca asked.

"Forbidden to cellfolk," Ms. Strepp said. "Forbidden to you. And me. And anyone you know."

111

BECCA

WAS THIS THE SAME STREPP who had tortured us, made us fight, tested us constantly? What was she doing? This had to be a trap somehow.

"Is this a test?" I asked flatly.

"All of life is a test," said Ms. Strepp, sounding like herself at last. "But look."

The image on the TV screen changed. It had been taken from an airplane. It flew over a cell, an ag cell like ours. I saw the houses, the fields, the cows, the boundary fence. The plane kept flying and went over dark-green trees that lasted a long time. It flew over another fence, much taller and thicker than a boundary fence, made of brick.

Next to me, Cassie gasped.

This was a cell of some kind, but like nothing I'd ever imagined.

"Those are not government buildings," Ms. Strepp said. "Those are houses."

The houses were enormous, the size of the hospital or our school. They had balconies and beautiful gardens filled with flowers and trees and bushes.

"What is that place?" Cassie asked.

"It's called Virginia. Another of the Forbidden Zones. Keep watching."

Now the images on the screen switched back and forth: a close-up of one of those gorgeous houses, its walls made of pale-red bricks. The next shot was of a big pit of red clay, then a cell factory where the clay was being made into bricks. Filthy, sweating men and women shoveled the clay into huge molds that got pressed by a machine.

The image changed again and we peered through an open window at a table. It had a lace tablecloth and beautiful plates and glasses. On the table was a loaf of bread. Abruptly, the next image was another cell factory. Huge machines were churning wet dough. Women wearing white coats and caps hauled the machines to and fro, dumping the dough onto conveyer belts.

"I don't understand what any of this is," I said. They looked real. But none of it made sense.

Ms. Strepp didn't reply, but clicked her remote again. Now the images flew by on the screen: a close-up of a rosebush, then a shot of gardeners toiling in the sun, growing rosebushes by the thousands. A view of a beautiful wooden desk, a shiny wooden floor, a stack of wood by an amazing marble fireplace—followed by a timber cell, where men using enormous saws were felling trees, and cranes loaded the trees onto long trucks.

Finally we saw some people who looked like they had never worked outside a day in their life. They were eating steak and corn on the cob. The next shot was of…

"That's B-97-4275," I breathed. "Oh, my God."

The screen showed farms I knew, reaping machines like the one Pa had used, trucks full of corn and wheat and pumpkins driving out through the boundary gates.

I stared at Ms. Strepp.

"You think this is a prison?" Her voice was oddly gentle. "The prison is your home cell. That's the prison you can't leave. That's the prison where people are held in slavery, making goods and products for these other people to enjoy."

"What people?" I burst out.

"The United," said Ms. Strepp.

112

"WHAT?" CASSIE CRIED.

"The rich. The powerful. Those at the top of the United," said Ms. Strepp.

"I don't understand," I said again. I felt so confused, and wished she would make me do push-ups or something I could wrap my head around.

"The people who run everything and control every facet of our existence," Ms. Strepp said. "They tell farms when to produce more corn or fewer tomatoes. They tell manufacturers to make more cars or different cars or trucks. They tell bakers to make white bread or rye bread or rolls."

"Why?" I asked.

"For their enjoyment," Ms. Strepp said. "The few in charge of the United keep the rest of us in slavery, so that they can enjoy life."

I glanced at Cassie. Her brow was furrowed and I could almost see her trying to decipher those words.

"They don't live in cells?" Cassie said.

"No. They live in Forbidden Zones," Ms. Strepp answered. "But they're allowed to go to any Forbidden Zone they want, anytime they want, without permission. Some of them have houses in three or four or more different places."

"What do they make?" Cassie asked. "What do they produce?"

"Nothing." Ms. Strepp's face looked hard and condemning. "They produce nothing. Even their music and art are made by people they control."

"Well, what do they *do?*" I still felt lost.

"They relax," said Ms. Strepp, and the way she said it made relaxing sound like it was about as worthwhile as incubating the plague.

"Why are you telling us this?" I asked.

"Because we—the Outsiders—are tired of being slaves. We're tired of being controlled. We want to play the game by our rules."

Wait—back up. Was Strepp saying she was an Outsider?

113

CASSIE

BECCA AND I BOTH SAT there looking like largemouth bass as Ms. Strepp went on with her mind-blowing revelations.

"Once I was a girl in a cell, just like you," she said. "And just like you, one day I was kidnapped and taken to prison and put on death row."

What?

"That prison was where my life really began."

My eyes were bugging out of my head, and I didn't dare look at Becca.

"In prison, I learned right from wrong. You know what death row is like. Facing death forces you to leave extraneous emotions behind. It focuses your thoughts, your energies, unlike any other situation."

No shit, I thought.

"In prison I learned to survive, much as you have done. I learned how to live free, as much as anyone can. Not free *outside.* Free *inside,* inside of myself. They had caged my body, but they couldn't cage my mind, or my soul."

Was this the same Strepp who had made me do push-ups until I fell on a bed of nails? I felt like I was having an out-of-body experience. The images from the TV were ricocheting around in my mind—the white sand, the huge houses, the fancy drink.

"You are two of the Outsiders. Pleased to meet you. I'm Helen Strepp, one of the heads of the Outsiders." She gave a smile that was so unexpected that it was almost scary.

"We—the Outsiders—are like a hydra," she said. "We have many heads. If one of us is cut off, others are ready to step into our place. Our mission is too important to risk a break in the chain of command. You see, we—the Outsiders—are preparing for the future. Life as we know it is about to change radically, and not for the better. We as a people will face great hardships, and almost certainly a terrible war." She let out another breath, as if even knowing this was a heavy burden.

"I'm sure you've wondered why you were taken. Basically, we try to take anyone who has shown curiosity or a willingness to break the rules. Cassie, you were put into a terrible situation—both parents gone, a farm to keep up. But you made perfect grades and never missed a day of school. You were holding it together in the face of great adversity, and that's the kind of people we need."

I didn't know what to say. I'd always thought of myself as really ordinary.

"Becca, we were planning to take Cassie first and you later," Ms. Strepp said. "We were thrown by you using the truck."

I turned and gave Becca the stink eye.

"But in you we found someone with a rebellious spirit. Someone willing to take risks. Someone who wasn't totally under the United's thumb."

This was the first time that those qualities had been seen as positive, I thought.

"You two have shown great—exceptional—potential. You *escaped*—the first prisoners out of thousands to do so. My job is to find the very best and to train them. This has been going on for almost twenty years. We take just a few kids from each cell. The cells don't communicate with each other, which works to our advantage. I was taken. Now I have taken you. You, in your turn, will someday take other kids."

"What?" Becca exclaimed.

"Yes," Ms. Strepp said. "Everything we've done, everything you've gone through has been calculated to make you stronger, tougher, smarter, and more likely to survive. Your training will continue here. You will learn how to use weapons, efficient ways to kill or disable someone, how to break into buildings, how to hack computer systems. Skills you'll need to take down the United."

I needed time to think all this through. I remembered telling Becca that they had trained us to be heroes. Now it sounded like they would train us to be assassins. Maybe in this case, those were the same thing.

Suddenly Ms. Strepp jumped up and slammed her hands on her desk.

"There's no time for dithering!" she shouted, seeming much more familiar. "It's time to act! With everything I've told you, shown you, do you know what the point of all this is?" She waved one arm as if to encompass all of creation.

"Do you know the most important thing that you've learned?" Her voice was loud and harsh. "Do you know what your real value is to us? It isn't your decision making! I don't care if you can make sense of all this! I don't care if you have feelings or thoughts you want to share! You!" she pointed one long finger at me. *"What is your value?"*

My brain raced, unable to formulate a coherent thought. Then suddenly it was there. The one thing I'd gotten out of everything we'd been through. I remembered that when they'd opened the van, Becca and I had been laughing.

I looked right into Strepp's icy eyes. "I'm not afraid to die."

"We're not afraid to die," Becca repeated. "That is our value."

Ms. Strepp sat back as if struck, an odd, cold glint of triumph crossing her face.

"Yes," she said quietly. "Exactly."

ABOUT THE AUTHORS

James Patterson received the Literarian Award for Outstanding Service to the American Literary Community from the National Book Foundation. He holds the Guinness World Record for the most #1 *New York Times* bestsellers, including *Confessions of a Murder Suspect* and the Maximum Ride series, and his books have sold more than 375 million copies worldwide. A tireless champion of the power of books and reading, Patterson created a children's book imprint, JIMMY Patterson, whose mission is simple: "We want every kid who finishes a JIMMY Book to say, 'PLEASE GIVE ME ANOTHER BOOK.'" He has donated more than one million books to students and soldiers and funds over four hundred Teacher Education Scholarships at twenty-four colleges and universities. He has also donated millions of dollars to independent bookstores and school libraries. Patterson invests proceeds from the sales of JIMMY Patterson Books in pro-reading initiatives.

Gabrielle Charbonnet is the coauthor of *Sundays at Tiffany's, Witch & Wizard,* and *Crazy House* with James Patterson, and has written many other books for young readers. She lives in South Carolina with her husband and a lot of pets.

Eager to find out what happens to Cassie and Becca in
their fight against the United?
Get a sneak peek of the even crazier sequel!

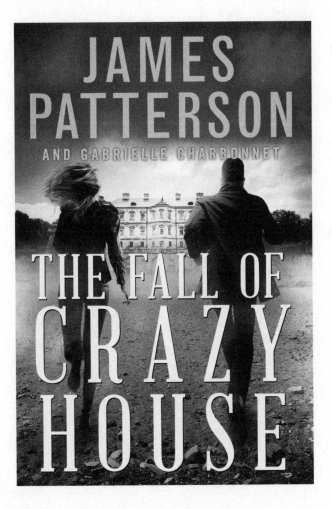

Turn the page to see what happens next...

CASSIE

HERE'S WHAT YOU HAVE A lot of in training camp: Pain. Injury. Grit. Adrenaline. Anger.

Here's what you don't have a lot of: Softness. Gentleness. Patience. Lightheartedness. Cute clothes.

So when Ms. Strepp announced that we would have a celebration that evening, it took me a few moments to process that concept.

"Our last leadership member has finally passed the crucial test," Strepp announced, without looking at me. "You've all been working hard. Tonight you'll be rewarded."

Warm, recognizable food? Check. Sweet, fruity, punchlike substance? Check. Dressing up in fun, sparkly partywear? No. But I did shower.

Recent rains had left the middle of our camp full of frozen, churned-up mud, but we threw down a layer of dried pine needles and danced there anyway. Someone had rigged up a portable sound system, like a boombox. It hung from a tree, blasting music we hadn't heard in forever. A cold, full winter's moon hung low in the sky, casting silvery shadows, disguising bruises and dirt, highlighting scars with fine white lines.

The whole camp was dancing in one writhing, disorganized clump, but Nate and I, and Becca and Tim, tried to stay together as much as possible. The music was too loud, its bass reverberating in my chest and making my ears ring. Someone had spiked the punch—more moonshine—and all of my aches and pains and injuries melted away into the night air. Despite everything, I felt exhilarated and intensely alive. Despite all the differences that Reckless Rebecca and I had, have had, and will have, there was no one I'd rather be with in this new, post-cell life of battle and secrecy, violence and fear. There was no one I trusted more.

Nate grabbed my arms and swung me around, pressing me close so that our bellies touched. He smelled like harsh camp soap, and I saw that he'd worn his least destroyed camo pants. After Becca, Nate was my closest second. He and Becca's boyfriend, Tim, had both easily passed leadership training, making hard life-or-death choices with no hesitation. I was thankful they were with the Resistance rather than the Uniteds. Nate looked down at me, his eyes shining despite a darkening bruise on his left cheek, and I smiled up at him and looped my arms around his neck.

"Attention!" Ms. Strepp had to raise her voice three times before someone shut off the music. She climbed on top of a wooden crate and looked at us, these hundreds of kids she'd mercilessly trained and beaten into some sort of a military force.

"Some of you have been here a year or more," she began. "Some of you have been here only weeks." A kid got a flashlight and aimed it up at Strepp, giving her a weird, statue-like appearance. "Some of you have a grasp on the broader picture of what we're facing, and some of you have simply learned to shoot." Her eyes, always frosty, raked over us. "But enjoy yourselves tonight. Feel young, feel free, feel hopeful. It's perhaps the last time you'll feel any of those things."

I frowned—this wasn't exactly the cheerful, "go get 'em" speech I was expecting.

"Tomorrow, and every tomorrow after that, will be uncertain," Ms. Strepp said. "Starting tomorrow, we will officially be at war with the United. We will be on the path to overthrow them, to seize their power, to topple their leaders. It will be the only path we know, and we'll stay on it until we succeed—or die."

My buzz was wearing off and my dance-fever warmth had ebbed, leaving me chilly.

"My troops, my comrades-in-arms, my soldiers—we will be free!" Ms. Strepp punched her fist in the air and shouted it again. "We will be free!"

The rest of us took up the chant, punching the air and yelling, "We will be free! We will be free! We! Will! Be! Free!"

BECCA

THANK *GOD* CAREFUL CASSIE HAD finally passed the last leadership test. I mean, *Good Lord.*

Having said that, the last three months of training had made our stint at the Crazy House look like summer camp.

"Here." Tim handed me a cup and I took a sip, then smiled up at him.

"Yay, spiked!" I said, draining it. We headed back out onto the dancing area and leaned together, arms wrapped tightly around each other, and swayed slowly to some sappy song about how love was like a walk in the rain.

"You feel good," Tim murmured against my hair. I rested my head on his shoulder, glad I'd taken the time to get most of the tangles out of my hair earlier. A lot of girls here had gone the crewcut route: easier to care for, keep clean, and gave enemies nothing to grab. So far, Cassie and I had both resisted, but I was weakening.

"You know what?" I said into Tim's muscled chest. "I hope when we're out fighting, we'll find one of those non-cell towns Strepp told us about."

"Yeah," Tim agreed. "Take it over, raid their food and medical supplies."

"Do you believe all that stuff she told us?" I asked him. "All those pictures and videos? It just seems . . . crazy. Not real."

"I guess I believe it," Tim said slowly. "I want to think that's what we're fighting for."

For seventeen years, Cassie and I had lived in a regular Ag cell, going to school, helping on our parents' farm. It had been boring as hell. Now, with the whole United ahead of us, our army rushing out to meet whatever might come, I was too excited to feel fear.

Tomorrow, everything—*my life*—would really begin. This party, this celebration, felt like the last night on earth as we knew it. Slowly I edged Tim and I over to the food table, where I refilled cups for us both. Tim threw his back and I finished mine in three gulps. Grinning at each other, we rejoined and clung together, barely moving our feet.

"Tomorrow we're getting our assignments," Tim said. "Strepp has been dropping hints for weeks."

I nodded. "Fingers crossed that the four of us end up on one team. She *has* to keep us together." Cassie, Tim, and Nate had my back, without question. We would fight more effectively as a unit. A unit of trust.

"I can't believe it's finally happening," Tim said, stroking my back. "All the shit we've gone through, the pain, the injuries—it was all leading up to tomorrow."

"I know," I said, not admitting that my throat felt tight and I had butterflies in my stomach. "Strepp better make it worthwhile, that's all I'm gonna say." Reaching up, I wound my arms around Tim's neck in the loud semi-darkness.

"Let's sneak away," I whispered, going on tiptoe to reach his ear.

Tim looked down at me, his fair eyebrows—one split in half—raising at me. "Out into the snow?" he asked.

I grinned. "You can keep me warm."

Tim smiled back, doing a decent wolf impression, and we slipped past the trees and out into the darkness. The world—our world—might end tomorrow. But tonight I was going to live.

Read more in

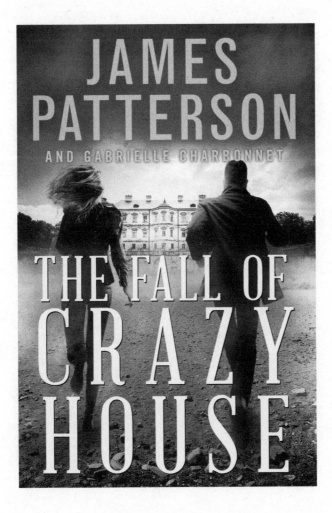

Available now!

Each year, eight beautiful girls are chosen as Paper Girls to serve the king. It's the highest honor they could hope for . . . and the most demeaning. This year, there's a ninth. And instead of paper, she's made of fire.

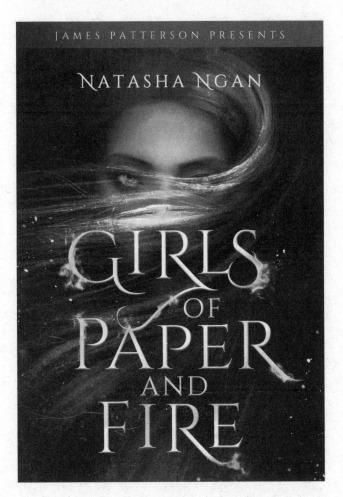

JAMES PATTERSON PRESENTS

NATASHA NGAN

GIRLS OF PAPER AND FIRE

Can't get enough of girls kicking butt? You'll love Lei. Turn the page for a tantalizing chapter of this exciting new fantasy!

There is a tradition in our kingdom, one all castes of demon and human follow. We call it the Birth-blessing. It is such an old, deep-rooted custom that it's said even our gods themselves practiced it when they bore our race onto the earth. When babies die before their first year, there are whispers like leaves fluttering darkly on the wind: the ceremony was performed too late; the parents must have spoken during it; the shaman who executed the blessing was unskilled, a fake.

Coming from the lowest caste—Paper caste, fully human—my parents had to save for the full nine months after the news of my mother's pregnancy. Though I've never seen a Birth-blessing ceremony, I've imagined my own so many times that it feels almost like a memory, or some half remembered dream.

Picture smoke-cut night and darkness like a heavy black hand cupped round the world. Crackling fire. Standing before the flames—a shaman, his leathery skin webbed with tattoos, teeth sharpened to wolflike points. He's bent over the naked form of a newborn, just hours old. She's crying. On the other side of the fire, her parents watch in silence, hands clasped so tightly their knuckles are white. The shaman's eyes roll as he chants a dao, painting its characters in the air with his fingers, where they hang above the baby, glowing softly before fading away.

As he comes to the crest of the prayer, a wind picks up. The grass stirs in a feathery rustle. Faster and faster the shaman chants, and louder and louder the rustle and the wind, until the fire whips upward, a whorl of orange-red flame dancing high into the sky before flashing suddenly out.

Blackness.

The starlit night.

Then the shaman reaches into the air where the fire had been for the object floating in its wake: a small, egglike golden pendant. But the pendant isn't what's important. What's important is what the pendant hides within.

The baby's fate. *My* fate.

Our kingdom believes words have power. That the characters of our language can bless or curse a life. Inside the pendant is a single character. One word that we believe will reveal a person's true destiny—and if my life will be blessed, as my parents hoped when they saved for my ceremony, or whether my fate is something far darker. Cursed years to be played out in fire and shadow.

In six months, when I turn eighteen, the pendant will open and its answer will finally be revealed.

Our shop is busy this morning. Not even noon yet and it's already packed with customers, the room bright with chatter, Tien's brusque voice cutting through the thick summer air. Sunlight streams in through the slatted windows, drowsy with cicada song. Sandals slap on the floorboards. Beneath it all, like the shop's familiar heartbeat, comes the bubble of the mixing barrels where we brew our herbal medicines. The six tubs are lined along the back of the store, so big they reach my shoulders. Five are full of pungent mixtures. The sixth is empty, filled instead with me—admittedly *also* pungent after an hour's hard work scrubbing dried residue from the buckled wood.

"Almost done, little nuisance?"

I'm working at a particularly stubborn stain when Tien's face appears over the edge of the barrel. Feline eyes rimmed with black; graying hair flowing softly over pointed cat ears. She regards me with her head cocked.

I swipe the back of my hand over my forehead. *Little nuisance.* She's been calling me that for as long as I can recall.

"I'm seventeen, Tien," I point out. "Not little anymore."

"Well," she says with a click of her tongue. "Still a nuisance."

"I wonder where I get it from."

A smirk rises up to challenge my own. "I'll pretend you're talking about your father. *Aiyah,* where is that lazy man? He was meant to refill our stock of monsoon berries an hour ago!" She waves a hand. "Go fetch him. Mistress Zembi is waiting for her consultation."

"Only if you say please," I retort, and her ears twitch.

"Demanding for a Paper caste, aren't you?"

"You're the Steel with a Paper boss."

She sighs. "And I regret it every day."

As she bustles off to deal with a customer, I smile despite myself at the proud flick of her neat lynx ears. Tien has worked for us for as long as I can remember, more family now than shop hand despite our caste differences. Because of that, sometimes it's easy to forget that there *are* differences between us. But while my father and I are Paper caste, Tien belongs to the middle caste, Steel. Somewhere between my plain human body and the animal-like strength of Moon castes, Steel castes have elements of both, making them a strange meeting point between human and demon, like a drawing only halfway finished. As with most Steels, Tien has just touches of demon: a tapered feline maw; the graying amber cat's fur wrapped around her neck and shoulders, like a shawl.

As she greets the customer, Tien's hands automatically pat down that messy ruff of fur where it pokes from the collar of her samfoo shirt. But it just sticks straight back up.

My lips quirk. It must have been a prank by the gods to give someone as fussy as her such unruly hair.

I climb over the side of the tub and catch a better look at the woman Tien is talking to. Her long black hair is pulled back, twining past a pair of elegant deer antlers as slender as vine. Another Steel demon. My eyes travel over her elegant kebaya glittering with silver threads and embroidery. It's clear that she belongs to an affluent family. The jewels dangling from her earlobes alone would keep our shop running for a year.

As I'm wondering why someone like her has come to our shop—she must be from out of town; no one here has that kind of money—her gaze glides past Tien and catches mine.

Her eyes grow wide. "So it's true."

I just about make out her murmur over the noise of the shop. My face flushes.

Of course. She heard the rumors.

I turn away, ducking through the bead-curtained doorway to the back rooms of our old shop building. The deer-woman's elegance has made me extra aware of the state I'm in. Clumps of dirt cling to my clothes—a pair of loose sand-colored trousers and a wrap shirt knotted at the waist with a frayed sash—and my ankles are soaked with the camphor liquid I was using to clean the mixing barrel. Stray hairs stick to my cheeks with sweat. Sweeping them back, I retie my ponytail, and my mind slips for a moment, remembering.

Other fingers looping a red ribbon through my hair.

A smile like sunshine. Laughter even brighter.

Strange, how grief works. Seven years on and some days I struggle to remember her face, while other times my mother seems so real to me that I almost expect her to amble in through the front door, smelling like peony petals in the rain, a laugh on her lips and a kiss for Baba and me.

"She's gone," I tell myself roughly. "And she's not coming back."

With a shake of my head, I continue down the corridor and out onto the sunlit veranda. Our garden is narrow and long, bordered by a mossy wall. An old fig tree dapples the grass with shade. The summer warmth heightens the fragrances of our herb plot, the tangled patchwork of plants running down the center of the garden, familiar scents rising from it to tease my nose: chrysanthemum, sage, ginger. Charms threaded along wire to keep the birds away chime in the breeze.

A cheerful-sounding bark draws my attention. My father is crouched in the grass a few feet away. Bao wriggles happily at his toes as my father scratches the little dog's belly and feeds him scraps of dried mango, his favorite treat.

At my footsteps, my father quickly hides the fruit behind his back. Bao lets out an indignant bark. Bouncing up, he snatches the last piece of mango from my father's fingers before running to me, stubbed tail wagging victoriously.

I squat down, fingers finding the sensitive spot behind his ear to tickle. "Hello, greedy," I laugh.

"About what you just saw..." my father starts as he comes over.

I shoot him a sideways look. "Don't worry, Baba. I won't tell Tien."

"Good," he says. "Because then I'd have to tell her how you overslept this morning and forgot to pick up that batch of galangal Master Ohsa is keeping for us."

Gods. I completely forgot.

I spring to my feet. "I'll go and get it now," I say, but my father shakes his head.

"It's not urgent, dear. Go tomorrow."

"Well," I reply with a knowing smile, "Mistress Zembi is here for her consultation, and that *is* urgent. So unless you want Tien to threaten to skin you alive..."

He shudders. "Don't remind me. The things that woman can do with a fish-gutting knife."

Laughing, we head back into the house, our steps falling in line. For a moment, it's almost like before—when our family was still whole, and our hearts. When it didn't hurt to think of my mother, to whisper her name in the middle of the night and know she can't answer. But despite his joking, Baba's smile doesn't quite reach his eyes, and it reminds me that I'm not the only one haunted by their memories.

*   *   *

I was born on the first day of the New Year, under the watchful gaze of the full moon. My parents named me Lei, with a soft rising tone. They told me they chose it because the word makes your mouth form a smile, and they wanted to smile every time they thought of me. Even when I'd accidentally knocked over a tray of herbs or let Bao in to paw muddy footprints across the floor, the corners of their mouths couldn't help but tuck up, no matter how loudly they shouted.

But these past seven years, even my name hasn't been able to make my father smile often enough.

I look a lot like her, my mother. I catch Baba startling some mornings when I come down, my raven hair long and loose, my short frame silhouetted in the doorway. But neither of my parents knew where I inherited my eyes.

How did they react when they first saw them? What did they say when baby-me opened her eyes to reveal luminous, liquid gold?

For most, my eye color is a sign of luck—a gift from the Heavenly Kingdom. Customers request for me to make their herbal mixtures, hoping my involvement will make them more potent. Even demons visit our shop occasionally, like the deer-woman today, lured by the rumor of the human girl with golden eyes.

Tien always laughs about that. "They don't believe you're pure Paper," she tells me conspiratorially. "They say you must be part demon to have eyes the color of the new year's moon."

What I don't tell her is that sometimes I wish I *were* part demon.

On my rare days off, I head into the valleys surrounding our village to watch the bird-form clan that lives in the mountains to the north. Though they're too far to be anything more than silhouetted shapes, dark cutouts of wings spread in motion, in my mind's eye I make out every detail. I paint their feathers in silvers and pearls, sketch the light of the sun on their wing tips. The demons soar through the sky over the valley, riding the wind in effortless movements as graceful as dance, and they look so free it aches some part deep in me.

Even though it isn't fair, I can't help but wonder whether if Mama had been born with wings, she'd have escaped from wherever she was taken to and flown back to us by now.

Sometimes I watch the sky, just waiting, and hoping.

Read more in

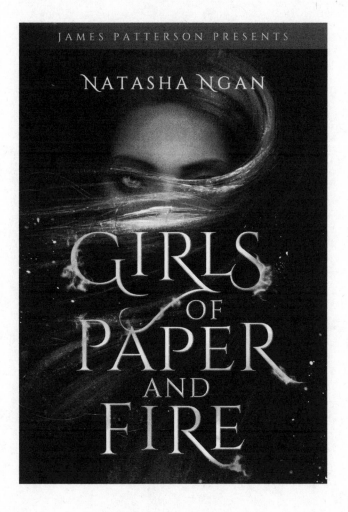

Available now!